# MAR Rising

Craig Brusseau

*Marion,*

*Thank you for sharing your unique and humorous way of looking at the world, and your unconditional, unwavering support.*

.

There is much more to be gained by exploring the shadows than running from them.

LHT

**Editors**

BubbleCow

David Hindin

Ashley R. Carlson at Utopia Editing &
Ghostwriting Services, LLC


**Cover Design**

Sanura Jayashan


**Cover Art**

Creations/Shutterstock.com
Jeff Thrower/Shutterstock.com
Russell Shively/Shutterstock.com
Vladimir Arndt/Shutterstock.com

# CHAPTER 1

# The Crater Creator

❖

With a subtle plop, a tiny pea-sized object entered a vast sea. And what would seem like an unremarkable moment, following a long succession of other unremarkable moments, was in fact quite the opposite.

In that instance, a new species was introduced into a fragile, yet quickly-evolving ecosystem. Had the current inhabitants of that planet possessed the capacity to understand the gravity of the situation, they would all have agreed to let the invader sink slowly into the cold, dark depths of the vast ocean. No harm, no foul, and they all could have moved on about their day. But this was not to be.

A small aquatic creature had heard the sound of the incoming morsel and quickly devoured it. Soon thereafter, as is the way on most inhabited planets in the universe, that creature was eaten by a slightly larger creature with the good fortune of being placed slightly higher on the food chain.

Immediately after being eaten by the first creature, the microscopic, mechanical inhabitants of this tiny invader began replicating in their new host. Through each subsequent step up the food chain, the tiny invader infested its new host. Roughly two hundred hours after its introduction into this new world, it resided inside a host that was at the top of this particular ecosystem.

Every part of the host would be composed of the invader, each tiny object perfectly mimicking the function of the cells it consumed. This new organism could exist indefinitely, as long as a source of protein could be found. Unfortunately for the other inhabitants of the planet, once fully-fueled it was stronger, faster and angrier than the original. Any – and all – creatures were fair game, even those of the host's same species, providing the need for protein was critical enough.

This new and improved beast was not so out of place in its environment. It was pretty much business as usual, since creatures at the top of the food chain tended to be killing machines to begin with. For the prey, the only option was to run away, hide, and hope it didn't find you. Fighting was a desperate last resort and, even then, was entered into with the knowledge that it would likely be the last thing the prey would ever do. Any victim that managed to beat the odds and live through the initial attack was quickly transformed by the mysterious invaders, from the inside, into a killing machine themselves.

This new ecosystem proved very suitable for the MAR, but their success was to be short lived. For the second time in a month, another not so unremarkable moment followed the first. From the depths of space, a new mechanical device, not quite so advanced as its predecessor, made its way to the surface of the planet.

Shortly after crashing into the soft, mossy surface, the device sprung to life and collected a sample of saliva from a fresh kill. A few seconds later, a small antenna extended from its metallic surface and transmitted a signal into the heavens.

The response to the transmission was immediate. It did not take the form of a return signal, as the original message was not a request for conversation, but rather an alarm. The action that followed was to mirror the urgency of the alert. An asteroid, roughly six miles in diameter and some six hundred thousand miles away from the planet, was nudged from its orbit.

Sixty days later, the asteroid exploded into a fireball that streaked across the planet's sky. It descended rapidly and collided with its surface, with catastrophic results. The impact scarred the planet's surface with a huge crater, ejecting ash and dust high into the atmosphere. A raging firestorm swept across the planet, incinerating everything in its path. As the dust settled and blanketed the ground, all advanced life ceased to exist.

This was sixty-six million years ago.

# CHAPTER 2

# World Of Shite

*Year 1588 - 118 lost souls - 90 men 17 women 11 children*

## *Washboard Gabs*

"Your husband's got the heart of an artist, and the arse of a painter," Anabel jabbed to Elizabeth across the washboard as she hopelessly scrubbed the brown streaks from yet another pair of long johns. "If William put as much time into being mayor as he does scratching his arse through his overalls, he'd be a member of Parliament by now."

Elizabeth, not new to the wash yard banter, shot back. "If we attached a sail to Albert's britches, he could propel this entire village all the way back to England. Thank the Lord he is too lazy to fix the gaping holes in the chinking in your cabin, or I dare say the fumes would overtake you in the night."

"By the smell of your breath, it appears the fumes came to rest on your teeth," added Mary as she walked up with another basket of dirties.

Anabel chortled at that one. The give-and-take at the washboard was never dull, and today was proving to be no different. She had long wondered how it was that her husband could produce so much gas. The more years that passed in their marriage, the more she thought it proved Albert had shite for brains – and that passing gas was simply his version of a profound thought.

Still, she had to admire the man she married. He was a strong, devout man, and a good provider. There was always food on the table and a fire in the hearth. He had a way of making her feel safe in an otherwise unsafe place.

Any safety Anabel may have felt was not shared by Elizabeth. Her husband, William, had left with three other men on a hunting trip nearly a week ago and none had yet returned. The game had been scarce lately, but even so - the men should have returned by now, their bags filled with bird and beast. She could see that, for all the outward show of strength that Elizabeth was displaying, his prolonged absence had to be weighing heavily on her.

"Well dearie," Anabel said, as she turned to Elizabeth with a warm smile, subtle in a way familiar only to women who have shared the hardships of adventuring to a new land. "When William and the rest walk into camp today, we will surely smell him before we see him."

Elizabeth, just for a second, dropped the adversarial facade and gave her friend an appreciative nod. Although the gesture of hope and camaraderie was much needed, she knew the realities of the harsh world in which she lived.

At least she thought she did…

## *Intruder Alert*

Smell was not the first thing that entered the camp that day. What did come came fast and without warning. The Whitestone's boy was the first to cry out and fall. Though only fourteen, with the exception of Albert, Clive was already larger than all of the other men in camp. The boy barely had time to lift his arm in self-defense before his throat was opened up to the backbone.

The ladies at the washboard cried out in vain for someone to help the poor child. Mrs. Whitestone instinctively ran toward the intruder with nothing but the stick she was using to beat the dust out of her well-trodden rug. It proved ineffective. She had barely reached swinging distance when the beast swiped at her midsection, spilling its vital contents on the ground.

The camp erupted into panic. Colonists ran in seemingly random directions, their judgment clouded by fear and adrenaline. In their minds an unconscious tug of war was taking place, as they struggled to choose between flight and fight.

For Albert, there was no such conflict. His own tug of war ended when he was eight and had tried, in vain, to save his father from a bear attack. Albert was perpetually stuck in fight mode.

And he had the bear skin rug to prove it.

Luckily for the colony, Albert and several others were already preparing to set out on a search for the missing hunters when the first shriek was heard. His musket was loaded and ready by the front door. Fearing an Indian attack, he was immediately on his way out the door, musket in hand, before the dying screams of Mrs. Whitestone finished echoing through the towering pines surrounding the colony.

Though he could not discern exactly who, or what, the foe was that was slurping the insides of Mrs. Whitestone, he knew it was time for this creature to leave its earthly embrace. As he lowered his musket and prepared to fire, a brief sliver of recognition entered his mind.

As he pulled the trigger, Albert's suddenly recognized this predator's true identity. It was the savagery and raw strength exhibited by the attacker that delayed the initial recognition, but now there was no doubt. This was Aldrich Lennox. The Lennox family was very close to the Whitestone's, having lived in the same town in England before relocating to the new world. He could not imagine the shock and horror Mrs. Whitestone must have felt as she was eviscerated by the very man who was godfather to poor Clive.

Albert's shot was true to its mark. And in that instant, any resemblance the attacker had once held to Aldrich quickly faded. His human form devolved into a roiling black mass. The boiling black ball approached the stout colonist, and in his mind, the best Albert could compare it to was a colony of fire ants caught in a flood. Fire ants will instinctively form a ball, each taking turns standing on the backs of the other ants, to get above the water and take a few precious breaths of air. This action gives the appearance of a boiling liquid. As damaging as fire ants can be, Albert knew this creature was far more dangerous.

For the first time in his adult life, the flight response was reignited, and Albert turned and raced back toward his cabin, prepared to bar the door from this unknown threat. Luckily for him, the roiling black ball that was initially licking at his heels gradually shrank as it rolled. The mass completely dissipated just feet from Albert's door, leaving behind an unsightly, coal-colored streak marking its path.

## Not So Lost Colony

From the safety of the cabin, Albert heard two gunshots. He stepped back out the cabin door and into the campsite. There were no more intruders, but rather Anabel and Elizabeth standing over the bodies of Clive and Mrs. Whitestone. The women had just ended the suffering of their longtime friends. Seeing the immediate threat was over, and in the absence of William, the mayor, Albert gathered the remaining colonists to the center of the campsite. He realized the colony needed to form a plan in the event that more attackers were stalking them.

"What we saw here today was an abomination. Clearly a demon sent from hell," Albert shouted to the concerned gathering around him. "This ground is unholy. We must make plans to leave this place at once."

Elizabeth cried out, "But what of William and the other men. They are still out there. We can't leave them to die."

Albert responded, "Aldrich was one of the men who went out looking for food with William. If the demon force that compelled Aldrich to do these unspeakable acts has also possessed the others, we will be no match for them if they return here. Food has been scarce these past few months and just before he left, William and I decided that in a fortnight's time we would move the colony to Croatoan Island. We will pack up camp and leave as soon as possible. Everyone, meet back here in two hours, ready for travel."

Immediately the camp sprung to life, bustling with purpose. Each colonist worked hard to gather his or her meager belongings and prepare for travel. No one wanted to be left behind after glimpsing the savagery that surely awaited. With one eye on the woods and one eye on their work, the colonists quickly broke the camp down.

Anabel and Albert had their belongings packed in short order and headed over to help Elizabeth get William's things together.

"I can't go without leaving word for my William," Elizabeth explained to Albert as he entered her door. "I must let him know I am alive and where I am going."

"I understand your reluctance, Elizabeth." Anabel responded, "I would feel the same if it were Albert out there in the woods."

"Why don't you and Anabel carve our new location in a large tree on either side of the campsite. If the men come back and are of clear thought, they should see that and understand its meaning. If they suffer the same possession as Aldrich, and regress into that animalistic state, I dare say they would not."

Elizabeth nodded in agreement. Once her belongings were properly packed for travel, she and Anabel set out to carve "Croatoan" into two trees on opposite sides of the camp.

Anabel set to work on her carving, choosing a large pine that boarded the west side of the campsite. She had finished the C R and O in short order when she heard commotion from the camp. Screams rose from men and women alike. Before she had a chance to stand up from her crouched position and run to the camp, she smelled it. It was foul and it was behind her. She turned quickly and saw William coming at her. Not on his feet, but in mid leap. Her last thought was, *"Wow, I really did smell him before I saw him."*

## *Lightning Warrior*

The Croatoan Indian population had a legend about the night the colonists disappeared. They called it the night of the lightning warrior. It was a tale of how the Great Spirit took revenge upon the white man for their senseless killing of their kindred brothers and sisters. The great lightning warrior shot spears of white light, striking down his enemy without a sound until not a soul was left. According to the legend, it was the one and only time the great warrior walked upon the earth.

# CHAPTER 3

# Of Ants And Men

❖

*Year 1867*

## *Chill*

*A**ces and Eights*, Samuel Losman thought to himself. He studied his counterparts across from him. *That should do it*. Boone Marsh slammed his hand palm down on the rickety table, nearly spilling Samuel's whiskey.

"Finally! This one's mine!" Boone bellowed. Dust rose from the table and fell to the floor, meeting with the thick layer of dirt, sawdust and stale beer that had already taken up residence there.

More than a few eyebrows rose around the saloon, and, instinctively, a few not-so-stable types moved their shooting hands slightly closer to their gun belts. After some brief scrutiny, the men realized death was not imminent, and just as quickly returned to their own affairs.

"Damn Boone, you keep carryin' on like that and you'll find yourself in a pine box if you're not careful," Samuel joked to his good friend.

"After this hand, I'll pay for that box with your nickel," Boone shot back.

Samuel snorted. "It would be the first nickel of mine that found its way into your pocket." Samuel had played cards with Boone enough to know when he was bluffing. Over-exuberance was Boone's first and most reliable indicator.

"Well, you'll have to put up a hundred nickels to see my hand," Boone shot back. With great emphasis, he dropped a five-dollar note into the pot in the middle of the table.

"Well, that does it for me," sighed the only other man at the table, the local stable hand, who had been quiet up until this point. "Might as well go back and feed the horses. By the way," the man smirked at Boone, "any nickels you take from Samuel tonight were most likely mine when this game started."

"Give Jasper an extra bucket of oats tonight - I think I'll be able to afford it," Samuel shouted as the stable hand made his way across the bar and out the door.

Samuel didn't feel too bad about how often he took Boone's money. Boone's mercantile business was booming lately, with all the new railroad traffic in town. Boone and his family were quickly becoming one of the wealthiest families around.

"Well, it is just you and me, and as much as I would like to sit here humiliating you all night, I have to get going myself. Let's make this easy. I'll see your five dollars and raise you another five. Judging by the bankroll in front of you, that will leave you with enough money to drown your sorrows, but not so much you are of no use to that beautiful bride of yours tonight."

"Call!" said Boone. "And you should be so lucky to have a woman as fine as she."

"That is the first intelligent thing you've said in quite some time," Samuel replied as he showed Boone his cards. Boone hung his head and threw his cards, face down, onto the table.

"Pleasure doing business with you, Boone," Samuel said. He folded his winnings into his billfold.

"Same time tomorrow?" asked Boone.

"I'm afraid not, my friend. Got some things to take care of for the railroad. I'll be out of town for a week or so. Say howdy to Annie and the little ones for me," Samuel added, getting up from the table. He shot back the last of his whiskey and headed out the door into the dry, chilled night air.

## *On The Job*

Samuel turned right out of the swinging saloon doors and began walking along the boarded sidewalk, back toward the Carson City hotel. He thought about how many bounty hunters had been showing up in town recently, looking to cut into his workload. Many of the jumpy patrons back at the saloon were part of the new crop of inexperienced, gun-happy wannabes. They were flooding into Carson City, every one of them looking for a quick payday - which Samuel knew was much more likely to instead be a quick death.

Before this new crew of competition, Samuel was enjoying the upswing in work and wealth, thanks mostly to the increase in commerce that the railroad work was bringing to his hometown of Carson City. Railroad work meant employees - and employees meant payroll. Stagecoaches were being robbed on a fairly consistent basis as every two-bit thug within a hundred miles was trying to get their hands on the bankroll funding the railroad's construction.

This new group of bounty hunters worked cheap. The railroad had begun hiring them at a fraction of what Samuel normally charged. He refused to work at a discounted rate. After all, he knew his life was too valuable to risk it for less than fair compensation.

He hadn't always been on the right side of the law. It wasn't that long ago that Samuel himself was robbing his share of stagecoaches. Many a time he found himself wondering how he had managed to stay alive after particularly dicey robberies.

The stress of that life finally convinced Samuel that, although there was no huge payday, going straight was his only option. He had chosen bounty hunting, as it would make the most of his skills and provide a stable income, not to mention being much better for his long-term health. That, and as a bounty hunter, he could work alone. It was unlike robbing stagecoaches, which required one to trust the very people who were amongst the least trustworthy on earth. Even in the unlikely event you were lucky enough not to get shot in the back by one of your coworkers during the robbery, you couldn't sleep again until the bounty was divided and you were long out of sight.

Samuel chuckled to himself. The whole concept of bounty hunting still struck him as a bit odd. The railroad paid the most fearsome retired gunmen in the county to hunt for the most fearsome active gunmen in the county. It was a true dog-eat-dog scenario. But as long as Samuel was the dog doing the eating, he was OK with the arrangement.

Christian "Dusty" Meeks, the acting sheriff in town, was leaning on the wall outside the bank - half-smoking, half-choking on a cigar - when Samuel walked by. Dusty pushed himself off the wall with his shoulder. He strode up alongside Samuel.

"Just when I thought this night was going to end on a high note," Samuel chortled as Dusty caught up to him.

"I heard you were heading out of town tomorrow. You sure you can handle this? This killer is picking off bounty hunters at a rather alarming rate. If you're scared, I will gladly take this one off your hands," Dusty said.

As Dusty spoke, Samuel took out his own cigar, pulled a match from a small pouch on his gun belt and swiped it across the back of his pant leg. The man had long been Samuel's nemesis in the bounty hunting business. Samuel preferred to have his bounties ride back into town to face justice, rather than dragging them in the dust behind Jasper. To Dusty, the printing company could just have well have saved the ink and left the posters at "Wanted, Dead."

"I think the railroad is done with amateur hour. Time for a professional," Samuel replied. He lifted the flame and took quick, hard pulls off of the cigar. Smoke circled his head and trailed off behind him as they walked.

"When you're dead, I'll only charge your bosses double to finish the job. I'll be waiting to hear from them," Dusty said. He quickly turned away, heading back in the direction they had come.

Samuel, cigar at his side, exhaled deeply. The night's chill caused his breath to form a cloud around his head as he continued down the sidewalk. He had to admit it: he was alarmed that no one seemed to be able to catch, or kill, this marauder.

Things had started to go poorly for the Central Pacific railroad several months ago, when workers, mostly Chinese, started to go missing from the work crew. Initially, this did not raise many eyebrows, as the losses were limited to the Chinese members of the crew: for every worker lost, there were ten more ready to take his spot.

But when construction began to lag behind schedule, the railroad's attitude changed. They were losing several crew members each week, with many more walking off the job out of fear. The railroad hired several discount bounty hunters. None of these men succeeded at catching the perpetrator. And worse, some were never seen again.

The final straw for the railroad happened the day before when the crew chief turned up missing. Making matters worse, the crew chief was the son of a close personal friend of the Central Pacific Railroad's founder. That's when the railroad turned to Samuel. They wanted this perpetrator alive so the founder could exact his own, personal revenge. This was all good news for Samuel, as he stood to earn more in the coming week than he usually made all year. The gravy train was indeed rolling full steam ahead.

## Reflections

Samuel was up early the next morning, making his way down to the stables just as the sun began to rise in the east over the vast plains. He walked into the barn, where Jasper greeted him eagerly. Samuel and his horse had a close bond. They had worked side by side for the past five years. He rubbed the neck and nose of this trusted companion, remembering the events surrounding his chance meeting with this four-legged friend.

Samuel had come across this magnificent animal grazing on a small patch of grass just off the main trail, six miles outside of Carson City. Back then, Samuel ran with a group led by Zeke McCoy, one of the most notorious bad guys roaming the Nevada territory.

Unbeknownst to Samuel, Zeke had killed the steed's previous owner in a holdup, just minutes prior. The horse had run off in a panic, managing to avoid several lead rounds fired in his direction.

As Samuel approach the grazing animal, Zeke came galloping up the trail in the opposite direction. Jasper seemed to sense his impending demise. He positioned himself behind Samuel.

*Smart animal*, Samuel had thought to himself as Zeke bore down on them.

"Just one second there, Zeke," Samuel said. "What do you mean to do with this horse?"

"What do you care?" Zeke replied. "Just give me a second to dispatch of this animal and we can be on our way."

But Samuel had already lowered his hand toward his holster, a move that had not gone unnoticed by Zeke.

"Well Zeke, the way I see it is that we have two choices here. You can make your move and see which one of us can draw the fastest. We both know who that will be. Or, you can go on about your business, head back down the trail thatta way, and consider this animal my cut of the last job."

Zeke's eyes narrowed.

"What's it going to be, Zeke?" Samuel growled, almost wishing the man would reach for his pistol. Zeke laughed. They both knew he had no chance of winning a gunfight with Samuel.

"You want the wretched beast? He's yours. Just know that the previous rider didn't have much luck with him, and yours is likely to be just as bad if we ever cross paths again. And his saddle - that will be going with me."

"Fine by me," said Samuel. Samuel had made his mind up for quite some time that he wanted to be out of the thieving business. That particular moment seemed like the right time to make it official: saving the animal from being shot dead was his opportunity to be done with the outlaw lifestyle. He had seen too many innocent people die for no good reason. Life had to mean more than that. It just had to.

Samuel unsaddled the horse and gave the leather seat, and all of the other wares attached to it, to Zeke. Without another word to Samuel, the outlaw piled the leather saddle on the back of his horse, spun around, and headed back down the trail.

Samuel tied a rope to the bridle of his new steed and watched Zeke ride down the trail and out of sight. "Looks like today is your lucky day, my friend," Samuel said and, after a brief pause, added "Jasper." The horse whinnied, as if satisfied with his new name. Samuel mounted the horse he had ridden up on, leading Jasper behind them back down the trail.

It was later that night, as Samuel and his horses made camp, that he decided bounty hunting was a profession that fit his skill set and would keep him on the right side of the law. Once his profession was decided, it did not take long for him to choose Carson City as a fitting place to make his start.

The next morning as Samuel made his way to Carson City, they passed the body of Zeke McCoy, twenty feet off to the side of the trail. It was stripped clean of all of his valuables. *Dog eat dog*, Samuel thought as he passed. *I got out of that business just in time.*

## Long Ride Ahead

Samuel turned his attention back to the job at hand. He was now packed and ready for the trail. He mounted Jasper, and they made their way out of the stable and onto the main street. The night's chill quickly subsided as the sun continued to rise. "It's going to be a long hot day, old friend," he said to Jasper as they made their way out of Carson City and turned to the north. A full day's ride lay ahead. Both he and Jasper set their minds to the trail. *Just like old times*, Samuel thought.

The trek out to the railroad camp was long and tedious. Samuel's mind wandered to the morning he and his horses first arrived in Carson City. He had been a law-abiding citizen for an entire day when he trotted down the main street, toward the only mercantile store in town.

When he arrived, Samuel had wrapped the reins of his horses to the post out front and entered the store. He looked around the room and could not help but notice how new everything was, right down to the counter and register. *Ahhh, the register*, he thought. Right there, next to the door with the till open. *Maybe he could start his law abiding days tomorrow*, he thought, as his eyes came to rest on a beautiful lady standing in the back near the shelves full of barbed wire and flour sacks.

"Is there something I can help you with?" the woman asked, noticing the stranger eyeballing the register. She walked to where the register stood open and shut the drawer. "A cold beverage, perhaps? It's on the house today. We are having a grand opening," she added.

"That would be swell, ma'am," Samuel replied. He was taken aback by her kindness. Surely he had to look a bit more menacing than the woman was letting on?

"You look a bit tired from the trail," she said to the stranger. "My name is Annie. My husband Boone and I just opened this place yesterday. I haven't seen you around before. Are you new in town?"

Samuel thought for a moment. He was not exactly new to the town, having been part of a raiding party that robbed the bank here eighteen months ago. "Yes, I am," he replied.

"Well," Annie responded, a pleasant tone in her voice, "welcome to Carson City. We have just about anything you could need here. If you're short on funds, there are plenty of jobs to do around this place and we would be grateful for the help."

*This was a fine woman*, Samuel thought. "I just may take you up on that. I am a bounty hunter by trade, but find myself between jobs at the moment."

Boone entered from somewhere in the back recesses of the store and shot out his hand. "I see you have met my better half already. My name is Boone. I couldn't help noticing you have a couple of fine animals out front. Any chance you would be willing to part with one? We are in need of a horse. Our trusty companion met his demise only a few days ago."

"It just so happens, I do find myself in the possession of an extra horse. The tall black mare is available," Samuel said. He pointed to the horse next to Jasper.

"Excellent. What do you say we discuss it over some cards and whiskey at the saloon?" Boone said to his new friend.

"Sounds swell. But I have some words of advice to you and your lovely wife. Put your register toward the back of the store and don't leave the drawer open when you are not behind it. Too many unscrupulous types around here. You never know when one such type is going to walk through your front door."

"Sam, you seem like a good, God-fearing man. Don't let my Boone talk you into drinking too much. And watch him, he is no stranger to the card table and will take you for everything you are worth if you let him," Annie said, as she went back to organizing the wares in the store. Samuel remembered an overwhelming feeling of acceptance that morning. It was then that he decided that Annie, Boone and their whole family were going to be his family, too.

## *Take Your Mark*

It was just before dusk when the trail-weary pair strode into the railroad camp they had set out for. Cole Earle was now in charge of this particular work camp, and he met Samuel just outside the command tent.

"I assume you are Samuel Losman, come here to do what many before you have failed to do?" Cole sneered at Samuel.

Samuel was in no mood for taking guff after his long ride. "Yep," he said. "Looks like you finally pulled your head from your chaps and stopped hiring boys to do a man's job. If you care for a shooting demonstration, I would surely oblige." Samuel tapped his revolver with his right hand.

"That won't be necessary. Let's take it down a notch. We've had enough trouble around here without adding to it. You can tie up your horse over there by the canteen where we have a tent set up for you," Cole said, pointing in the direction of the canteen. "In your tent you'll find fresh water for drinking and bathing if you want, for both you and your horse. When you're ready, head next door to the canteen and tell the boys inside you are here courtesy of the railroad. They'll make you whatever we got handy. When you're done, come on back here and we can discuss how you are going to go about taking care of business."

Samuel nodded. He dismounted Jasper and led the horse in the direction Cole had pointed. Once at the tent, he got Jasper a large bucket of water and a handful of oats before he washed and headed over to the canteen for grub. It was an hour later that he made his way back to where he had met Cole. Cole was not alone when he entered the command tent. An American Indian stood by him, discussing a plan to catch the killer that had been stalking the camp for many weeks.

"Running Wolf, meet Samuel Losman. Sam here is from Carson City and is being paid quite a sum to catch our killer."

"Evening" said Running Wolf.

"Paiute?" Samuel inquired to his new acquaintance, trying to ascertain the man's Native American tribal affiliation.

"Yes," said Running Wolf.

"Is this going to be an issue?" asked Cole.

"Not at all, just wanted to know a little more about my new friend here. You do know I work alone?" said Samuel, looking back at Cole.

"That is understood," said Cole. "Running Wolf is here as an expert tracker and is very familiar with the area around this camp. Use him however you must to get this taken care of."

Samuel was secretly glad to have the help. Though his tracking skills were top notch, they were nothing compared to the skill possessed by the native people of this area. Samuel had developed a great deal of respect for native tribes. They lived off the land, killed only what was necessary for their own survival, and had deep respect for all forms of life. He wished there were more people like that.

"Running Wolf, I will leave you to fill Samuel in on the details of what we are dealing with. I'll be in the canteen having a whiskey. Join me when you have him up to speed and have finalized a plan."

With that, Cole exited the tent and left them to their business. Samuel turned back to Running Wolf.

"Running Wolf is quite a mouthful. Can I call you Running or would Mr. Wolf do," Samuel joked.

"My friends call me Levi. Mr. Earle is not among them. He and his ilk have no respect or mercy for my people or our ways. He needs my help and he knows in order to get it he must refer to me with my proper Indian name. I'm ashamed to admit it but I get a certain pleasure from watching him twist in his britches every time he has to show me that respect."

"You think it is too late to get him to call me Mr. Losman?" Samuel chuckled as he replied to his new friend. "Well Levi, it looks like we have a job to do here. Whaddaya say we get down to it?"

Levi spent the next half hour describing the grisly murders and disappearances that had taken place in camp recently. Although no bodies had been discovered, one could assume the worst given the amount of blood left behind at each attack site. Levi had tried to track the killer - or in his opinion, killers - but each time, the trail was lost before the attackers could be found.

They made a plan to lay in wait just outside the main camp in the hopes of catching the killer, or killers, as they approached for their next attack. Once decided, they found Cole in the canteen and filled him in on the details. After a few rounds, Levi and Samuel headed out to a position a rifle shot away from the western edge of the camp, atop a small swell in the landscape. It afforded them a clear view of where most of the workers slept for the night.

Just before dawn Samuel awoke with a start. As the sleep was leaving his eyes, he saw a distinct flash of light, something like lightning, shoot away from him to his right. It flashed out in the direction of the sleeping workers. He could hear the Chinese workers hollering and could just barely make out their silhouettes pointing off to the north. The words they were yelling were in Chinese, so he did not understand them, but it seemed pretty clear judging by the panicked tones what was happening. Just then, Levi ran up the small hill from Samuel's right yelling.

"Samuel, there has been another attack. Let's get moving!"

Samuel was disappointed in himself. He got to his feet. Falling asleep on the job was an unprofessional move. The full day's ride yesterday had proven to be too much for him to make it through the entire night without sleep. Quickly Samuel joined the pursuit. He was now just a few short strides behind Levi, running in the direction of camp. As he ran, a strange thought crossed his mind. He had seen lightning, but did not hear thunder. Looking up, he did not see clouds either. *As strange as that was, it was actually a good thing*, he thought. Rain would wash away any hope of tracking the assailant, or assailants, through the desert.

Levi and Samuel ran up to the area where the crowd of workers was pointing. The rising sun began to shed light on the ground. It was just enough to make out pools of fresh blood in the sand.

"Just like the others," Levi said, shaking his head.

"I make out four sets of tracks coming, and three leaving." Samuel added. "Our victim appears to have walked out to this spot on his own."

"To relieve himself," Levi added and pointed to a clear wet circular spot in the sand.

"And then what? I don't see his tracks leaving. He certainly didn't fly out of here." Samuel said puzzled. "Strange as it sounds, he must have been carried."

They studied the three sets of footprints leading away from the site. One was headed back in the direction that Samuel and Levi had just come from. They followed those tracks for fifty yards back toward the hill that Levi and Samuel had occupied the night before. Abruptly, the tracks stopped. Some black residue had settled onto the ground and continued for another ten feet or so, but then nothing else. *Very strange indeed*, thought Samuel. *Were they headed for us? And if so, what happened to them?*

Samuel turned to Levi. He shrugged his shoulders. "No sign

of a body, so one of the other assailants must have carried away our victim." Samuel and Levi doubled back, following the other two sets of tracks a hundred yards or so to the north. At that point, the two tracks diverged, one east and one west.

Levi and Samuel agreed they would each follow a set while they were fresh, giving the men their best chance of catching both killers. Samuel quickly returned to camp, threw his saddle on Jasper and headed out to follow the tracks to the east.

In short order, Samuel was hot on the heels of his prey. As he followed the footprints, he could not fathom how a man could make the strides he was seeing in the sand, let alone do it carrying a person on his back. He guessed that Levi was tracking the man carrying the worker and he was following the accomplice. After two hours, the tracks led him to a small cave. It was set in a rock outcropping, deep in the Nevada desert.

Samuel was sure the person he was looking for was in that cave. He surveyed the landscape, trying to pick the best possible vantage point. He decided on a nearby rock formation that would afford him both cover and a clear view of the cave opening. The formation was too small to hide Jasper, so he tied his faithful companion behind a larger formation a couple of hundred feet to his right. From his position, he could see Jasper, but the horse was not in view of the cave. Samuel took a prone position. He steadied his rifle on a small rock outcropping in front of him.

With every neigh and whinny that came from Jasper's direction, Samuel anticipated the appearance of the man from the cave. After an hour in the baking sun, he was about to change tactics when he saw movement in the cave entrance. At first he just saw the head of a man appear. *Not Chinese*, he thought, *most likely Mexican*. The man's head turned in the direction of Jasper as if he were trying to pinpoint the exact location of the animal. What Samuel saw next was right out of a nightmare. The man, in one short stride, leapt eight feet in the air and landed on a rock above the cave. In all his years, he had never seen such a feat of human agility. More shocking was the look on the man's face. Pure rage. And even more terrifying to Samuel, was that the rage was being directed at his best friend.

Without further hesitation, Samuel fired one well-aimed round. The echo of the shot reverberated off of the nearby rocks and Jasper jumped back with a start. The round struck the man in the head, right near the spine. He went down immediately.

## *Into Obscurity*

It was two days later that Samuel walked Jasper back into Carson City. He led his companion to the stable for a well-deserved feeding and rest. Boone and Cole Earle, the railroad representative, caught up with him as he headed for the saloon. Cole had ridden to Carson City in search of Dusty when Samuel failed to reappear in camp.

"Levi said he killed a man in the desert but was unable to retrieve the body. Something about it falling into a river and being swept away. I see you had no luck either," Cole quipped.

"I killed the man responsible for those attacks," Samuel replied, "but I have no body to prove it either."

"Without a body, you don't get no bounty. Even if you ain't lying and you did kill the man, you were supposed to bring him in alive," Cole shot back.

Cole could not believe his good fortune. He was sure neither Levi nor Samuel was lying about killing the assailants, but without bodies, he didn't have to pay them a dime. Cole dropped back and headed in the direction of the stable, presumably to gather his horse and head back to the railroad camp.

Samuel lived out his remaining years in relative obscurity. He quickly got over the loss of the bounty, but it was the hit his reputation took that was not so easily swallowed. Dusty was relentless in his comments. More and more work went Dusty's way in the wake of Samuel's perceived failure.

It wasn't until his death bed, some twenty years later, that he handed Boone his very worn necklace and recounted the events of that day. Although his friend chalked it up to heat stroke, Samuel told the story with such intensity that he could not help but think that there was some hint of truth in his words.

There was a reason Samuel could not bring back the body. There was none. When the man went down, he neither stayed down, nor stayed human. As the killer's body fell toward the ground, it transformed before his eyes into a roiling mass of black. Samuel was momentarily paralyzed as he attempted to process the scene before him. The roiling mass began moving in the direction of where Jasper was tied. Samuel, snapped back into action by fear that his steed was in danger, fired at the mass. It had no effect. However, as the rolling ball progressed toward its prey, Samuel noticed it was getting smaller, leaving behind a black residue. The mass managed to cross the seventy-five feet of desert toward Jasper, before finally dissipating mere feet from some very nervous hooves. Samuel raced to where Jasper was standing and reassured his horse, taking the opportunity to gather himself.

Still unable to believe his eyes, he worked his way back to the cave opening. He did not find the body he was hoping would still be there. What he did find was a necklace made of leather and what appeared to be a large quartz crystal. Knowing this belonged to the killer, he put the necklace on, where it would remain the rest of his days as a personal testament to his abilities as bounty hunter. Samuel knew that no one else would believe his story, and he would rather be known as an average bounty hunter than a crazy one. Though he had taken the trail back to Carson City countless times, he never remembered it taking quite so long.

# CHAPTER 4

# Beantown Blues

## *Just Another Day*

Madison Jaques was awakened by the sound of thunder. The deep, penetrating bass rumbled through the three foot by two-foot grate that stood shoulder height on the cement wall. Light entering the grate from the alleyway beyond, only dimly illuminated the small boiler room.

She checked the cheap watch on her wrist: 9:10am. Darn - she was late. The morning rush was mostly over, and she was missing out on her chance to avoid yet another soup kitchen dinner. She shivered as she rose from her cot, noticing her breath forming a cloud in front of her. *Once again, the furnace didn't come on last night*, she thought. *I wonder if I will get another visit from Juan.*

Juan was the building maintenance worker who was responsible for this particular boiler. Madison had met him on her second night of residence, some four months ago. She had made the mistake of turning off a leaky valve that was causing the small room to become unbearably humid. Juan, in a not so jovial mood, had appeared thirty minutes later, having received dozens of complaints about the hot water situation. She was caught completely off-guard. Her only option was to come clean about her living situation and then show him the valve that she had turned. Juan turned the valve back on and studied the leak, while Madison tried vehemently to convince him that she could be trusted not to mess with the pipes in the future.

"OK, OK," Juan gave in. "You can stay, but this was your one and only screw up. If my manager ever found out I knew you were in here, I would lose my job."

The next day, she returned cautiously through the wall grate, fearing Juan may have tipped off building security to her presence. She quickly realized she had nothing to be worried about. Juan had placed a small, canvas-covered cot along the wall near the grate. On it was several bottles of water, a small package of saltines and a note that read:

"Sleep as close to the grate as possible. These boilers have a way of sucking the oxygen out of room. Don't leave food in here; it will just attract the rats. There is a drain in the floor on the far side of the room. You'll see a shower-head directly above it. The valves on the wall directly below that control the water to the shower. These are the ONLY valves you can touch in this room. Be safe."

Heat, running water, shower, all at no cost. Juan had made her mental list of good guys.

The boiler had not run for a few days. Madison was worried that Juan could be in trouble after all. Surely he should have been down here by now to fix things. She glanced at her watch again, and realized she had no time to worry about that right now. There was no time for a shower either, unfortunately. She quickly changed out of her sweat pants and into an old pair of Levis. Madison's bare feet were cold, but she did not want to risk wearing socks, as they would only soak up the puddle water she would surely be encountering today. Reluctantly, she pushed her bare feet into her beat-up canvas Converse sneakers, her only choice of footwear. Those were certainly going to take a beating today. Madison wasn't sure how many days like this they had left in them.

Reaching under the cot, she pulled out a box of garbage bags and extracted one from the roll. She made holes for her arms and head and then pulled the makeshift raincoat over her pink hoodie.

Now ready for the day, Madison stepped onto the blue plastic milk crate located directly below the grate. She tugged the heavy piece of metal inward on its hinges. It made an angry, screeching sound as it swung open and came to a stop against the wall to her right. Some rust flakes dropped to the floor below. She waited a few seconds for the sound to stop echoing down the alleyway outside, then poked her head out and peeked first left and then right.

The alley carved an eight-foot gap between the two soaring

buildings on each side. To her left, ten feet of dumpsters ended in a brick wall. To her right, twenty feet down, was the walkway that passed in front of the alley.

Madison could see the normal throng of people the city belched forth at this time of day. Like usual, no one bothered to look down the alley as they passed. The asphalt was wet from the storm that had just passed overhead, but the rain had stopped, at least for the moment. She pulled her head back in, lifting her most prized possession in the entire world - a guitar she had named "The Reaper" - through the grate. She quickly followed behind it.

The heavens opened up again as she spun around, reached back into the boiler room, and pulled the metal grate closed. Rising to her feet, Madison tilted her head skyward and remained motionless, letting the large drops of water pound her cheeks and roll off down her neck. *Today I will go by Rain,* she thought to herself.

This habit of giving herself a new name every day had started the first morning of living on the streets. That day, she gave someone a fake name, fearing her real identity would be discovered. However, she found it empowering and chose to continue the practice. It reminded her, each and every day, that her fate and her destiny was in her hands - and her hands alone. She based the name on whatever musing crossed her mind on a given morning.

Fearing that the case the Reaper was in would not successfully repel the downpour; she decided to hustle. She turned and headed down the alley toward the sidewalk. As she reached it, she had to duck under some yellow police tape that had been placed across the alley entrance and around the front of the building. *Wow*, she thought. *Looks like something bad happened out here last night.*

She hadn't heard anything out of the ordinary. She would have to be extra careful returning tonight - not just for potential assailants, but for nosy policemen as well. With the Reaper in hand, Madison headed out into the city.

## It's Me, Rain

Madison walked briskly down the rain-soaked sidewalk. She decided that, even though she was late, she was going to take the long way through Faneuil Hall on her way to the Aquarium T stop.

The Aquarium stop on Boston's blue line subway system was one of her favorite spots to work. Not only did it unload many travelers on their way to the tourist havens of Faneuil Hall and the Freedom Trail, it also serviced the Aquarium itself.

The Aquarium meant families, and families meant food money. After all, what parent could look at the poor, guitar-playing girl, dirty and living in the subway, without a twinge of guilt that their own children's circumstances were far better. It was usually enough for them to throw a few coins into her guitar case.

The rain, which had been coming down in torrents just moments before, was back to being little more than a drizzle. Birds were collecting in many of the large puddles, taking the opportunity to bathe in the clear water. As she passed one large towering building, Madison caught her reflection in a large display window of a shop occupying the ground floor. The window reflected all five foot eight inches of her. Her clear complexion and facial subtleties were lost in a thin layer of grime. She could clearly see how ragged her long blonde hair was, completely soaked from the rain and very much tangled. *Good thing I can't afford makeup, or it would be streaking down my face right now*, she thought, passing by.

The trash bag made quite a fashion statement as it reflected back at her, side by side, with some of the latest fashions out of Italy. A beautiful young girl dressed in bags and rags juxtaposed against inanimate, plastic silhouettes covered in the most beautiful, expensive clothing available. *Someday*, she thought to herself as she reached an intersection and crossed a busy street.

Within minutes, Madison was entering the long courtyard between the two main merchant buildings that make up the Faneuil Hall marketplace. Immediately she heard the familiar sounds of a harmonica.

Fifty feet ahead, sitting on a five gallon bucket and playing to a packed crowd consisting of an Asian couple and their two daughters, was Jeremiah Church. Her spirits lifted as she approached the six foot four black southern gentleman in the derby hat.

The downpour that had soaked her had managed to somehow miss this tall, skinny man. He was dressed in his old blue sports coat, white turtleneck and jeans. Despite the heavy cloud cover, he wore dark sunglasses.

When she got within earshot Jeremiah greeted her, without turning his head in her direction. "My dear Maddie, how are you this fine morning? Slept in a little, I see. That cushy lifestyle of yours must be getting the better of you."

"First of all, kind sir, you need to eat better. Not even the raindrops can find such a skinny target. Secondly, I'm not sure who this Maddie girl is of which you speak, but she sounds like a perfect angel. My name, sir, is Rain and I'm just visiting for the day," Madison replied in her best southern drawl.

"My apologies, my 'pour' girl, my mind must be clouded and soaked with gin. Please, let me drop everything and shower you with gifts from one of these fine establishments," Jeremiah joked back, adding as many puns as he could.

They were not lost on Madison, and she laughed out loud. "You should save your breath for that piece of tin you blow through. I thought that last number was a bit slow and sloppy."

Nothing could have been further from the truth, and she knew it. Madison loved listening to him play. Without his knowledge, she had spent many a day sitting thirty feet away from him, listening to him entertain the masses passing by his bucket. Sometimes she would read, if it was particularly beautiful that day and the hardships of the world decided to leave her alone for a while. And on the days when the world was picking on her particularly ferociously, she would just close her eyes and let the music swallow her whole.

It was important to Madison to not let him know how often she felt the need to be near him. It would seem needy, and she didn't want to be a burden to the man.

It was obvious to her that Jeremiah had his own issues with life and the situation he found himself in. But he was simply the kind of man that would take it upon himself to try to carry the burdens of a sixteen-year-old along with his own.

She liked the relationship they had right now. It came free and easy, without any strings attached. It was shortly after meeting Jeremiah that he told her about the small "apartment" that had recently become available. It had free heat and water and an amazing view of the city. How could she refuse!

"Well, sir. Unlike some lucky souls who get to sit on their brains all day, I have a job to do. You should go back to offending the ears of these unsuspecting people with that godawful noise. By the way, why is your harmonica pink?" she giggled, knowing there may be some part of him that would wonder if someone secretly painted his harmonica pink.

"Well, dear Rain. If you should happen to meet a girl named

Madison, tell her there is a sale at Guitar Center and she should stock up on strings for the Reaper. Now, you should be off as I am about to begin an opus of immense length and volume. It contains such complex harmonies that it would absolutely blow a feeble mind such as yours."

She gave Jeremiah a peck on the forehead and headed off toward the Aquarium, still chuckling over the pink harmonica gag.

## *Mean Girls Suck*

Madison descended into the subway, swiped her Charlie Card, and breezed through the turnstile. The Charlie Card was also courtesy of Jeremiah. Due to his blindness, he qualified for a fifty percent discount on a monthly MBTA pass. She would give him the twenty-nine dollars once a month and he would purchase a pass for her. Every little bit helped.

Madison ducked into the public restrooms to take care of business before descending the final set of stairs that led to the long concrete platform running the length of the station. She chose a spot ten feet or so from the stairs from which she had just descended. She opened the beat-up black case and let the Reaper out to play.

The Reaper was a Martin HD-28, built in the late seventies. The serial number had been scratched out long ago by an unknown perp, who had obviously come by the guitar in some unscrupulous manner. It came to be in Madison's possession thanks the woman Madison considered to be the closest thing to a mother she would ever have: Nana Jean.

Nana Jean's real name was Lorraine Waldo. She was the aunt of the woman, Deena, who provided foster care to Madison when she was eight. It was Madison's third foster care home since she entered the system at age four.

Nana Jean was an aunt in name only. In reality, she was the house cleaner who came to clean the home three times a week. Listing her as an aunt made Deena's home seem more family-oriented and gave her favorable treatment when it came to placing children in the system.

Favorable treatment meant she had first shot at the children with the least emotional baggage when they were processed. To Deena, it was easy money. At five hundred and twenty-three dollars per month per child, her five foster children got her a tidy two thousand six hundred a month in payments. As long as she kept the costs down, and she was an expert at that, she could use the other fifteen hundred on cheap wine and cigarettes.

It was fortunate for Madison that Deena did not take much of an interest in her. That type of attention would not have led to good things for her. Instead, it was Nana Jean who nurtured the child.

Early on, Madison had taken to following Nana Jean around the house as she cleaned, asking every question under the sun.

It wasn't long after their meeting that Nana Jean would find herself staying hours longer than was actually necessary to clean the house. In short order, Madison would find Nana Jean at the house even on the days she was not scheduled to work.

Nana Jean's health had been declining steadily over the past few years. After all, she was eighty-two when they first met. When Madison was ten, she began noticing Nana Jean would repeat the same story several times during the course of the week, often forgetting large pieces or changing the details of the story from one telling to the next.

It was one cold Christmas Eve when Madison was eleven that Nana Jean brought over her most precious Martin acoustic guitar. She had told Madison stories of the many campfires and singalongs that she participated in over the years, recounting the memories in such detail that Madison felt like she could have been watching the events as they unfurled.

"Promise me, my dear, that you will look after my friend Rico here. It has lifted my spirits and soaked up my tears many a time over the years. I trust it will be as good a friend to you in the years to come. Rico was a name that meant a great deal to me. It was the name of my late husband, who passed away a few months before you and I met. We were married for sixty-two years, and we never let an opportunity go by to share a laugh or a smile. Now, you must find a name befitting of this spectacular instrument. Once you've named it, I will teach you to play it."

A week later, Nana Jean asked Madison what name she had come up with. Madison had nothing. She had gone through every name she could think of. None of them seemed to fit. It was a lot of pressure. She was fearful that any name she chose would not be worthy of the instrument or her Nana Jean.

"Well," Nana Jean said. "Let's just sit here for a minute and something will come to us, I'm sure."

Quietly, they sat. Secretly, Madison was not at all sure what the old woman was expecting to happen. Her mind wandered and she began tuning into the sounds coming from other parts of the house. She heard a radio in the distant background. A Blue Oyster Cult song was playing. She had heard the song many times, but in the quiet of that moment she really heard the words for the first time.

"Love of two is one. Here but now they're gone."

As the song continued, she realized it was a song of loss and of acceptance.

"How about The Reaper?" Madison said.

"I think that is a fine choice. Now, let's get to teaching you how to make the Reaper sing."

Back on the train platform, Madison started playing the Blue Oyster Cult song "Don't Fear the Reaper" to the small gathering of travelers around her. She had begun to play the song almost subconsciously. Madison was lucky to have been born with a good singing voice. Perhaps not the most delicate of voices, but it was filled with soul.

Over the years, she had become less and less bashful about singing in public. Now, it made no difference to her at all if she was singing to herself in her room or in front of hundreds of people who would show up in the courtyard in Faneuil Hall over the Christmas holiday. Her music took her over - and when it did, it flowed out of her effortlessly. When she was playing, the rest of the world, everything but the Reaper, seemed to drop away.

Madison was brought back to reality by a loud thud and the scratching sound her guitar case made as it slid several feet to her right. Standing over it was a tall blonde-haired girl in her late teens.

"Jesus, Rat Girl, keep your garbage out of the aisle."

Ingrid, her red-headed side-kick chimed in, "Careful Michele, it might be rabid."

"You ladies have yourselves a nice day," Madison responded and reached out to pull the guitar case back in front of her.

"Whoa," Michele said, "looks like Rat Girl has an attitude. Wait a sec, Rat Girl, I've got a little something here for you."

Michele took a step closer to Madison, now standing directly over the guitar case. She leaned her head forward and released a large glob of gum from her mouth. It landed square in the case with a thud.

"A little something for dinner later tonight."

Ingrid prepared herself, expecting to have to rescue her

friend from yet another altercation entirely of the girl's own making. She was getting tired of having to stick up for Michele, and was becoming increasingly aware that she was not, in fact, a good person.

"Looks like the train is leaving," Madison said and gestured to the platform. "Just keep this in mind. It appears the universe is already starting to gang up on you, seeing as you're here, with the rats in this tunnel, and not up there riding around in your brand new BMW. It won't be long now before you are here, beside me, singing for your supper."

"It was just a flat tire, not some huge apocalyptic event that brought me here, Rat Girl. By the way, it's a Mercedes – 2014, to be exact. I think the universe actually loves me!" Michele turned to catch the train that was, indeed, ready to leave the platform.

Ingrid, on the other hand, stood looking at Madison for a moment. She could see how pretty Rat Girl was behind all of that ragged laundry. In that moment, she wished that she could trade Michele for the Rat Girl. The sound of the train doors closing quickly snapped her back to reality and she turned to follow her blonde leader, who had held the train doors open.

As they shut, the pair sat in the only two remaining seats on that car. The train started with a jerk. In front of them, a pregnant young Asian woman stumbled.

Michele let out a quick giggle and poked Ingrid in the ribs. Rather than play along, Ingrid rose and offered her seat to the grateful woman. Michele did not make eye contact with her for the rest of the ride.

## *Out Go The Lights*

*AAAAAAAAAAAAAARRRGGGGG,* Madison screamed in her head. She would never understand people like that. What possible pleasure is there in kicking someone when they are so obviously down? She needed to call it a day and get her Jeremiah fix.

Madison put the $6.80 that was in her guitar case into her pocket. She searched a nearby trash barrel for a napkin. She found an old doughnut wrapper that was somewhat clean and tugged at the gum stuck to the crushed velvet-like fabric that lined the bottom of her guitar case. Most of it came out, but there was a small, sticky residue that would probably always remain there.

Madison tore off a small piece of the wax-covered paper and stuck it over the gum residue. It remained in place and would hopefully provide enough protection to keep the Reaper from sticking to it. She threw the remainder of the wrapper back in the trash and put the Reaper to bed.

The smell of doughnut on the wrapper reminded her that she had not eaten at all that day. She decided lunch was in order. A little over six bucks was not much for a full day's food requirement, so she would have to settle for a cheap meal. *McDon-*

*ald's dollar menu again*, she thought. The next train heading south was just pulling in, and Madison hopped on. She switched trains twice, once to the Orange line and once to the Red line until she reached South Station.

Madison enjoyed hanging out at South Station. With so many people coming and going, the place somehow felt alive with possibilities. She got three burgers, a soda, and some fries from the dollar menu and sat down to eat. She managed to get down only one of the burgers, and most of the fries by the time she was full.

Madison stuffed the other two burgers and what remained of the fries into the pocket of her hoodie. *Time for some real home cooking*, she thought to herself. She made her way back to Faneuil Hall the same way she had come.

*** 

It was dusk by the time Jeremiah finally called it quits. On and off during the course of the afternoon Madison would glance over to where he was playing. Only rarely was anyone interested enough to stop and listen.

Most days, if the action was that slow, he would pick up and find a more lucrative spot. But not today. Today he spent his time playing for the universe itself, and she was thankful for it.

As he rose up and picked up his bucket, he was facing in her direction. He lifted his head and she swore he was looking right at her. For just that split second she wondered if he knew she was there. But just as quickly, he began tapping the sidewalk in front of him with his walking stick, sauntering off across the courtyard and out into the unknown.

Madison was going to call it quits herself. She stood up from the bench she had occupied for way too long that day, making her way back home. As she reached her building, she noticed the yellow tape was still stretched across the alley, but there were no police present and no menacing-looking types lurking anywhere, at least none that she could see.

Madison ducked back under the tape and made her way down the alley to her home. Bending, she opened the grate, causing the usual screech. It drew no attention. She tucked the Reaper in the hole and dropped it gently onto the cot. She quickly followed and shut the grate behind her. The air was already getting chilly again and still no sign that the boiler had started that day. *If this went on much longer, she would have to find a new residence*, she thought.

An all too familiar squeak came from one of the many large pipes running the length of the ceiling. She kicked off her shoes and changed back into her sweat pants. She discarded her hoodie in favor of a sweatshirt lying at the end of her cot.

Today she would risk turning on the light. She wanted to read a bit before going to sleep. She reached up to tug the string attached to the lone light bulb hanging above her. Nothing. Darn bulb must be burnt out. Well, candles it was.

Madison lit the large candle she kept at the head of her bed. She pulled the burgers and fries from the pocket of her now-discarded hoodie, grabbed the well-worn copy of Harry Potter and the Sorcerer's Stone from under her cot and lay down. She was soon joined by Mr. Twitches, the Mac Daddy of all the rats that Madison had ever seen. The rat made his way down from the pipe above her and now stood at the foot of her cot. As she ate one burger, she pulled large pieces from the other and tossed them to her friend.

One of the many pearls of wisdom Nana Jean had passed on to her was how to overcome ignorance. "Listen to me child. Sometimes smart people say dumb things and dumb people spout words of wisdom. You can't stop people from talking, but you can decide what to do with those words. Best thing is to chew on 'em till you find their truth. Discard the rest. That's just as important as findin' the truth: it keeps you from carrying around a heap of garbage your whole life

In her head, Madison began chewing over the day. *So where is the truth in Rat Girl? Let's see, not showered for two days, soaking wet, sitting on the floor of a filthy subway and living in a rat-infested boiler room. Yup, they nailed me. I'm no longer Maddie, I'm Rat Girl, Queen of the Rats.*

She heard her Nana Jean's voice in her head saying, "Keep chewing."

*OK, why was Rat Girl so insulting? Rats are industrious, they work*

*hard, are resourceful, don't go looking for trouble but they are ready when it comes their way. Not so bad, I think.*

Now out loud, Madison said, "What do you think, Twitches? Am I your Queen?" The large rodent made no indication that it had heard her as it chewed on the remainder of the burger.

As nonchalant as Twitches seemed at the moment, Madison knew he watched out for her. At night, she could hear him fighting off his hungrier, less fortunate comrades. He kept her from being nibbled on while she slept and she kept him fed with cheeseburgers. It was a well-balanced ecosystem.

Madison could not be sure if the rat did this out of some form of friendship or if the connection was no deeper than, "Hey, I need to protect my food source." She had decided long ago that it didn't matter. Since there was no way to know for sure which was true, she was free to pick whichever version of reality made her happier.

Madison chose the friendship version. "That makes two friends now. Watch out Facebook, two and counting." Twitches had now moved up to her chest. She handed him a French fry. Madison had chewed on things long enough, Queen Rat it was.

## *Things That Go Boom In The Night.*

Madison woke the next morning to the sound of a whistle and a man's voice yelling, "One minute everyone. Clear the area." As the remnants of sleep slowly released her brain from its dream state, a million possibilities raced around in her head. She remembered the yellow tape at the end of the alley. Could this be the police, finally catching the perp? Had there been another attack?

Madison decided to collect her things and leave them by the grate on the off-chance she needed to make a quick getaway. She put her jeans and sneakers back on and leaned the Reaper on the wall near the grate. As she went to collect her hoodie from the floor, she saw Mr. Twitches there, and with him was a whole bunch of little Twitches.

"Well, well, well, looks like him is a her," Madison said to her friend.

At almost the same time, she noticed a great number of other rats had made their way into the small boiler room. Queen or not, this many rats had her a bit nervous.

"My kingdom is now yours, madam," she said, giving Twitches a quick curtsey. "And it looks like all of your friends have come to witness your coronation."

Unfortunately for Twitches, her reign would be brief. Very brief. The building suddenly shook violently. The grate fell from its opening. Madison lunged for the Reaper and tossed it out into the alley.

Another explosion shook the floor as Madison tossed her knapsack, filled with everything she owned, out of the window.

Just as her foot hit the milk crate the entire building began to crumble around her.

Out of the cloud of dust that had filled the room, a hand reached through the opening where the grate was. It grabbed her by the arm, and tugged her out into the cold morning air. She felt a warm fluid running down her face as she lost consciousness.

# CHAPTER 5

# WHO Are You?

—————— ❖ ——————

## *This Job Rocks*

Nicholas Moore used the end of his stone tweezers to nudge a few of the smaller rock samples laid out on his desk. He leaned over, using his free hand to lower the jeweler's loop from his customized headband. Nick depressed the plunger on the stone tweezers to produce the four small wire prongs from the opposite end of the instrument.

With dexterity developed through many repetitions, he snatched up one of the more promising specimens and drew it closer to the jewelry loop protruding from the front of his eye until it came into clear focus.

Every color of the rainbow was visible in this semi-transparent white stone. Nick could not help but marvel, again, at its innate beauty. Unfortunately for him, he did not find what he was looking for.

He dropped the stone into the discard box next to his chair marked, "Diego, Do Not Discard." He raised the loop again and rubbed his tired eyes. For the last hour, perspiration had been collecting in a line down the center of his back and under his arms. It was becoming very uncomfortable.

The temperature in December on Isla Holbox, on the Yucatan peninsula, reached the mid-eighties during the day but dropped to just below seventy at night. The complex Nick worked in had air conditioning. In fact, it had been originally built by the World Health Organization for study and containment of Level 4 biohazards - the worst bugs on the planet. Climate control, containment and security were all high on the list of design considerations.

When the WHO pulled out of the building, it was repurposed as a worldwide research facility. Due to its proximity to the Chicxulub crater, it brought climate scientists and geologists from around the globe. "Camp Holbox," they called it, with sandy beaches and abundant wildlife in every direction.

The tourism industry had not yet discovered this part of the world and, as a result, you could often walk one of the many beaches while only seeing a handful of other people. If the laid-back lifestyle wasn't for you, Cancun was just a two-hour ride away.

Nick leaned back in his office chair and stretched his arms to the ceiling. His desk lamp was the only light left on in the room, and it cast long shadows across the twenty or so other desks just like his. *Time to call it a day*, he thought, just as his phone began to ring. He reached for the receiver of the military-grade black office phone on his desk.

"Hello Ami," he said, reading the caller ID on the phone and then using his shoulder to cradle the phone against his head.

"Hey Nick, glad I caught you," she replied. "I tried your cell phone several times with no luck. I don't have much time as I am coordinating the last minute details of my trip down there. I need you to listen very carefully."

A slight twinge ran up Nick's back as she spoke. She sounded very businesslike and none of the usual jovial tone was in her voice.

"Have you found any more anomalies in your latest samples from the crater?" she asked.

"No," he replied. "I have spent the last two days going over almost every rock in the box, in detail, and it is still just the two stones that I initially called you about."

Nick looked back down at his desk, still littered with stones of various sizes and shapes.

"OK, now I need you take those two samples, along with all of the material the dig team brought to you this week, and lock them in your filing cabinet. Do not take them out again until I get there tomorrow," Ami said.

Concerned, Nick asked, "Is there something I need to be worried about?"

"No," Ami Knight replied. "Not at this point. We are not sure what, if anything, it is that you found. I received a call from another geologist working in your facility who apparently found some of the same anomalies you have. However, whereas you found yours in the shocked quartz samples, she found hers in a quarter-sized Tektite stone."

"What I am hearing is the boss telling me to close shop for the night. I am all for that," he said, trying to lighten the mood a bit. "Anything else? Maybe we can have lunch when you get here."

"Unfortunately, my plane doesn't land in Cancun until 11:30 and even with driving above the limit, I will be lucky to make the 2pm ferry to the island. I'll give you a ring when I land," she said and hung up.

Nick didn't even have a chance to say he would be glad to pick her up in the small Boston Whaler he had at his disposal, before the dial tone rang in his ear.

It was only six weeks ago that Nick had met Ami, back on the campus of Pennsylvania State University where he was earning his graduate degree in Earth Sciences. Ami, twenty years his senior, had been asked by her Alma Mater to do a series of lectures on deadly biological agents, their prevention, containment, and potential use for bioterrorism. She had been happy to oblige.

Ami felt it was her personal responsibility to educate as many people as possible on the very real threat posed by these biological agents and their potential use as weapons. It was after one such lecture that she found herself talking to a particularly bright but uninspired graduate student in the campus bookstore.

Ami had told Nick of an opening in the Holbox facility, and of the building's proximity to one of the world's most interesting geological features. Seeing his excitement over the possibility of studying the crater, she said she would be happy to put in a good word on his behalf. A week later, Ami called to let him know that he would begin in a months' time.

It was that set of circumstances that had brought Nick to this point: staring down, puzzled, at the dozen or so shocked quartz and Tektite stones on his desk. He did as she had asked, and carefully boxed up the remaining samples, locking them in the filing cabinet adjacent to his desk. Once locked, he wondered if he should have been wearing gloves just in case. He sighed as he realized he had some bad news to give to his friend Diego.

Nick left the facility through one of the concrete-lined hall-ways, and stepped out into the muggy night air. He walked the short distance to the dock where his boat was moored, fired up the engine, and headed across the lagoon to his small apartment.

## *What's For Lunch?*

The weather the next day was not good. Heavy rain and thunderstorms in the morning gave way to more heavy rain and thunderstorms in the afternoon. Nick waited for a break in the lightning. He jumped into his boat to head across the lagoon to his office. He passed several whale sharks along the way, and was quickly reminded how truly special this place was and how lucky he was to be here.

It was just before noon when he pulled back his office chair and turned on the desk lamp. *Darn*, he thought. He just remembered he was supposed to meet Diego for lunch today. He had almost forgotten, preoccupied by his upcoming meeting with Ami later that afternoon.

Nick got back up from his chair, walked down the center aisle that divided the square room in half, and entered the hallway leading toward the middle of the complex.

The facility itself was circular in shape with the center being the windowless security room. This security room was surrounded by a circular hallway, from which other hallways jutted out perpendicularly. To get from one point in the building to another, you would first go to the center hall and then circle until you found the hallway leading to where you needed to go.

Nick had never seen inside the security room. Each entry door to the room had a card reader that controlled access, and he didn't have a card that allowed him in. *Curiously*, he thought, *he never did see anyone else with a card either.* He would have to ask Diego over lunch if he knew the particulars of that room.

Diego was on the building maintenance staff - surely he would know something. Nick had met Diego on his first day at the facility after he called building maintenance to get the keys to his desk and a desk lamp. Diego was a likable fellow, easy to talk to. He was kind of guy who would tell you his whole life story in one sitting if you let him. In the past two weeks, he had come to know more about Diego's life than he did his own sister who lived just a few hours from him, back home in Pennsylvania.

Nick reached the central, circular hallway, walked a quarter of the way around, and took a right down the next hallway leading to the cafeteria. He entered the cafeteria and scanned the room, looking for Diego. He found him sitting alone in a folding chair at one of the long narrow dining tables. His friend had already picked out his lunch and was eating. Nick grabbed an apple from the fruit basket, paid the lady running the register, and sat down opposite Diego.

"Sorry I'm late, the weather today was not very cooperative," Nick said as he took a bite of his apple.

"No worries," said Diego, just loud enough to be heard over the din of other lunch conversation going on around them. "I just got in myself. I missed a mandatory meeting this morning and I'm not looking forward to seeing the boss today. I thought it best to face that music on a full stomach." he chuckled as he patted his belly.

"Unfortunately, I have some more bad news for you," Nick responded. "I can't get you any more stones from my lab. Evidently there are some issues with this latest batch and there are some fairly big hitters coming in today to take them away."

"Not a problem, my friend," Diego replied. "My sister is no longer in the jewelry-making business. She now thinks her road to riches runs through eBay. She has been selling everything in sight, often for less than she paid for it. That girl has no business sense whatsoever."

Last week, Diego had described his sister to Nick over a lunch much like this. Her goal in life was to get rich and to travel the world. The problem, however, was always the get rich part. She jumped from one idea to the next, never really giving any of them a chance to succeed. It was just last week that Nick had begun to give his friend the stones that were of no use to him in his research. Diego, in turn, would give them to his sister to make into various pieces of jewelry and sell to tourists in Cancun.

"She actually boxed up every stone she had and sold it to a lady from the US. She sold the entire lot for fifty dollars. Had she made them into necklaces, she could have earned ten times that amount in Cancun," Diego said, shaking his head in frustration.

As Diego spoke, a shapely brunette in her late twenties approached their table and said, "Excuse me, is your name Diego?"

"Yes," Diego replied.

"Diego from building maintenance?" she continued.

"Yes," Diego replied. "What can I do for you?"

From the look on Diego's face, Nick could not help but think he meant "to you."

"Well, I just got in today and it seems the door to the research lab where I work is shut - and I don't have an access key. We were never given keys, but it hasn't been an issue before as the doors were always open."

"Well, that is strange," Diego said. "Let me see what I can do about that. Nick, we'll talk later?" he said, turning to Nick and raising his eyebrows several times in a row.

Nick chuckled, "Absolutely, enjoy the rest of your day."

As he watched Diego leave the cafeteria with the brunette in tow, he was shocked to see Ami appear through the door with two heavily armed gentlemen. Though not in uniform, the way they carried themselves made it quite obvious they were highly trained military professionals. Nick rose from his chair as Ami scanned the room. She made eye contact with him and quickly, along with her escorts, crossed the large room to his position.

"We need to get your samples right now," she said.

If Nick wasn't uneasy already about their appointment today, he certainly was now.

"Sure," he said. "Absolutely. They are locked in the filing cabinet next to my desk. Is something the matter?"

"Yes," Ami replied. "Let's walk while we talk." Ami continued as they walked through the cafeteria, heading back towards his desk. "Remember I told you about the other researcher who found anomalies similar to yours in her rock samples?" Not waiting for an answer she pressed on. "Diane is her name. Well, it appears Diane has contracted an unknown illness that has caused her to become quite violent and unpredictable. We don't want to raise any unnecessary alarms at this point, so that is all I am willing to say about it for now. We do, however, need your samples so we can attempt to determine exactly what might be causing her illness."

"Is she still in the building?" Nick asked. "Are we safe here?"

"Yes, she and her team are currently quarantined in their research lab. And these gentlemen are here to ensure our safety," she said, gesturing to the two men beside them.

Just as they reached the central hallway, they heard a female scream coming from down the hallway in the opposite direction where Nick's office was. It was quickly followed by several grunts of a male voice, sounding as if it was under great duress. *Diego*, Nick thought. Nick began putting the pieces together very quickly. The door that was shut must have been the research lab that Diane, and the brunette, worked in. Unfortunately for Diego, he had apparently been successful in getting the door open.

Events unfolded quickly after that. Before Nick could explain the situation to Ami, three fast-moving human figures came into view around the circular hallway. They fell upon Nick and Ami's group in fractions of a second, moving at an unnatural speed.

Two of the forms tackled the military man to the right of Nick. The other one attacked the man next to Ami. The creatures slashed at the men before they had any time to un-holster their sidearms and defend themselves.

The screams and commotion had brought more people out of the cafeteria. The assailants lunged quickly and violently at their new prey. Nick was frozen in place, unable to make sense of what was going on around him. Ami, on the other hand, quickly lifted her access card from the end of the lanyard at her waist and swiped it against the card reader of the door leading to the security room. As she opened the door, she grabbed Nick by his shirt collar and pulled him in with her.

The door closed with a sharp metal clank. Inside, the room was dark and quiet. No noise of the massacre that was happening outside made its way into this room.

## *A Really Bad Day.*

"I think that was Diane," Ami said, clicking the wall switch that activated the overhead lights.

They were both shaken, although Ami was much more composed than Nick. The room contained many wall-hung monitors, which gave the appearance of windows in the otherwise windowless room. A waist-high bank of switches, keyboards and smaller electronic gadgets was situated in a circular formation in the center of the room.

A small break in the circle allowed Ami and Nick access to the two chairs within the inner open area. This was clearly the brains of the building. Ami began to toggle switches and push buttons in an attempt to bring the security monitors online and broadcast a warning to the surviving researchers in the building to lock themselves in their respective labs until further notice.

While Ami struggled with her task, Nick was still trying to grasp what he had just witnessed. Was he going to turn into what Diane had become? He had handled the same rocks and discovered the same anomalies.

"Give it to me straight, Ami. Am I going to turn into one of those? Diane and I handled rocks with the same anomalies."

"At this point, we don't know what caused that to happen to Diane, but I intend to find out. However, I don't think just handling the rocks would cause that. If it did, you would have shown signs by now," Ami replied.

What Nick did not know - what nobody could have known - was that Diane was not a geologist by chance.

Diane Skelly suffered from a poorly-understood condition known as Pica, a rare disorder that caused a person to have an appetite for substances that are non-nutritious. In Diane's case, her substance of choice was small stones.

For Diane, the affliction had begun a young age. It began with picking up small bits of gravel from the back yard and putting them in her mouth. Initially she spit them back out, but it was not long before she began swallowing them.

Diane became fascinated with rocks of different colors, wondering if each tasted different. This curiosity and fascination naturally progressed into her academic pursuits, eventually resulting in her degree in earth sciences. Although her habit was not as prevalent as when she was a small child, she never fully outgrew it. Yesterday, the urge to put one of these small, anomalous stones into her mouth had become unbearable. It ended up being her last meal.

Ami methodically worked her way through the controls and, finally, one by one the monitors in the room sprang to life. The images they displayed were much worse than what Ami and Nick had experienced moments before.

In fully half of the labs throughout the building, infected humans were tearing at their uninfected counterparts. In one room, a rather large man had just been pulled down from behind and his arm was bitten into. The attacker leapt from that gentleman to rip the throat from an older lady who was running ahead of them in the hallway.

As the attacker ran off camera, the heavy man started twitching, lumps forming and disappearing under his skin. Then, in one quick motion, he was back on his feet, racing down the hallway with a speed and agility eerily unnatural for a man of his size. One by one the two watched as the infected spilled into previously unaffected labs.

Ami knew she had to get a distress call out to her fellow WHO employees. Her vast experience with infectious disease told her that this outbreak was special. It was unlike any she had seen before in the speed and violence with which it spread from one host to another. For the first time in her career, Ami felt she was seeing a disease that, if unleashed on the general population, would mean no less than the total annihilation of humankind.

Ami tried in vain to log in to the terminals that lay before her. Since the facility had been repurposed, it was no longer attached to the central computers at the World Health Organization. As a result, her login account was not working.

Attempting to access email was of no use. Although internet access was available elsewhere in the building to facilitate the research, it had not been wired into this room. And since the room contained the critical building command and control, general internet access was firewalled and prohibited. General internet access would have exposed the facility to hackers, malware, computer viruses and other malicious electronic threats.

Cellular phones were useless in here. Her only hope was to use the landline and try to contact her counterparts. Unfortunately, lifting the handset on the phone produced no dial tone. The lines had most likely been rerouted to one of the many labs in the building. With no way to leave and no way to contact help, it was clear the two were stranded in the room.

Ami realized her next task had to be sealing the building. It would give her some time to work out the details of a plan. Luckily for her, the security measures, and the various mechanisms to activate them, were identical in all WHO facilities. As the director, she was fully-trained in all of them.

Ami found the emergency terminal and began the lockdown procedure. Once activated, outer doors throughout the circular complex began shutting and locking. Monitors at each exterior door confirmed that the building was entering lockdown mode. *And not a moment too soon*, Nick thought, as more than one hallway that led to the exterior doors were filling with these hostile, rampaging beasts. The monitors had so far confirmed that no one had left the building.

A red light began to blink above a monitor labeled 'west entrance.' The west entrance led to the facility's designated smoking area. To their horror, Ami and Nick both saw the reason for the alarm. The door had been propped open with a small red brick. An infected individual had already spilled into the adjacent hallway and was heading quickly toward the door. Ami looked at Nick and her heart sank. Only one option now. She knew there was no way she could let this infection out of the building.

Ami prayed for two things in the split second it took her to key in the activation code for the building's emergency destruct mechanism. The first was that the mechanism had not been disabled. The second was that her friend Nick had led a fulfilling life, and that if she had the time to explain their predicament, he would have agreed with her decision.

The resulting shock wave was felt as far away as Cancun.

# CHAPTER 6

# South For The Winter.

— ❖ —

## *Melody*

Madison awoke with a gasp. The room was dazzlingly bright around her. A tube ran from her arm into a bag hanging just above her head, and wires sprung from her chest to destinations unknown. She heard an alarm beeping slightly behind her and to her left. Panic set in when she realized she was in an unfamiliar place and the Reaper was nowhere to be seen. She ripped at the wires, causing more alarms to sound.

"Easy darling," Tiana, the nurse on duty, urged as she hurried into the room and reached out for Madison's hands. "Calm down. Everything is OK. You need to calm down and not pull at the wires."

Madison, still in full panic-mode, asked, "Where is my guitar? Where is my stuff?"

"It's all here, in the closet. All your stuff is here. You need to calm down," Tiana urged her young patient.

Madison stopped struggling and laid back in the bed.

"There you go. Do you know where you are right now?" Tiana asked.

Madison shook her head no. Wow, did she have a headache.

"You are in Mass General Hospital. You've had quite a day. People around here are calling you the miracle child. Fifty-two stories of brick and mortar fell thirty feet from you and the worst injury you have is a bump on the head and a mild concussion."

"Did a bomb go off?" she asked. *Like the one going off in my head right now,* she thought to herself.

"All your questions will be answered in just a few minutes. There are some folks here who want to talk to you. Are you up for that?" Tiana asked.

Madison shook her head no. This was bad.

Tiana motioned for the two officers at the door to enter.

"These men really need to speak with you and time is of the essence. I'm going to run to the cafeteria and bring you back some ice cream. You like chocolate?" Tiana asked.

Madison nodded slightly, still reeling as she realized her current situation. How had she managed to get out of the building before she was crushed? More importantly, how was she going to be able to answer the police's questions without landing herself back in foster care. There was no way she could let that happen.

"I'm Officer Rowe and this is Officer Phil Senior," Joe said as he sat on the side of Madison's bed. "I know you have had quite a day, but I really need to ask you a few questions. It is important that you are truthful with me as more lives may be at stake. Do you know if anyone was actually in the building?"

Madison shook her head no.

"I'm asking because we have search and rescue personnel combing the rubble looking for your parents or anyone else that may have been with you," Joe continued.

"I was alone. No one was with me. But there must have been other people in the building. It was over fifty stories tall," she replied.

Phil keyed the mic attached at the shoulder of his uniform. "Unit 23 to Dispatch. Be advised the unknown female indicates she was alone in the building. Over."

A voice returned with, "Unit 23 acknowledged. Over."

Joe tried to reassure the girl. "There was nobody else in the building. It had been evacuated three days ago in preparation for the demolition. What was so important in there that you needed to disregard all those warnings?"

It all became very clear, very fast: the yellow tape, the furnace, and the electricity being turned off. They had been preparing the building to be demolished. And she slept right underneath it while it was all happening. Her mind turned to Twitches and her new family. In her great big world of what the heck else could happen, this was all just a bit much. Her emotions began to well up inside her but she pushed them back down, as she had so many times in her life.

"Crying over death is wasted energy," her Nana Jean had told her many years ago. "The deceased aren't around to see it, and, even if they were, they already knew you cared enough about them and wouldn't need your blubbering as a reminder. Tears are weakness, my girl. They tell the world that you are sorry about something. Either something you did, or something you wish didn't happen that you had no control over to begin with. Well, if it was in your control, show you're sorry by being better and not making the same mistake again. And if it wasn't, then your time would be better spent helping the needy through their troubles and not drowning them with your tears. Find a more productive way to let that energy out. Write a song, bake a pie, anything. Nope... nothing ever got accomplished by crying."

Joe could see the girl's demeanor had changed and tried to comfort her. "It's going to be OK, I promise. No one got hurt and you're going to be just fine. By the way, I haven't even asked, what is the name of the luckiest girl I've ever had the privilege of meeting?"

Madison paused, probably too long to be believable, she thought, but managed to sputter, "Melody, Melody Church."

Her voice was an octave higher than it had been previously. Another dead giveaway. Wow, she was a bad liar. In that brief instant, Jeremiah was the only person she could think of. He may not have been her actual father, but it was as close as she had come to one in her young life.

"I'm sixteen and it's just me and my dad, Jeremiah. You can find him playing harmonica outside Faneuil Hall," Madison continued. "We lost our apartment a few weeks ago and have been staying at the Pine Street Inn shelter on Harrison." She did not actually know where Jeremiah stayed, so she made up what she hoped was a believable lie. She also hoped that Jeremiah would go along with her story when they did find him.

"I know him," Phil jumped in. "I've listened to him many times since he moved to town back in July. We normally keep the street performers out of the courtyard but him - we let him play as long as he wants. He's always well-dressed, doesn't harass anyone and plays a mean blues harmonica. I didn't know he had a daughter. Adopted, I assume."

"Yes adopted, obviously," Madison said, sounding a bit snider than she had intended. She couldn't help it. She was scared and was trying desperately to think on the fly. She found it strange that Jeremiah had told her he'd lived in Boston for the last fifteen years, having left his home state of Alabama in search of top-notch medical care that promised to regain his eyesight. He certainly would not have started playing the courtyard just five months ago.

"Officer Senior and I are going to go look for your father and bring him back here to you. Your job is to sit here, rest, and not worry about anything for the next couple of days," Joe said, getting up from the bed. "I believe this fine lady has some ice cream waiting, if I am not mistaken." He motioned to Tiana as she stepped back into the room.

"Take care, young lady," Phil said as he and his partner left the room.

"Well, Ms. Melody, here is a little treat for you," Tiana said, handing the young girl a small bowl of ice cream. "I will be around with something more substantial for dinner in a few hours. There is a remote for the TV beside your bed, if you want it." Tiana could not help but notice the girl was not relaxing at all.

"Would you mind opening that door so I can see my things?" Madison asked.

"Of course, dear," Tiana replied. She leaned over and opened the tall thin closet door.

There was the Reaper, leaning up against the back wall. Ragged and worn square, white stickers were clearly visible on the guitar case. Each sticker contained a bold black letter, the kind you would find on a mailbox post identifying a house address. The letters spelled out "The Reaper." Tiana did a double-take at the guitar case and turned to Madison.

"Looks like luck may not have played as big a part in this as everyone seems to think." she said.

"No, the Reaper didn't save me," Madison replied. "At least not this morning anyway. Someone reached into the building and pulled me out. Didn't they tell you?"

"Are you saying there was someone else there? Did you lie to the police earlier?" Tiana asked the young girl, already reaching for her cell phone.

"No, no, they were not with me. I didn't know they were there until their hand reached in and grabbed me. Surely someone saw us in the alley after the building came down?" Madison replied.

"But you were not in the alley when they found you. You were out on the sidewalk. You and all of your things. You didn't run out the front of the building when it came down?"

"No, you are not listening. I lived in the boiler room under the building. The only way I had in and out was through the alley," Madison replied.

*Darn again*, she thought. She'd basically just admitted to being homeless and living on the street. *Really not good.*

*The bump on the girl's head may be worse than we initially diagnosed,* Tiana thought to herself.

"Melody, we are going to have the doctor come back and take a look at what fine progress you are making. I really want you to get some rest now," the nurse said, heading for the door.

Tiana had seen the news that morning. She knew the alley was completely covered in fifteen feet of debris. If this young lady had been in the alley, she wouldn't have made it out alive.

Madison lay in her bed, wondering whether she had imagined the hand reaching in to save her. There was a lot going on at that moment and she did get hit in the head with a brick, probably more than one. But even if she imagined the hand, she knew there was no way she had made it to the sidewalk with all of her things before that building landed on her. She looked toward the closet and wondered, however briefly, if her guitar actually had something to do with it after all. She chuckled to herself. *Yup, that brick definitely knocked something loose.*

## Juan, My Friend.

On the walk back to their patrol car, Phil and Joe shared their suspicions that the young girl was lying. Not about being alone in the building. On that one they had no doubt she was telling the truth. But there was no way Jeremiah Church was her dad. He was, at best, homeless and had no obvious way to take care of a young girl. They were still going to go find him to see if he had any idea of who the girl's guardian really was. She would be safe in the hospital for a couple of days, but they were going to need to do something with her when she was released. How would the police department look if they sent an underage runaway back out onto the streets - especially one whose rescue and subsequent trip to the hospital had been all over the morning news?

Officers Senior and Rowe searched the marketplace. They checked all of the obvious spots a street musician might be playing, but had no luck locating the elderly musician. They returned to the station and were immediately met by their boss, Sergeant

Dunbar.

Sergeant Dunbar had been in charge of the police detail that was supposed to have secured the fifty-two story monster of a building that almost crushed a young girl. On this day, he was not a happy man. He had spent his morning coordinating the search and rescue operations at the site. What little time he had left over was spent answering questions at various press conferences.

"Gentleman," he barked as the two officers attempted to pass by his office door unnoticed. He motioned for them to enter. "Shut the door behind you," he continued. They filed into his office and stood in front of his desk.

"Let me ask you a question that I have been answering all morning. How does a police force with some of the best and brightest officers in the nation let a fifty-two story building nearly crush an unsuspecting sixteen-year-old girl? Don't answer. It's a rhetorical question. But rest assured, I will find that answer - and when I do, there will be repercussions. And they will be severe. Dismissed," he said, without looking up.

Joe looked at Phil on the way back to their desk. "Who had the alley detail this morning?" he asked.

Before Phil could answer, the officer who sat at the desk closest to them shouted out, "Hey Joe, a guy has been calling the precinct all morning. He says he used to work in that building that came down. He was asking if the young girl made it out alright. I left his number on your desk."

Joe had reached his desk and picked up the paper with the number on it.

"01152. What kind of area code is that?" he asked his partner.

"I think this guy is calling from somewhere in Mexico," Phil responded. Joe began punching in the numbers.

"Hola," a male voice answered.

"Hello. I am Officer Joe Rowe of the Boston, Massachusetts police department in the US. We've been receiving calls from this number in regards to a missing girl?"

"Si, si. I mean, yes. My name is Juan. I used to work in that building a couple of months ago. There was a young girl living in one of the boiler rooms on the ground floor. A very nice young lady. She couldn't have been more than twenty-years-old. The news showed the building being imploded this morning - I need to know that this young lady is accounted for."

"Can you describe this woman?" Joe asked.

"About five foot eight or so. Long blonde hair, blue eyes," Juan responded.

"Yes, and could you tell us her name? We could check it against our list."

Phil looked at him as if to say, "What list?"

"Maddie," the man said. "I believe her last name was Jakes, or something like that."

"Well, Juan, we don't have anyone by that name as a resident, but there was a young lady brought to the hospital this morning who fit that description."

"Wait, wait," the man on the other end of the phone said. He had obviously stopped listening. On the other end of the line, they could hear someone turning up a television in the background. Juan's voice came back on the line. "There! They're showing it again now on the TV. Wow, they really brought that sucker down. Yes, the girl going into the ambulance. That's her. Maddie. Is she OK?"

Phil and Joe looked at each other without speaking. Phil sat at his computer and began punching on his keyboard.

"Yes, Juan. The girl is fine. Just a bump on the head. I appreciate you calling to check up on her. I'll personally let her know you were asking about her."

"OK, glad to hear it. Adios."

Joe hung up the phone and swung around the desk. He looked over Phil's shoulder as the man searched the child services database. After trying several variations of the name, the screen spit back several pages of information - on a Madison Jaques.

"Wow, this girl has been in the system since she was four." Joe skimmed through the reports, no longer thinking Madison was the luckiest girl in the world.

*2003-2004 - Jaques residence Plymouth MA. 4 other foster children in house. Placed back into the system due to unfit conditions of the household.*

*2004-2010 - Rosario residence. Alias "Madison Rosario," Deena Rosario and Lorraine Waldo. 4 other foster children in the house. Mary 4, Melody 6, Nora 9 and Betty 11.*

*2010-2012 - Devonshire residence, Saugus, MA. Alias "Mary Devonshire." Foster Care. 4 other foster children in the house. Timothy 11, Tomas 14, Trevor 17 and Mona 9. Reported missing in April of that year.*

"Looks like she ran away just before her fourteenth birthday. That is really young to be on the streets," Phil said.

"Dollars to donuts the seventeen-year-old, Trevor, knows why she ran," Joe spat out in disgust. "But it only goes back to 2003. That would put her at five years old. What about before then? Shouldn't we be able to see the birth parents, or at least the adoption notice?"

Phil responded, "Yea. Usually. Odd that the first foster care home listed has the same last name as Madison. That is a pretty big coincidence."

"Yeah - too big," Joe replied. "Let's try some long shots. Assuming she didn't lie about her age, she would have been five or so when she lived at the Jaques' residence. Let's run a search with the following parameters: Female, residences within one hundred miles of Plymouth, MA; entering the system sometime between 1997 and 2003 and with the last entry in 2003."

Phil clicked several links and buttons on his screen until he found the correct combination of search criteria. He was not yet familiar with the new searchable database his department had recently deployed.

Just a year prior, the city was given access to the US Department of Health and Human Service's new searchable database of foster care and adoption information. All state and federal agencies that dealt with the health and wellbeing of children were tasked with entering their records online. The initiative started a decade ago, but due to budget pressures, many cities and towns were years late in processing the huge volumes of data. It was only through the federal pressure of losing future funding that this backlog had finally been resolved.

Within seconds the screen showed a handful of results. A quick inspection of the data left the officers with only one possible match: Madison Wolfe.

*1998 - Born May 21st in Wilton, NH to Willow and Levi Wolfe. Father reported missing in 2000. Mother deceased, 2002. Cause of death: brain tumor. There were no known relatives on either side.*

*2002-2003 - Dorman residence. Bill and Terrie. Nashua NH. No other children. Foster parents died in a car accident.*

"Well, well, well. Look at the last date for a Madison Wolfe and the first entry for Madison Jaques," Joe said. "They line up. Looks like whoever entered Maddie's information for her stay with the Jaques accidentally started a new file on her under the last name of her foster care family, instead of adding this to her existing file as Madison Wolfe."

"Not so fast there, chief," Phil interrupted. "Part of adding this data included scanning the original documents. The paper-work that was filed still lists her as Madison Jaques. It wasn't a data entry issue. The original paperwork was filled out incorrect-ly. Her records were added seven years ago, but the Wolfe records were only entered this month."

"Must have been going through the filing cabinets alphabet-ically," Joe suggested.

No sooner had the words come out of Joe's mouth, then the realization of what this could mean suddenly hit him like a freight train. "Phil, take a quick look through missing persons for a Madison Wolfe."

Phil saw where his partner was going and was already keying in the new search. His screen brought up one record.

"Unbelievable," Joe gasped. "Someone has been looking for this girl for more than eleven years. It seems Madison had an aunt - a sister on her mother's side who lives in Charleston, South Carolina. Not only that, looks like Madison has a twin brother, too."

Joe and Phil printed the results and headed straight to Ser-geant Dunbar's office.

"Come in," the sergeant said as they banged on his door.

The officers entered their sergeant's office, but found that he was not alone. A tall, white-haired gentleman sat in one of the chairs across from the sergeant's desk.

"Officers Senior and Rowe, I would like you to meet Wilfred

Ashley. He works for the Department of Health and Human Services. The chief has instructed me to provide him with whatever assistance he deems necessary. It seems the federal government has taken an interest in Ms. Church and sent Mr. Ashley here to take temporary custody of her and to liaison with the local child protective services on her behalf. Luckily, he was only a few hours away on Cape Cod when all of this went down."

The gentleman rose from his chair and greeted the officers.

"Well, sir" Joe said as Mr. Ashley returned to his seat, "we have some new information that you need to hear." He proceeded to explain the history of Madison Wolfe to his sergeant and Mr. Ashley. When he was done, the room fell quiet.

Mr. Ashley was the first to speak. "Nice work fellas. You have made my job a lot easier. Sergeant Dunbar, I will coordinate with the local child protective services agencies and personally escort Ms. Wolfe down to Charleston. Charleston happens to be my home town, and as my vacation was ending tomorrow anyway, I have travel plans to return there in the morning. We should be able to wrap up the paperwork in time for Ms. Wolfe to join me then."

"Excellent." Sergeant Dunbar replied, happy to be relieved of the additional responsibility and headache's that Madison represented.

"I would like officers Rowe and Senior to join me tomorrow morning when I explain all of this to Madison. They have already met the young lady and it may make it easier on her if they went with me." Mr. Ashley said to the sergeant.

"Done." The sergeant replied. He glanced at Phil and Joe, adding, "you will both report to my office at 0900 hours tomorrow morning to accompany Mr. Ashley to Mass General. Is that all?" he said, swinging his gaze back to Mr. Ashley.

"Not quite." the southern gentleman responded, now addressing them all in a low, serious voice. "I feel it necessary to remind you all that Madison is a minor and has undergone and incredible amount of stress already today. I would hope that you will all respect that and keep the details of her situation confidential. The last thing she needs is more media attention."

"You heard the man." Sergeant Dunbar said to Joe and Phil. "This information does not leave this room. Understood?" Both officers nodded and replied "Yes sir."

"That is all, then. Excellent police work gentleman. Dismissed." the sergeant said to the two officers.

"Let's get this girl home," Mr. Ashley said, turning to follow the officers out of Sergeant Dunbar's office.

## *Like A Ton Of Bricks*

Madison woke to Tiana sliding back curtains that covered the window to the right of her bed.

"Good morning," she said to the girl. "How are we feeling?"

"Much better. I think I can go back to my dad now. He must be worried."

The truth was, she *was* a bit worried. She knew the police had gone out looking for him, but he hadn't shown up the previous day. She feared the man was in trouble.

"We'll have to let the doctor make that decision. My orders are to remove this IV from your arm and those leads from your chest. That should make you a bit more comfortable," Tiana said. She went about removing the IV line being used to keep the girl hydrated, and then turned her attention to peeling off the stickers that held the heart monitor leads in place on the girl's chest.

"I need to use the restroom," Madison said as Tiana finished removing the last wire.

"OK, it's right over there. Take your time - you might still be a bit woozy."

Madison swung her legs over the bed and stood up. The room spun slightly before she steadied herself. *There goes Plan A to escape*, Madison thought. If she had this much trouble getting to the bathroom, she wouldn't make it very far outside. On her way to the bathroom, Madison opened the closet door, taking another peek at her friend. Still there. She closed the door and shuffled toward the bathroom.

"There's a bath tub and a shower in there. If you feel up to it, you can take a bath - but no showering, young lady. We don't want you to fall and hit your head again! Everything you need is in there, including some hospital pajamas. You can get out of that Johnny. I'll come back in ten minutes to check on you."

It wasn't until Tiana said "Johnny" that Madison realized her backside was exposed in her current garment. She reached around and pulled the two sides of the garment closer together. "Thank you," Madison replied. She closed the bathroom door behind her.

Madison looked around the small bathroom. Everything she could need was, indeed, right there. She felt like royalty - royalty with some seriously bad morning breath. She opened the hot water valve to the tub and began filling it, then went about the task of brushing her teeth. The tub was filled by the time she finished rinsing the toothpaste from her mouth. She turned to the bath and thought, *when was the last time I had one of these?* She removed the hospital gown and lowered herself in. Heaven.

Ten minutes had passed when she heard a knock on the door.

"Everything OK in there?" It was Tiana, coming back to check on her.

"Everything is beyond OK. I could stay in here all day!" Madison called out.

"Well, young lady, I understand where you are coming from, but you have some visitors coming in half an hour. You can have another fifteen minutes, but I need you back in bed before they get here. Deal?" Tiana asked.

"Deal," Madison said and went back to enjoying her soak.

If the bath had not been so relaxing, she would have been more concerned about the word visitors. For now, nothing was going to ruin this bath.

Twenty minutes later, Madison was back in her hospital bed, TV remote in hand. It had been months since she last watched television. She began eagerly clicking through the channels.

"Lose twenty pounds in a week," the infomercial announcer promised in an energetic voice. Click. The last thing she needed was to lose any weight.

"You are the father," a grey-haired man was saying to a skinny man with three teeth sitting in a row of chairs on a stage. Two rather large women jumped up from their chairs and started yelling at him, "Told you. I told you. You're worthless." This continued for thirty seconds. Madison clicked the channel again.

"An explosion rocked Mexico's Yucatan peninsula this morning. There is no official word on the cause of the explosion, that decimated a small research facility studying geography and climate change. It is feared that the lives of more than four hundred researches have been lost." *Those poor people*, she thought, just as Tiana reentered the room. Madison turned off the television.

"Well, I see you kept your part of the bargain. Looking fresh as a daisy," Tiana greeted her. "Officers Joe and Phil are back to see you," she continued as the officers entered the room. Behind them was a well-dressed man in his sixties. She was hoping Jeremiah would be with them, but he was not.

"Someone looks like they got their beauty sleep last night. How are you feeling, Madison?" Joe asked.

"Much better, thank you. Did you find my dad?"

She suddenly realized her mistake. She did not correct the officer when he used her real name. Stupid! All that soaking in the tub must have turned her brain to mush.

"That's what I thought. Do you remember Juan, the building maintenance worker that you met in the boiler room? He called, wanting to know that you were OK. He gave us your name. It's Madison, Madison Wolfe, isn't it?"

Madison was now really confused.

"No, it's Madison Jaques," she replied, figuring it made no sense to continue to try to lie to the man.

The two officers looked at each other, each realizing the young girl was no longer pretending to be someone else. It was Mr. Ashley that now addressed Madison.

"Madison, my name is Wilfred. I have been granted temporary custody of you until we can get things sorted out. I work for the federal government, and my only job here is to ensure your safety and well-being. I know you have been through a great deal over the past day, and month, and years, for that matter. What I need to tell you will come as a bit of a shock. Your real name is Wolfe, not Jaques. Jaques was the name of your foster care providers when you were four. There has been a missing person's alert out for you for some years now. The DNA provided with that search matches yours. Of this, there is no doubt."

She lay there, taking all of this information in. "DNA sample? From whom? Are my parents still alive?" she asked.

Wilfred responded. "No, I'm sorry to have to tell you that they aren't. But your mother had sister named Marion who is - and she has been looking for you since you were five. And there is more. You have a twin brother. Connor. He is the one we compared DNA samples with. Nurse Tiana got your DNA from a strand of hair you left on your brush yesterday."

*A brother?* she thought. *I have a brother? I have an aunt? People are out there that may look like me and talk like me?* Madison was excited, but only for a moment. Now deep in thought, she wondered, *if these people wanted me so bad, why did it take eleven years for them to find me? I've been in foster care for most of my life. They have records. How hard could I be to find if someone were really trying to find me?*

Once again, Wilfred broke the silence. "I can only imagine the confusion you must feel right now. This must all be tremendously difficult to take in. I think it best if we leave you in nurse Tiana's care for now and give you some time to chew on things."

Madison looked at the man inquisitively. Her Nana Jean was the only other one she had ever heard use that expression to indicate "think things over."

"I'll be back later today and will be available to answer all of your questions. In the meantime, I'll need to take care of the details related to our upcoming travel."

He placed a bag containing new clothes on the bed next to Madison, put the Trilby hat he had been holding in his hand back on his head, and turned to exit the room.

"Wait," Madison said as they all reached the doorway. "Travel?" she asked.

"Why yes, my dear," he replied. "Your brother and aunt live in South Carolina, just outside the city of Charleston. If you have never been, you are going to very much enjoy it. It is a beautiful, peaceful city. I've lived there my whole life."

With that, they were gone down the hallway.

"Madison," Tiana began gently, "if you need or want to talk to someone, we have people here who can help you sort this out. I'm going to send someone by in a bit to chat with you."

"I don't think I need that," Madison replied. "I just need some time to make sense of all of this. If I could just have an hour or so, I'm sure I'll be OK."

"OK. I'll be back around in an hour to check on you." Tiana said, leaving the room.

## *Those In Need*

Madison lay in bed for almost an hour chewing the new information she had been given. She really wanted to believe there was a family out there who wanted her and had been looking for her all these years. But what of it? She was an adult now. She could take care of herself. She didn't need anyone telling her how to live her life. She was doing just fine. And a brother? The last young boy in her life tried to take advantage of her in the middle of the night. *Nope - I don't need any of that.*

But what if it was awesome? People to care for, who cared back. They could be like Jeremiah. The very thought brought a light feeling inside. *I just don't know. What I do know is that the Reaper must be hungry.*

Madison got out of bed and opened the door to the small closet. She pulled the Reaper out, opened the case, and slung the well-worn strap over her head. She sat back down on the side of her bed, and began playing "Prelude from Bach´s Cello Suite No. 1." It wasn't a conscious choice of music – it was just the first song that came into her head. Sound filled the room and spilled into the hallway, catching the attention of everyone on the ward. Soon, heads were poking inside her doorway. The brave ones came in to stand by Madison's bed. But as usual, she was too deep in her own world to even notice. Tiana was one of those who had gathered in the hallway, which was now getting crowded with enthusiastic onlookers.

"Wow, you are really good on that thing," Tiana said to Madison as she entered the room. "Unfortunately, I can't have you pulling all these nice folks out of their beds. Everyone, back to your rooms," she said to those who had gathered. "Mr. Wilson, your Johnny is open all the way up your backside. Go on now.

Back to your rooms."

"Sorry," Madison said, with her head turned slightly down toward the floor. "I forgot where I was for a minute."

"Don't be sorry, young lady. In fact, I'd like to ask a favor of you. Would you mind taking the Reaper down to pediatrics? I'm sure there would be some grateful young faces that would like to have music played for them."

"Sure," Madison smiled. The brief moment she had played was not nearly enough. *Besides*, she thought, *I can look at all the cute newborns.* She had once seen a movie that showed the couple of a newborn gazing through a large, glass window at row upon row of babies in clear-sided beds. She had always wanted to see that for herself.

Nurse Tiana led Madison, still in her hospital pajamas, down to the pediatric ward. They walked into a large open room with many beds lining the walls. There was a child in every bed. Their ages varying widely. The oldest appeared to be a girl not much younger than herself. She learned the girl was undergoing radiation therapy for some form of cancer.

"This young lady is named Madison. She brought her guitar with her today and has graciously volunteered to play some songs for all of you," Tiana said, introducing Madison to the group.

"Hi," Madison said, looking around at all the eager faces.

She walked over to the girl not much younger than herself and sat on the end of her bed. Madison took the Reaper out of its case and began to play. When she was done, she had played for almost half an hour. Her young audience was all smiles, and when the final note hung in the air they began clapping at the same time. Those who could walked up to her. There were many hugs - both given and received.

As she looked around the room at the kids who could not get out of bed, Madison saw one small boy, about eight or nine, with his parents by his side. He was very sickly-looking. Madison's heart sank. She got up from the bed and walked over toward them.

"What's your name?" she asked the child, as she made eye contact with each of his parents.

"Bobby," he said, his voice soft as though he had a cold.

His face was all smiles and she could see that inside that sick little boy was a kid who just wanted out of that bed and back onto a ball field somewhere. His parent's faces told a different story. They were tired, sad, frightened. The hope seemed to have drained from their smiles. They were wearing them for his sake.

Madison sat on the edge of the bed next to him and said, "Do you mind if I play one more song for you?"

He nodded in agreement while his parents smiled at her, as if to thank her before she even had a chance to play. She played "Three Little Birds" by Bob Marley. By mid-song, the entire room was joining her in the chorus. "Don't worry about a thing. 'Cause every little thing, is gonna be alright!" When she was done, Bobbie's mom was in tears, her head buried in her husband's shoulder.

"That was really cool," Bobby said, "but you made my mom sad."

"No, Bobby, she didn't," his mom replied, looking at her son with unconditional love. "She made me very happy. Just like you do, my beautiful boy."

The woman leaned over and kissed her son on the forehead. Madison got up from the bed and waved bye to the little boy. She looked into the tear-streaked face of his mother in a way that conveyed her sympathies. In Bobby's dad's face she found unimaginable sadness, indomitable strength, but no tears. *A kindred spirit*, she thought. She took the Reaper off over her head, walked back over to where she had set the guitar case down and placed it back in. *Time for a plan*, she thought, as she and Tiana made their way back to her room.

Tiana thanked her several times on the walk back. "How did you ever learn to play the guitar so well?" she asked.

"I have my Nana Jean to thank for teaching me to read music. And pretty much everyone who works at Guitar Center for giving me all of the clearance sheet music after no one else wanted it. Lots of classical stuff. I just retain music in my head. Once I play a song, it kind of sticks up there. I could kick myself for ever learning the "Barney the Purple Dinosaur" song."

Tiana laughed. "*I love you, you love me...* Yup, that would be a killer."

They reached Madison's room and Tiana let her enter alone.

"I have some rounds I have to catch up on. You going to be OK?" the nurse asked.

"I'll be great," Madison replied, thinking that this may be her chance.

Madison put the Reaper on her bed and opened the small closet again. She pulled out her knapsack and was about to rummage through it for a change of clothes when the bag of clothing Wilfred had given her fell out at her feet. She had forgotten about until just now. A pair of jeans and a belt had spilled out and lay sprawled across the floor. She picked up the clothing, and the bag, and placed them on her bed. The bag was not yet empty. Madison reached in and pulled out a shirt, a jacket and pair of boots. *Wow*, she thought. *This is all for me?* Madison scooped up the clothes and headed into the bathroom.

When she came back out, she looked at herself in the full length mirror that was attached to the closet door. *I clean up pretty nice*, she thought. Whoever picked out the clothes obviously had teenage children her age. Fashion-wise, everything was spot-on. *Michele from the train would be jealous*, she thought to herself.

Madison stuffed the hospital pajamas and her Converse sneakers into her knapsack. She briefly wondered what had become of the clothes she was wearing on the day of the building collapse. Wherever they were, the ones on her back seemed more than a fair trade. She threw the knapsack on, and with Reaper in tow, approached the door of her room.

Madison peeked out of her door in both directions. Not seeing anyone in the hallway, she quickly made her way to the elevator. It wasn't until the sunlight hit her face as she stood on the landing in front of the hospital that she felt the events of the past few days were finally behind her. She didn't need family, or anyone else for that matter. She had the Reaper. That was good enough for her, as it had been for so many years.

"I see the clothes fit you," a man's voice, thick with a southern drawl, sounded from behind her. Madison turned to see Wilfred approaching her side. "Are you ready for our trip?"

## *Fly Away Home*

Madison's first instinct was to run, but she hesitated. Being in front of the hospital, there were several ambulances and a few police officers within shouting distance. If she ran, she certainly would not make it very far. The southern gentleman seemed trustworthy enough, and she had no reason to believe that he was not genuine in his intention to deliver her to her newly discovered relatives. Surely there would be better opportunities to give him the slip on their trip down south. *Might as well bide my time and wait for a better opportunity.*

Wilfred hailed a taxi, not taking his eyes off the girl, knowing she could bolt at any time. A cab pulled up without incident, and Wilfred opened the door for Madison. She entered the cab and he took his seat beside her. "South Station," he said to the cabbie as he closed the cab door.

"Mr. Ashley, can we go by Faneuil Hall so I can say goodbye to my friend?" Madison asked.

"Sure we can. Driver, would you circle down by Faneuil Hall on the way?" Wilfred asked. The driver nodded. "And, Ms. Madison, you can call me Wilfred. I want to let you know the officers have been looking for Jeremiah since you mentioned him yesterday. In fact, every officer in the city has been looking for him, knowing your particular circumstance. I don't want you to get your hopes too high that you'll see him there."

Madison knew what he was saying was the truth, but she had to look all the same. As they passed by Faneuil Hall on Congress Street, Madison rolled down her window, straining to hear the harmonica that she had become to depend upon so deeply. Hearing nothing, she rolled the window back up.

"Do you want to get out to take a look?" Wilfred asked.

"No, that's OK," she replied. "I know he's not there." Madison looked down at her hands in silence.

*Why would he be? That would just be too convenient*, she thought to herself. If there was one thing she had learned over the years, it was that nothing in her life ever approached convenient.

The driver negotiated the city traffic, eventually pulling up in front of Boston's South Station. Wilfred paid the driver. He and Madison exited the cab and entered the train station.

"Why are we not at Logan airport?" Madison asked, talking for the first time since they left Faneuil Hall. "South Carolina is like a gagillion miles from here."

"I never pass up an opportunity to see this great country of ours," Wilfred replied. "You can't see anything from thirty thousand feet. Now we have to be quick - our train leaves at 11:10, and that is only five minutes from now. We have just enough time to get to the platform before it leaves."

The pair hustled their way through the station and out onto the concrete platforms that reached outward like fingers before them. They found their platform and boarded the train with barely more than a minute to spare.

"It's a good thing you came out of the hospital when you did, I was about to go in after you. If I had we would have missed our train," Wilfred said to his young travelling companion as they made their way to a row of empty seats.

Wilfred found a quarter on his seat as he let Madison pass him and sit by the window.

"Look, I found a quarter on the seat. It's all yours." Wilfred said, showing Madison the coin in the palm of his outstretched left hand. Instead of giving it to her he passed his right hand palm down over his left and then curled both hands into a fist before finally spreading his hands wide open, palms up, and showing her that his hands were now empty.

"Wow, you made the quarter disappear like magic," Madison said in a mocking tone, although somewhat amazed that she did not actually spot what he had done with the quarter.

"It wasn't like magic, it was magic. The quarter is gone." Wilfred said.

"Really? I'd be crazy to believe that." Madison responded, wondering what point the man was trying to make.

"You don't know that it hasn't, do you?" Wilfred replied.

Madison realized the man was not going to let this go. She began to play along. "I have two choices here: assuming I had searched everywhere on this train and didn't find it, I could believe that you are indeed magical and made it disappear, or I could believe that you are just really good at hiding things." Madison said. "Either way I'm out a quarter, but one way doesn't make me sound crazy."

"You seem very cynical, young lady. The world is a very special place if you allow it be," he said.

"I think you have me all wrong," Madison replied. "I would love for there to be real magic in the world, but I've come to realize that hoping for something to be true is a lot different than believing it is actually true. Believing the quarter actually vanished is far more fun and interesting, but I'd bet another quarter that it is in your pocket."

"I think you are too smart for your own good," Wilfred said.

He reached over and pulled the quarter from behind Madison's ear.

"If I am so smart, how did you know I would try to make a run for it?" Madison asked.

"Well, I figure you have been on your own for a while now, and that the thought of losing some of your freedom could have scared you a bit," Wilfred replied. "That and the very common fear of the unknown. South Carolina is a long way away. You are going to end up living with people you have never met."

"Well," Madison replied, "you were in the right place at the right time - for all the wrong reasons. I was not afraid of any of that. I just didn't..." she paused, "...don't want it. I don't want or need a family at this point in my life."

"You seem like a very bright girl, not at all unsure of yourself. Let me ask you. If your intention was to run, why didn't you take the chance when I offered to let you search Faneuil Hall for your friend Jeremiah? We both know you wouldn't have found him there, but you certainly could have given me the slip had you wanted to," Wilfred said as he lowered his Trilby over his eyes.

The train shuddered slightly as it began to pull out of the station.

"That was a rhetorical question, my dear. We both know the answer. Somewhere inside you, you want to meet this family of yours. This brother of yours. You owe yourself the chance at happiness."

Wilfred adjusted his posture in an attempt to get more comfortable. "There is something you should know," he said, not opening his eyes. "I have not contacted your aunt and brother. I was in charge of all communication as it related to your case, so as far as Child Protective Services is concerned, your case is closed. Whether or not your family finds out about you is completely up to you at this point. As it has been for the past few years, your future is entirely in your hands. But make no mistake, I did not make this decision for you. I did it for your aunt and brother. Imagine the grief and sorrow they would feel if they knew you were on your way back to them only to disappear again."

Wilfred cleared his throat and readjusted himself in the seat yet again. "Now that we have that out of the way, from now on we are traveling on the honor system. I am not going to babysit you. You are far too old and far too competent for that. If you decide to run, I will not chase you. If you do decide to stick around past lunch time, and not exit the train at the first stop, you will find fifty dollars in my jacket pocket. Feel free to visit the dining car if you get hungry. When the conductor comes around, our tickets are in the ticket holder on the seat in front of us."

With that the man went quiet, and began to fall asleep. For the second time in two days, Madison had a lot of chewing to do. She did have a perfect opportunity to ditch the man but she let it pass by. He was also correct in that part of her did want to meet these people who evidently truly were related to her. Her desire for a family had temporarily overpowered her distrust of their motives and intent. Why had they not tried harder to find her? The question weighed heavily on her.

The conductor had made his way down the car and, as he reached their seats, Madison handed him the tickets Wilfred had placed in the seat in front of them. The conductor saw the gentleman sleeping beside her. He asked quietly, "Charleston, South Carolina? You have quite a trip in front of you. You won't be getting in until a little after 5am tomorrow morning. There is food in the dining car three cars down. We have some sleeper cars still available, for an additional fee."

"Thanks," Madison said. "Is my stuff going to be safe here?" She motioned to her guitar.

"Absolutely, young lady. There is no way someone would take that while we are travelling between stations. There is simply nowhere they could hide it. Just make sure you are back at your seat before pulling into each station. That is really the only time an item like that would be vulnerable."

"OK. Thanks," she replied as the conductor finished punching their tickets with what Madison thought was an absurd number of holes.

Madison watched the conductor as he slowly made his way from seat to seat, punching tickets and making small talk with the other travelers. When he exited their car and proceeded to the next, she was left to look out the window at the passing scenery.

She marveled at how fast the world was going by outside. That brought on a bit of vertigo and she quickly brought her gaze back inside the car.

She soon grew tired of listening to Wilfred's tempered but consistent snoring. She gently reached into the side pocket of Wilfred's jacket (which he was now using as a blanket), and pulled out the fifty dollars from his pocket. She rose and made her way down the aisle towards the direction of the dining car. Halfway down she turned and went back to her seat, grabbed the Reaper, and turned again to head back down the aisle. *I'm not taking the chance*, she thought.

An hour later, fully fed, she quietly slipped back into her seat and placed the fifty dollars back in Wilfred's pocket. The folks in the dining car had been very impressed with her rendition of "Charlie on the MTA" and were falling all over themselves to buy her lunch.

As the last few chords were strummed, the conductor entered the dining car and heard her playing. He kindly requested that she stow the guitar for the remainder of their journey. It was policy of the railway not to allow live performances, as this discouraged the homeless and street musicians from bothering the riders during transit.

Not long after she had returned, Wilfred awoke. He tipped his hat back onto the top of his head, got up, and stretched.

"Are you hungry?" he asked.

"Nope, already ate - thank you very much," Madison replied.

Wilfred reached into his jacket pocket and found the fifty dollars. "Very resourceful young lady," he smiled at his young friend. "I'll be back in a few. Don't try jumping; we are going way too fast for that." He winked and made his way down the car.

Madison leaned back in her seat and closed her eyes. She must have fallen asleep, for when she opened them again, Wilfred was back in his seat.

"So, you seem to know a whole lot about me - but I know nothing about you. What's your deal? How did you get the honor of escorting me to Charleston?" she asked him.

"It actually came about quite by chance," he replied. "You see, my career was in the Coast Guard. I spent nearly three decades captaining ships on oceans all over the world. That is my passion. I am out on the water any chance I get. On one occasion early in my career, we received a call from the U.S. Embassy in Bermuda. A 14-year-old runaway from Wisconsin had been detained and needed to be escorted back to the states. It was my duty to get him back safely, and I did so to the best of my ability. There is an old proverb that says *Don't do a job well that you don't want to do twice* - and I can say, there is some truth to that. Over the years, I became the go-to-guy in these types of situations. When I retired, I agreed to continue performing these duties, provided they were not so frequent as to mess up my charter business."

"Charter business?" Madison asked. "What is that?"

"That is my passion. In my retirement, I now run a small sightseeing boat out on Charleston harbor. I take tourists around the waterways and point out the many historically significant spots along the way. It's very relaxing in its monotony, if that makes any sense to you. It keeps me on the water. There is nothing afloat I can't keep afloat and pointed in the right direction," he smiled.

"So I should be flattered. They called in the best just for me." Madison replied.

"Well, yes and no. As I mentioned, this one was more by chance. My contact in the agency knew that I was out on Cape Cod on vacation, and was the closest agent to Boston when your case came up. I simply happened to be in the right place, at the right time."

Madison's curiosity was getting the better of her. She finally asked the question she had been wanting to - and not wanting to - all day.

"You grew up in the Charleston area, right? Have you ever been to the neighborhood where my aunt and brother live?" she said, the words aunt and brother stumbling from her lips. How foreign a concept they seemed to her.

"I have. And it is beautiful. You'll see." Wilfred replied.

*We'll see*, Madison thought. How was she going to fit in there? She became overwhelmed thinking about it, and quickly regretted asking. She decided to change the subject.

"So, you don't mind being hundreds of miles from land on a boat bobbing in the ocean, but you're scared of being a few miles above it in an airplane? Riddle me that, Gilligan."

Wilfred laughed out loud. "I see you didn't buy the line of wanting to see the country pass by, huh?"

"Nope. I didn't buy it then - and I certainly don't now. I've been on this train for two hours and have never wanted to be off of something more in my life. We still have another sixteen hours of this. I pray to God we don't break down, or we may be stuck here forever."

"Do you?" Wilfred asked.

"Do I what?" Madison replied.

"Pray to God?" he said.

*Oh no*, Madison thought, *here we go*.

"If you're asking if I get on my knees and recite the Lord's Prayer, then no, I don't. If you're asking if I am thankful when good things happen to me or I don't die when a very large building nearly falls on me, then yes, I guess I pray in my own way," she said.

Wilfred responded, "I saw you, back when I was checking you out of the hospital, playing to those children. That was a very kind thing you did, and it could not have been easy. That one girl was not much younger than you are now. You also made it a point to go to that small boy's bed and play him a song. I know my eyes were pretty moist when you finished."

Madison said, "I didn't play that song for the boy, I played it for his dad. He needed it the most."

Wilfred shook his head slowly, noticeably in awe of the young girl.

"Are you going to give the Bible speech now? Are you going to tell me how the Kingdom of Heaven is only open to those who repent and get on their knees and ask forgiveness for every time they fart in public?" Madison replied, trying hard to kick the conversation to the endgame and avoid playing around in the middle.

"Quite the contrary, Madison Wolfe. There is nothing I can add in this area that you haven't already figured out for yourself."

"Good," Madison said, still not used to hearing her real last name. "And sorry in advance," she added with a grin. Wilfred appeared confused by her apology and looked quizzically at her. Before he had a chance to speak again, it hit him. It was by no means a thought, but an ill wind that had overtaken his senses. A stench so powerful that he thought it might still have some ca-loric value. He looked at Madison who could not help but burst into laughter.

"Maybe that taco in the dining car was not a good idea." She said between bouts of laughter.

"Maybe you should get on your knees and pray for forgive-ness for that," Wilfred gasped.

The pair spent the rest of the trip in relative silence. Madison alternated between reading and attempting to sleep. As if on cue, the locomotive pulling the long line of passenger cars had mechanical problems in Washington, DC delaying their trip by a full five hours. It wasn't until nearly 11am the next morning that their train finally pulled into the North Charleston, South Carolina station.

# CHAPTER 7

# Resolve

O peh Fiel walked slowly along the cobble path. She inhaled deep breaths of the calming, floral scents that always permeated the air in this part of the public botanical garden. She locked eyes with her nine-month-old baby girl, lying peacefully in the cloth sling that hung around Opeh's neck. It had been another long night and morning. Baby Roez's seizures were becoming more frequent and more severe with every passing day. The end was not long, now - and Opeh knew it.

She looked up and stared skyward, as if to ask once again, why? The question hung in the ether, joining the million or so other such queries she had made over the past two months. And just like the others, it went unanswered.

Now, walking through the garden on her way to work, she further resolved herself to the fact that she was not going to leave her baby's fate in the hands of an unseen and seemingly uncaring God. Though she did not have the power to intervene, her life partner did - and once she gave her consent, she knew that together they would do everything in their power to save their precious little girl.

As Opeh made her way down the path, the garden suddenly darkened and she entered the shadow of a large, expansive building arching several hundred feet overhead. No matter how many times she saw it, the structure always filled her with a sense of pride at what humans could accomplish when they set their minds to it.

The Domi was an engineering marvel of human endeavor. It arched over the half kilometer-wide Eaunet River which separated the twin cities of Merca and Belsic. The garden that Opeh was walking through was located on the Belsic bank of the great river, nestled between the water's edge and the building's main entrance.

The Domi was enormous, containing over two hundred floors. The bottom floors boasted an expansive collection of retailers. There was a well-deserved saying that "If you couldn't find it for sale in the Domi, then it wasn't for sale anywhere on the planet."

The residential floors housed the wealthiest one percent of the population. And then there were the government floors, which contained the offices of every major branch of government that presided over Opeh's home country of Sapientia.

Feeding this retail behemoth was a series of underground service tunnels containing several hundred maglev cargo trains that ran continuously each and every day.

The facade of the building was made entirely of a clear, smoke-tinted skin that allowed its occupants unobstructed views of the cities below and the countryside that spanned out beyond. The only flaw in this otherwise pristine building appeared directly in front of Opeh as she neared its entrance.

A one hundred meter-tall, fifty meter wide section of the building's skin had been peeled away, exposing the carbon fiber core beneath. A construction crew was working day and night to repair the damage and erase the remnants of the large blast that had shaken the building, and the nation, just a little over a month ago.

Opeh remembered that day clearly. As assistant deputy in charge of building security, she had been at her desk on the one hundred and sixtieth floor of the building, combing through background checks of the nearly one thousand workers that had applied for the various construction and maintenance jobs available within the Domi building. Her department was on high alert, as there was mounting evidence that the country of Kre Norta had managed to infiltrate the building's security and was stealing technology from her home country.

Under particular scrutiny was the crew responsible for laying the cable that fed the Ministry of Health offices on the one hundred and thirtieth floor. Her life partner, Etaf, was a brilliant scientist, who had risen to managing director of that department just eighteen months prior. In fact, it was Etaf's latest promotion that granted the couple the Certificate of Procreation that had ultimately resulted in little Roez's birth.

On that fateful day, Opeh was scrutinizing the application of one particular worker, who apparently had family living in Kre Norta, when the building beneath her suddenly swayed and shuddered. Instantly, alarms in her office began to wail. The large monitor in her office immediately switched to the camera covering the main entrance outside the Belsic base. Smoke billowed from a gash in the exterior of the building. Under the image on her screen, readings indicated the sensors, embedded in the sidewalk outside of the arch entrance, had only moments before detected explosive material in the vicinity.

Opeh rewound the camera footage one minute, to the point where the sensors first issued a warning. She watched as a tall, bald man approached the building's entrance wearing a hooded sweatshirt and a backpack. Moments later, when the suspect was still ten feet from the entrance, the protective screen slammed down in front of the entryway. The sensors had done their job and prevented the explosive material from entering the building. The man, realizing he would get no closer to the building, reached into his pocket and detonated his device.

The damage to the building was mostly cosmetic, but the blast and shrapnel killed more than fifty people, eight of whom were children under the age of ten. The nation mourned the loss of life and wondered what possible motive this individual could have had to orchestrate such an attack.

Opeh's boss had been fired over the incident. Although the

security measures had worked to perfection, public opinion was that no one should be able to get close enough to the building to inflict the kind of damage that was seen on televisions throughout the country. Opeh had been asked to replace the outgoing security director, a job that came with its own Certificate of Procreation. It was very rare that a single couple have the privilege and honor of two Procreation rights. Even with all of the stress and heartache each was under dealing with the illness of little Roez, Opeh and Etaf agreed she should take the promotion.

Opeh realized she was late for work. It was nearing second breakfast when she and Roez approached the entrance to the building. As the door swung open in front of her, baby Roez began convulsing in an uncontrollable body spasm. Opeh ran her hand over Roez's head in long soothing strokes. Her feelings of ineptitude were only slightly overshadowed by her deep, fierce anger at whatever it was that could be causing her child so much agony.

In the lobby of the building, she tried to calm her child as the small girl's entire body shook. A full minute passed before the seizure subsided. Opeh breathed a sigh of relief as she and Roez passed through the building's security screening procedure. This procedure was exceedingly thorough for individuals attempting to access the government floor of the building.

When the officials were satisfied that Opeh was indeed who she said she was and was not carrying anything prohibited into the building, she carried Roez to the entrance of the people-mover car used to access the floors housing the government offices. Due to the lateness of her arrival, the car was empty as she stepped inside. As the doors closed behind her, a tear rolled down Opeh's cheek. Each seizure her small child endured brought on a new wave of panic in her mother. The stress was unbearable.

"God, if you are out there, please let Etaf be successful today."

# CHAPTER 8

# Holy City

## *Sneak Attack*

The delta force commando leader moved quietly, his back against the smooth wall, sliding easily as he progressed down the hallway due to the fine fleece material making up his camouflaged pajamas. Preston Pierson motioned to his second-in-command, who had chosen Sponge Bob over the more appropriate commando wear, as he approached from the other end of the hall. Preston would deal with this obviously wedgie-able offence later. Right now, he had to keep his focus on the task at hand.

The young soldiers reached the mission entry point simultaneously. The door was slightly ajar. "*That was fortunate,*" the boy thought, as he did not have a free hand to turn the knob. His brother and fellow commando, Joel, had proven in the past to be completely inept at performing that particular task quietly. Joel raised his Nerf Rapid Fire in anticipation of the breach. Preston had chosen a more aggressive weapon. He carried two softball-sized water balloons, filled with water as cold as it would come from the tap in the kitchen. Just to be sure they had achieved the desired temperature, he slid an ice cube into each projectile before tying the balloon.

Preston eased the door open with his foot, and studied the room inch by inch as the door creaked to its fully opened position. They were in luck. Their prey had not yet awakened, and was lying motionless in bed. Even better was the fact that the sleeping female was facing them, covers kicked down to the bottom of the bed. Her Elsa nightshirt would be no match for what was coming her way.

Without warning, Preston and Joel unloaded on their unsuspecting sister. *Olaf's about to pee all over you!* Preston thought as he cocked his arm and fired. Each of his balloons found their mark, one after the other, landing on his older sister's forehead. Joel wimped out, as usual. He fired only one shot, missing the target entirely, before tearing out of the room.

The girl in bed was no longer sleeping and instead was screaming, "I'm going to kill you, Preston. Get out of my room!" Her face, pillow and bed were soaked from the assault. "Mom!" she yelled, over and over again.

Preston was rolling on the floor laughing when he noticed the red trickle of blood coming from his sister's forehead. His laughter stopped immediately and he himself turned and tore out of the room. He raced down the hall and into his room, realizing he may have gone too far with the ice cube.

Mrs. Pierson came in and sat next to her daughter.

"Quit your whining or I'll give you something to whine about," she barked at the young girl.

She noticed the small, bleeding bump on her child's forehead.

"What have you children been up to this morning? I swear it is always something with you kids. I'm sick of it. Birthday or no birthday, you keep this up and you will be grounded for the entire day. I can't deal with this anymore."

Mr. Pierson appeared in the doorway, making sure everyone's limbs were still attached.

"You," her mom said, focusing her attention on her husband. "Go knock some sense into those boys of yours. And you," she said, returning her attention back to Morgan, "get in the bathroom and put a face cloth on that head of yours before you bleed all over your sheets."

Morgan rose from the bed and made her way to the bathroom, leaving wet footprints in her wake. *Why should today be any different?* the girl thought. *It's not like there is any magic to turning thirteen.* As she wiped a small amount of blood from the cut on her forehead, she could hear her father spanking the boys further down the hall. *That should keep them off me for at least the rest of the morning,* she thought.

When the trickle of blood had subsided, Morgan returned to her room to get dressed for the day. She wondered if she was going to get a cake and ice cream at dinner. Last year, money was too tight for such luxuries. This year should be different, she thought. Her dad had begun working at the new Boeing plant and her parents were not fighting nearly as much about the bill collectors.

Morgan made her way into the kitchen to get a bowl of cereal and found her brothers were already there. Preston and Joel each had a bowl in front of them, with the box of Lucky Charms and the carton of milk already on the table. Jake, her eighteen-month-old brother, was on the floor playing with a not quite empty container of Fruity Pebbles, eating each colorful nugget as it managed to escape the box. Preston hopped up and pointed the arrow on his "I'm with Stupid" t-shirt right at Morgan. She stuck out her tongue at him. Preston adjusted his stance so the arrow was continuously pointing at his sister as she crossed the room.

"Give it a rest already," she groaned. She pulled a clean bowl from the cabinet, got a spoon from the drawer, and sat down for breakfast. She filled her bowl with cereal, picked up the milk and began to pour it over the top. A few drops were all that came out. She looked at Preston in disgust as she noticed his bowl full to the brim with milk. The boy smiled widely. Morgan ate her dry cereal and plotted her brother's untimely death.

Morgan's parents entered the kitchen, and Mrs. Pierson immediately noticed the overfull bowl in front of her eldest son and began yelling at the boy.

"What have I told you about wasting the milk? Did you save enough for my coffee?" she screamed, lifting the empty milk container.

"It wasn't me, Morgan used it last," he said, not completely lying to his mother.

Without skipping a beat, Morgan dumped her bowl of dry cereal onto the table. Not a drop of milk came out.

Whack. The sound echoed in the small room as Preston's cheek became instantly red where his mother's hand had made contact.

"What have I told you about lying to me?" she said. "It is your sister's birthday. You couldn't even find it in you to let her have some milk this morning?" She turned toward Morgan. "I know we were not able to celebrate your birthday last year, but your dad and I want to make it up to you. We're going downtown to the City Market and you are going to have twenty dollars to spend on anything you want. Does that sound good?" she asked her young daughter.

Morgan jumped up from her chair and gave her mom a big hug.

"Thanks Mom! Can we go now?"

"You're welcome, honey," her mom replied. "But we can't go until later this afternoon. I know it's Saturday, but your dad has to put in some time at the plant. While you are waiting, you can clean this kitchen and that nightmare of a room of yours. Boys, you do the same. Morgan, keep an eye on your younger brother. I have a bit of a headache and am going to sit down for a while."

Morgan knew what that meant. She was going to sit on the couch, grab the TV remote and start drinking one of the many bottles of vodka stashed around the house.

Even so, Morgan couldn't help but be excited about the adventure she would have later that afternoon. She quickly went about cleaning the kitchen, not wanting to anger her mom and risk losing the chance at a trip downtown. When she was done in the kitchen, she grabbed Jake and headed off to her room. A smile crossed her face as she pondered the many treasures she would be able to choose from at the market.

## *Hostel*

Madison grabbed her knapsack and the Reaper and followed Wilfred off the train.

"Well, that was fun," she said as her foot hit the platform.

"We're not quite there yet," Wilfred smiled. He stretched momentarily on the concrete walk. "Charleston is ten miles or so south of here. I left my car at the marina there, so we still have a short bus ride to take us into the city. Or we could just take a cab from here?"

"I think I can handle a bus ride. We made it this far - what's a little more?" She hoped her words sounded sincere enough that the man would believe her intention to follow him all the way to Charleston. The truth was that she had decided during the night not to go directly to her aunt's. She needed more time to figure out what her next step was going to be. She wanted to live on her own for a while and get to know this new city a little bit.

As she and Wilfred stood on the train platform, Madison was surprised at how warm it was outside. It was forty-three degrees when they left Boston and it was at least sixty-five degrees and sunny now. It would be nice not to have to worry about freezing to death at night. That would open up a whole new set of possibilities residence wise.

"Let me use the restroom and we will be on our way." Wilfred said. He turned and headed for the door marked "Men." Madison watched him enter the restroom and said a silent goodbye. She wasn't sure if her travelling companion was serious when he said it was the honor system, but decided not to chance it. She quickly scanned the area for a good hiding spot.

Madison found a small, open room off the main corridor and ducked inside. She positioned herself so she could see the building's exit and crouched and waited. After ten minutes, Madison saw the last of the stragglers from the train leave the building. She wondered why she had not seen Wilfred pass by when a familiar voice spoke, not loudly, but clearly audible.

"Take care of yourself, my dear. If you ever need anything, you know where to find me."

Madison saw Wilfred pass through the exit doors as the other travelers had done before him. As she waited to be sure the coast was clear, she flipped through a local newspaper that she had found on the floor. It was appropriately marked, The Charleston City Paper. One of the articles was about the one and only hostel in the entire city. At a little over twenty dollars for the night, she figured the NoSo Hostel would be her first destination.

When five minutes had passed, she figured the coast would be clear. Madison had some money left from the appreciative riders in the dining car, but it wasn't much. She would need another ten bucks or so if she was going to have enough for a bus ticket to town, a small meal and a night at the hostel.

Not wanting to risk running into Wilfred, she decided to kill some time before walking the block south to where the bus stop was located. She exited the train station and set up shop on the sidewalk out front. An hour later she was riding the route 10 bus to downtown Charleston, twelve dollars richer.

The bus ride was uneventful. She soon found herself bounding up the stairs of the hostel. She found the woman who managed the place and paid for a night in a common room that slept four.

The very friendly woman showed Madison to the room where she would be staying. Madison plopped eagerly on an open bed. She opened her knapsack and took inventory of her possessions. Other than the clothes on her back, the only thing even remotely clean were the hospital pajamas she had taken with her. She went into the common bathroom and changed into them.

Madison was shocked at how tired she was, given it wasn't even 1pm in the afternoon. The train had not been very conducive to sleeping and exhaustion was quickly overtaking her. As much as she wanted to go out and explore this new city, her eyes were becoming heavier by the minute. It was not long before she fell into a deep sleep.

## *This Little Piggy*

Mr. Pierson got home around 3pm and it was not soon enough for Morgan. She had Jake dressed and ready and was waiting by the front door when her father stepped through. Her father was surprised to see Preston and Joel waiting beside her. *That's a first,* he thought, calling for his wife.

He wanted to leave pronto in order to be back in time for the kickoff of the Gamecock football game, scheduled for 6pm that evening. He looked down again at Preston, wondering what the boy was up to. He was never ready to go anywhere. Little did he know that Morgan had bribed her brothers with the promise of candy if they didn't do anything to mess this up for her.

Morgan and her family piled into their old minivan and made their way downtown to the City Market. Preston was sure to sit to the right of his sister so the arrow on his shirt pointed at her for the entire trip. Morgan didn't mind. She was not going to let him ruin this. They lived just west of the downtown area of Charleston, and made the trip in just a few short minutes. And in an extraordinary bout of luck, they even found street parking.

They all climbed out of the van, crossed the street and entered the market from the southern end. The market building had high ceilings, and it was open to the outside along both sides. The ceiling was held up by brick columns along each wall, spaced fifteen feet apart. This allowed a cross breeze that, in the middle of summer, was the only thing that made the heat bearable. The city had installed gargantuan, industrial fans that spun slowly along the ceiling - but in the brutal August afternoons, it was not nearly enough. However, this was early December and the mild sixty degree weather was ideal for outdoor shopping.

Morgan set about finding the perfect birthday gift. Her mother had handed her a wrinkled twenty dollar bill in the car and she gripped it tightly in her pocket as she browsed table after table of never-ending treasures. Amazingly, her brothers had left her alone for a while, taking the time to instead pry some attention from their father. Mrs. Pierson browsed leisurely from table to table, never letting Morgan get more than ten feet away.

Morgan noticed a young girl from her class at one of the tables selling jewelry. She maneuvered closer, and got within earshot without actually being seen by her classmate. This particular girl was not her friend. She reminded Morgan of a female version of Preston. The lady selling the jewelry was telling the girl how exceptionally lucky she was to have picked up the last of the quartz "diamonds" she had for sale.

"That is a fine piece you are holding. It came all the way from Mexico. You have a very good eye for fashion, young lady! Here is what I can do. For you - and you alone - and because that is the only one of those I have left for sale, I will give it to you for the low price of fifteen dollars," the lady said.

"Well, I don't have any money on me," the girl replied, disappointed. "It is really pretty. I am going to go ask my mom." She put the necklace back down on the table.

As the girl walked away, Morgan thought, *Now's my chance!* and swept in.

"I'll take that necklace," she said. "It is my birthday and I think that would be perfect."

"Well, young lady, we have a deal. Good thing you came by when you did. That is my last one."

Morgan paid the lady and got her five dollars in change back. She slung the leather cord of the necklace around her neck and marveled at the colorful translucent stone hanging from the end. She would definitely be showing this off at school on Monday and, boy, would her classmate be jealous.

Unbeknownst to Morgan as she walked away with her purchase, the sales lady reached under her table into a box marked "Diego" and pulled out another necklace, placing it on the table in front of her.

Morgan found her mother a couple of tables away. As she approached, she saw her father was also there and the two were arguing about the time.

"Look, Mom!" she shouted with joy. "Look at my beautiful necklace."

"That is really nice, Morgan. I might have to borrow that from you the next time your father takes me out to dinner," she said. "In other words, never," she added, giving her husband dagger eyes.

"Excellent," her father said. "Since you are done, it's time to go."

"Wait," Preston said. "Morgan promised to buy us some candy."

"Did you now, Morgan?" he said, looking down at her, finally understanding why the boys were so eager to go shopping. "I saw a table full of candy back the way we came."

There was indeed a table full of candy on the way back to the van. Morgan kept her promise and used her last five dollars on enough candy to fill all of their pockets. As Morgan paid for the sugary merchandise, her classmate passed behind her, unnoticed, admiring the necklace dangling from her own neck.

"Don't eat that until we've had dinner," Morgan's mom said to all of her children.

Once again, the family piled back into the van and headed

back home. Morgan couldn't take her eyes off of her jewel. This was already the best birthday ever. Once they were back home, Mrs. Pierson reheated some spaghetti from the night before, and they all sat down to dinner - all except for Jake, who took up his usual position on the floor.

Morgan dove into the pile of pasta on her plate, knowing that if she finished, the wide assortment of sugar-laden delights awaited her. She was halfway done with her meal when she realized the stone was no longer dangling from the leather strap around her neck. She pushed the remaining spaghetti around her plate in a frantic attempt to find the missing rock. Having no luck, she pushed back her chair and began searching the floor. Just under the table she saw Jake, sitting upright and staring at her.

"Jake, did you see the stone from my necklace?" she said, hoping he got the gist of what she was saying.

"Canny," Jake said back. That was the answer he gave to most questions.

"Did you find candy?" Morgan asked him, now really worried about the fate of her stone.

"Morgan, you probably lost it in the car. Serves you right for not being more careful with your things," her mother slurred, taking a large sip of her third drink of the evening.

Morgan started crying loudly. Her father, fed up with the day, began to yell.

"You kids have it made and all we hear is whining and fighting," Mr. Pierson yelled as he pounded his fist on the table. "I am sick of the constant noise in this house. You should count yourselves lucky to have a roof over your head. Young lady, if you are going to continue with that wailing, go to your room where I don't have to listen to it."

Morgan jumped up from her seat and stormed down the hall, slamming her bedroom door behind her. She threw herself on her bed, crying uncontrollably.

## *Open Mic*

Madison woke to the sight of a long-haired boy in his early twenties rummaging through the clothing at the end of her bed.

"Hey, what are you doing?" Madison shouted, grabbing the boy by the forearm. "Those are my clothes!"

"Hey man, chill. I wasn't stealing them. I had to do some dirties and only had half a load. I saw yours needed washing so I threw them in with mine. No harm intended," the young man replied, in a thick Australian accent. "My girl and I are bunking over there," he added, pointing to a pair of beds on the opposite wall. "My name is Jack and my girl's name is Melinda." He extended his hand.

"Dixie," Madison replied and shook the man's hand. The name seemed appropriate given her location south of the Ma-son-Dixon line. "Sorry about that. It was very nice of you to do that for me," she said as she shuffled through her belongings, making sure they were all there.

"No worries. You were out cold - I didn't want to wake you up to ask," Jack replied. "I see you got a guitar there – do you play much?"

"Only all the time. I don't know what I would do without it. It's the only thing keeping food on the table," Madison responded.

"Naw," said Jack. "YOU put food on the table. The guitar is just your tool of choice. And a fine one at that. I already miss mine. I started out this trip with an old Fender, but had to sell it to get us here from New York. I have a bunch more at home in Melbourne, but that was my travelling buddy. Hey, you got plans tonight? Lily and I are going to take the bus out to Folly Beach. You're welcome to join us. Or, if you would rather make some cash with that guitar of yours, I know there is an Open Mic night at the Holy City Pub on King Street. One hundred bucks to the performer the audience chooses as the best of the night. You'll have to hustle though, I think the last act is at 10:30."

"The beach sound like fun, but I really need some cash. I think I'll go to the Open Mic contest. You guys have fun, and thanks again for the laundry! I owe you one," Madison said, wondering if everyone she was going to meet in this town would be that friendly.

"Break a leg," Jack said. He turned and walked out of the room.

Madison checked the time. 9:50pm. *Wow,* she thought. *I slept for more than eight hours. I really will have to hustle.* She was now alone in the room and so, for the sake of time, she threw caution to the wind and changed her clothes right there. She quickly got out of her pajamas and into her old jeans and pink hoodie. She guessed, correctly as it turned out, that the bar she was going to was not a fancy place.

Madison jammed the rest of her clothes back into her knapsack and stowed it beneath her bed. She hoped it would be safe, and if her interaction with Jack was any indication, she thought she could chance it. She grasped the Reaper's case by the handle and strode out into the night.

Madison walked the half mile or so down to King Street, where a great many bars with live music were located. She counted down the numbers until she reached the darkened alley behind the "Holy City Pub." *This is dicey,* she thought, shifting the Reaper to her other hand. Madison scanned every nook and cranny of the black, menacing pavement ahead as her breathing quickened. She had walked many an alley back in Boston, but there was something about this unknown alley that raised the hair on her arms. She found herself mentally dodging imaginary specters that seemed to attack her from all sides. The damp, heavy air reeked of rancid meat and urine.

Madison crossed the thirty feet of alley quickly, reached for a large metal door marked "backstage" and gave it a hard tug. Nothing. Her one hundred and twenty pound frame simply would not budge the heavy door. She gave it several short but firm kicks with her sneakers, but was met with only silence.

Reluctantly, Madison turned to begin walking the gauntlet back out to the main street. After taking only two short steps, she heard a heavy latch disengaged on the backside of the door and she turned to see it swing open. She rushed for the entrance, just catching the door with her right hand before it closed again.

Moving inside, Madison caught a glimpse of a young woman's backside, and the protruding dark green body of a guitar, as it moved through another doorway at the other end of a short hallway.

"Thanks," Madison called out as she moved just inside the hallway. The heavy door shut behind her. After receiving no acknowledgement, she slowly made her way down the hall to the doorway where the unknown girl had disappeared. As Madison approached it, she began hearing muffled voices of several people engaged in conversation. Under the voices she could hear an unamplified electric guitar being strummed in some unrecognized pattern.

"Hello," Madison said, as she reached the door and took a step into the small, cluttered, dimly-lit room. Inside, she saw two boys and two girls scattered about the room. A small Japanese boy was in the far right corner sitting on an upside down five gallon pail holding a pair of drumsticks. In the other back corner a tall, beautiful black teenage girl stood looking at some sheet music. Just to Madison's right was a skinny teenager with pale skin and blonde hair that went halfway down her back, highlighted with bright pink streaks. It was obviously an at-home dye job as she'd managed to get quite a bit of the pink substance on each earlobe. The remaining boy was to Madison's left. He was bent over an open guitar case.

"Greetings, fellow human," replied the Japanese boy, as he sat quietly tapping out the drum solo from Rush's Tom Sawyer on some adjacent pails and a mop bucket.

"Hey there. Don't mind the weirdo with the sticks. His name is Mako. We think he got hit in the head with some much bigger lumber when he was a kid. I'm Brooke," said the blonde girl with pink streaks to Madison's right. Brooke had a sea-foam green Fender P Bass slung over her shoulder. Madison recognized her as the girl who had opened the door for her.

"The chick with the sheet music there is Riley and the grumpy dude with the guitar is CJ," Brook continued.

"I'm Dixie. Thanks for getting the door for me."

"No problemo. You're lucky someone was back here to hear you. We just now finished up our set," Brooke responded.

"More like limped through our set," grumbled CJ. He was about Madison's age and there was something about him that looked familiar. Without warning, he closed the cover of his guitar case with unnecessary force, startling Madison. He stood and glared at Riley.

"Riley, the new tune is in D, meaning the C's are sharp in the bridge. If you had made rehearsal this week we could have gone over that," he barked at the girl.

"Hey there, buddy boy, studying for my Trig midterm is way more important than rehearsing for an open mic contest. Maybe we should have skipped the movies last night instead? It seems possible that dating isn't such a good idea for us. After all, I wouldn't want your music career to suffer," she shot back, with a wry smile.

"Sorry about that. I just hate getting things wrong on stage. When you finally become a doctor and don't need to study so hard, I will expect perfection on those keyboards." He joked, giving the girl an apologetic smile. "In the meantime, we can run through this again at rehearsal tomorrow. 10am, my house. Everyone good with that?"

Everyone in the room nodded.

"Good, now give it a rest, lovebirds. You're making me sick," Brooke laughed and turned back toward Madison. "What brings you down here, Dixie?"

"Well, I was hoping to go on for open mic night. I was told there is a hundred buck first prize and I could really use the cash," Madison replied.

CJ studied the young girl for a second. Madison realized that she must have looked like she just rolled out of a sleeping bag in a back alley and was more likely looking for a soup kitchen than an open mic night.

"Well, you went through all the trouble of getting down here and you brought your own guitar, so let me see what I can do. I know the bar manager really well. Let me run out there and check things out."

CJ left the room and Madison looked at Mako. "There are worse things than getting hit in the head with lumber. Trust me."

"I was struck with the tree of knowledge and wisdom, which is often harder on oneself than a two by four," he replied.

Brooke joined in. "Mako, whatever it is you smoke on a regular basis, you need to start sharing with the class."

Madison placed the Reaper on the floor near where Riley was standing and opened the case. She strapped on the guitar and ran a few scales to warm up.

CJ returned and was immediately drawn to the guitar in Madison's hand. He had not expected to see such a fine instrument come out of that tattered case.

"Our roadie Tanner, as usual, is taking his time packing up the gear and it just so happens that it is still on stage and live. The manager says you can have ten minutes if you start now," CJ said to Madison. "Be careful walking down the hall with that - it's kind of narrow." He pointed to Madison's guitar.

"Thanks. I'm sure I'll manage just fine," Madison replied. She found herself briefly annoyed by the implication she could not handle the Reaper responsibly.

"I'll show you the way," said Brooke. She led Madison out the door and down the hall to the stage.

## *Superman*

Morgan awakened to find her face lying in a cold wet spot on her pillow. She was not sure if that was from her crying or if her pillow was still wet from the water balloon incident earlier that morning. The digital alarm clock on her bureau said it was past 10pm. The house was quiet. *Too quiet,* she thought.

She got up and opened her bedroom door. Morgan could hear the TV playing in the living room. From the sound of the announcer's voice, a football game was on. What was absent was the constant barrage of cuss words coming from her usually inebriated father.

Morgan had decided to go out to the car and look for the stone from her necklace. Quietly she walked down the hall, intending to sneak through the living room and out the front door.

As she reached the end of the hall, she surveyed the living room as it opened up before her. To her left was her father's recliner and she saw him sitting there with her brother Jake on his lap. On the floor in front of Mr. Pierson, between the chair and the TV, were her brothers Preston and Joel.

At first she thought they had gotten into the finger paints as they were covered in red paint. *Wow, that was a lot of paint*, she thought. *Why is Dad not screaming at them?* She looked back at her father and noticed Jake, face down on the man's chest. He was making slurping sounds and both were covered in the red substance.

Jake turned and looked at his older sister. Skin, and what Morgan though to be part of an intestine, was dangling from the small child's mouth. The room was not covered in paint after all, but blood.

She looked to her right and saw her mother sitting at the kitchen table, her head dangled upside down from her neck, connected only by the thinnest thread of skin. Morgan screamed loudly and began running and stumbling toward the door that lead outside.

She managed to reach the door and open it slightly when she heard Jake growl and leap from her father's chair. She turned back around to see little Jake take one large pounce and land upon the entertainment center at the front of the room. He was looking right at his sister, dressed in his superman shirt and pull-ups.

"Jake, it's me, Morgan. I have candy," she said as the child made one last lunging jump in her direction. As the young child went airborne, Morgan managed to slip out the door and slam it shut. An instant later, she heard a thud as the toddler's small frame made contact.

Morgan began running wildly down the sidewalk as fast as her legs could carry her. She knew the police station was only a couple of blocks away and she wanted to get there as quickly as possible. Surely they would be able to help her family. In her haste to reach help, she neglected to pause and check for traffic at each intersection. That oversight caught up with her when she was crossing the street in front of the station.

Seeing an officer standing in the station's front door, Morgan began to yell. At that moment, she was struck by a Prius that had entered the intersection. She tumbled over the hood and struck her head hard on the pavement on the other side of the vehicle.

She came to in the back of an ambulance. She heard the paramedic saying "we have a Jane Doe on route. ETA 5 minutes." Before she could explain her situation, she slipped back into unconsciousness.

## A Bump In The Night

Brooke led Madison to the far end of the hall where the entrance to the stage opened up on the left.

"Your public awaits," she said. The girl motioned for Madison to climb the three stairs up to the stage. Madison did so, passing a dingy curtain that hung from parts unseen in the dark ceiling above. Ahead of her, she could see the drum set, keyboard and various amplifiers still sitting on the stage.

Patch cords ran from the various mic stands to monitors at the front of the stage. Beyond that, all of the cords joined into one large snake extending outwards to the back of the room.

To her right, twenty or so tables were littered throughout the room, situated between the stage and a large bar that ran across the far back of the room. Smoke filled the air along with the distinct smell of stale beer.

A hundred or so customers were clumped in smaller groups, engaged in various conversations. A short stool had been placed at the center of the stage, and with it, a microphone positioned at guitar level and a second positioned at head level.

Madison looked to the back of the room and saw a DJ booth. Inside was a lone man, looking down and adjusting what she assumed were the controls of the sound board. He looked up and motioned her toward the stool.

Madison was uneasy as she crossed the short distance to the stool. It had been quite some time since she had played on an actual stage. There were open mic nights in Boston, but they didn't often pay money, so she rarely bothered to participate.

A voice came quietly through the monitor. "I'm Tanner. I'm here to help you make music. Just play a little something before you start your set so I can get a good mix on your guitar mic. No need for a vocal check, we have that pretty dialed in already."

"Thanks Tanner," she said into the vocal mic, knowing the large man in the booth would be monitoring the mic but would not yet have the house volume turned up.

Madison chose a sonata by Bach to get her fingers loose and to give Tanner the needed time to adjust the levels. As she played the audience began to take notice. The rock and roll crowd was not used to classical music being played at the bar, but they didn't seem to mind.

Backstage, CJ, Brooke, Riley and Mako took notice as well. They bolted for the stage, gathered in the wings, and listened for a full minute to the complexity and beauty they heard coming from the Reaper.

"I hate to interrupt, but I think I have you dialed in," Tanner said through the monitors. His voice snapped Madison out of her trance and she stopped playing. The faces in the crowd stared at her for a moment and then a smattering of applause broke out.

"Thanks," Madison said into the mic. "That was probably a bit different from what you usually hear in here, huh? This one is one of my favorites."

Madison began playing the intro of the Evanescence song "Bring me to Life." CJ and his band looked at each other in recognition. It was a song they had attempted a year or so ago but didn't have a strong enough female voice to pull off.

As Madison moved through the intro, CJ, his guitar already strapped on his back, plugged into his onstage amp and pulled up behind one of the background vocal mics. Brooke followed suit on her bass with Riley heading to her keyboards and Mako seating himself behind his drum set.

When Madison reached the chorus, CJ jumped in on the male vocal part "Wake me up" and the entire band jumped in without skipping a beat. Madison, who had been drifting into her own world again, was momentarily stunned and stumbled over her lyric, "Wake me up inside." She looked back over her shoulder at CJ who nodded at her, motioning for her to continue. Madison had never really played with a band before. The experience rushed through her like a wave of electricity. The song built as she and her fellow musicians put their hearts into it.

When the final notes were played and hung, reverberating through the small venue, the crowd erupted in cheers, whistles and applause. Tanner, from his perch in the DJ booth, was doing a full bow with arms extended over his head. Madison was consumed by the experience and spiraled into a complete freak out.

She bolted from the stage, ran back down the hall, quickly placed the Reaper back in its case and headed out the back door. She was halfway down the alley when she stopped suddenly. Although her brain was reeling from what had just happened on stage, her primal senses for self-preservation made her instantly aware of her surroundings.

Madison sensed movement behind her, back down the alley the way she had just come. Unlike her paranoia on the way in, this was not her imagination. A fast moving form came with alarming speed from the back of the alley. She turned back toward the street and began to run with everything she had, but soon realized she would never get to the street before this unknown form overtook her. Her fight response took over and she decided to stop running and make her best attempt to defend herself from this attacker.

In the poorly lit alley, she could make out a small form as it parkoured its way toward her. It appeared to be a very small child dressed only in a diaper and a superman t-shirt. The small boy had an animalistic, crazed expression on his face.

With no more than four strides to go before what appeared to be certain death, a bolt of light came shooting in from behind her. It barely cleared her shoulder and struck her attacker. The boy dropped down immediately and vanished into the darkness of the alley.

Had the alley been better lit, Madison would have seen that a round black mass had indeed continued toward her, dissipating only inches from her feet.

Not waiting to see if there were more of these coming for her, Madison turned and quickly ran toward the street. As she reached it, she scanned the sidewalk for the person who had saved her from her assailant. A dumpster on the corner partially blocked her view of the person she thought might responsible as he entered a line of people passing by on the sidewalk. Madison could just make out the form of young man with long hair before the individual blended into the crowd and was lost to sight.

Madison stood on the sidewalk, out of breath and utterly shaken. A few passersby gave her pitiful glances, assuming she was just another overindulgent MUSC student out on a Friday night bender.

Madison regained her breath and quickly made her way back to the hostel. She glanced back over her shoulder repeatedly, knowing that additional assailants could be coming at her from any direction.

As she entered the house and quietly made her way to her bed, she placed the Reaper beside her and pulled the covers up over her head. Tonight, she was grateful to be surrounded by a room full of other people. There was safety in numbers.

The thought of a large house in a quiet neighborhood far outside the city suddenly seemed like a really good option as she lay shaking in her bed.

From across the room, she heard Jack whisper, "Hey Dixie, you OK?"

"I'm good. Thanks for asking. Goodnight," she lied. For the first time in quite some time, she was really not sure that she was OK.

# CHAPTER 9

# Lucky Winner

—————— ❖ ——————

*E*taf Fiel sat at her desk in the new, state-of-the-art, laboratory. It had been built to her exacting specifications. As head of the Ministry of Health, she spearheaded the Mechanical Autonomous Replication program that was revolutionizing the health care industry.

Their technology was unlike any other in the world, using carbon-based nanobots to repair damaged or diseased tissue. Advancements in this technology had progressed rapidly since its discovery just three years prior. After only a year of testing on animals, it was approved for human use. For the wealthy, and the lucky, this treatment had been proven one hundred percent successful in curing known diseases in almost every part of the human body.

The last remaining barrier was diseases and conditions of the brain. The team of researchers was able to get the nanobots to recognize the cells in the brain that regulate basic motor function and sensory input, but had been unable to duplicate their function. More frustrating were the more complex parts of the brain governing memory and complex problem solving. These were still a complete mystery.

The nanobots currently used in treatment were being instructed to gather as much information about these and other unknown cells as possible, and to carry that data back out with them when they were collected in the patient's saliva at the end of each treatment.

*Requests for treatment far surpassed Etaf's ability to fulfill them. Waiting periods were extending to a year and beyond, even with the huge price tag the government placed on each treatment.*

*Public pressure, mostly from the middle and lower class citizens, forced the government to implement a random lottery in which each citizen was eligible to win a free treatment session and jump to the front of the line. Drawings were held weekly and televised as part of a thinly-veiled propaganda show used to "educate" its citizens on just how special and privileged they were to live in such a wholesome and righteous society.*

*It was one such lucky sweepstake winner who currently sat grinning on a hospital bed in Etaf's lab. He was one of the thirty patients Etaf had to see that day. It would take her well past first supper to get through the list.*

*"So, Medith, what are we going to treat today? From my preliminary health scan, you have two primary issues that need to be addressed. Your liver is severely damaged, most likely from some sort of substance abuse," Etaf said. She leveled her gaze on the overweight man in his sixties. He reeked of alcohol, and she had no doubt he had consumed more than one drink already that morning.*

*"You also have a tumor growing in your abdomen. My preliminary scan seems to indicate this is benign, but I cannot make any guarantees of that at this time."*

*"Fix them both doc. I won the lotto, didn't you hear? You're supposed to fix me for free," Medith said, slightly slurring his response to the doctor.*

*"I'm sorry, sir. As it has been explained to you already, we can treat only one ailment per session. You must choose one specific condition. My rec-*

*ommendation is that we treat your liver today. You can follow up at a later date with your normal doctor to discuss more conventional treatments for the mass in your abdomen. As I said, it appears to be benign and not nearly as life-threatening as the issue you have with your liver. But it is your choice. You can choose either one or any other condition you may feel you need to address," Etaf responded.*

*"OK, OK. Unless you got something in there to make me irresistible to the ladies, let's do the liver. How long will this take? Will it hurt?" the man asked.*

*"You won't feel a thing. You will go to sleep for about thirty minutes and when you wake up, we will be all done." As she finished her explanation, Etaf crossed the room to a sterile refrigerator containing vials of un-programmed nanobots suspended in a clear liquid. She picked out a vial from the refrigerator and carried it over to the programming pod located in the center of the lab.*

*The programming pod was about the size of a coffee can and similarly shaped. Etaf placed the vial containing one hundred thousand of the microscopic nanobots into the pod, sliding shut the lid with a soft click. The pod glowed red, indicating the nanobots were not yet programmed.*

*Etaf punched away at the keys on her keyboard and started the program marked "Liver." As the program began, the pod turned to a yellow color. A few seconds later, it glowed green, indicating the programming was complete.*

*Etaf picked up the vial. She returned to the refrigerator where she selected a different container containing a yellow liquid marked "125-130 ki-*

*lograms.” It was an anesthetic used to render the patient unconscious, thereby sparing them from the pain that would otherwise accompany the half hour long procedure. She opened it and poured the contents of the nanobot vial into the yellow liquid. The liquid in the container turned from yellow to green.*

*"OK, Medith. You need to lie back on the bed. Once you drink this, you will almost immediately fall asleep. When you wake up your liver will be good as new," Etaf said. Medith lay back in the bed and Etaf raised the container of green liquid to his lips.*

*"Drink it all down at once," she said as the man gulped the concoction. He immediately fell into an unconscious state. Etaf placed a suction tube into Medith's mouth and looked down at her newest patient. Every time she administered this treatment, she marveled at how easy it was to perform.*

*Right now, inside this patient, her nanobots were busy doing their job. They were inspecting every cell of the man's body, leaving behind a unique chemical marker that prevented a cell from being inspected twice. If the cell happened to match the target cell type, in this case a liver cell, and that cell was found to be abnormal, the nanobot would consume it. Once consumed, the nanobot would create a mechanical replication of the cell's function and leave it in place of the destroyed cell. If for any reason, the nanobot could not identify the target cell, it was programmed to leave the cell in place but collect as much information about as it could for later study. When all of the cells in the man's body had been analyzed, the nanobots migrated to the saliva of the patient's mouth for collection.*

*With her nanobots hard at work, and the suction tube slowly suctioning out the excess saliva from Medith's mouth, Etaf returned to her worksta-*

*tion. A nanobot collection device was attached to the other end of the suction tube and would sound an alarm when all one hundred thousand nanobots had been recovered. This would take, at most, thirty minutes. Most of the time, the alarm went off after only fifteen minutes.*

*Etaf sat at her workstation reviewing the latest set of unknown cell data returned from yesterday's treatments. There were two new cell structures that were classified as unknown. A quick look at the data indicated these were yet another variation of brain tissue. She catalogued the results, added them to the growing list of unknown brain cells that required further study.*

*Ten minutes had elapsed and no alarm yet. Etaf tapped at her keyboard and reviewed her outstanding communication requests in her inbox. One communication immediately drew her attention. It was from Opeh.*

*"You win. Tonight," was all it said.*

# CHAPTER 10

# Meet The Peeps

— ❖ —

## *Bringing It All Home.*

M adison stared at the three-story house in front of her, unsure of how this was all going to go. It was a beautiful home, with palm trees in the front yard, and flower beds lining the driveways on each side of the house. Parked there, beside a large magnolia tree, was a red Jeep Rubicon with chrome accents and a beat up white Ford Econoline cargo van.

From her vantage point on the street, it seemed like heaven - and exactly the kind of place she would not fit into. It already seemed to reek of rules and order, not at all the life she was used to. *Nope,* she thought, *this may be someone's paradise, but not mine.* Just as she was turning to return down the street the way she came, she noticed a woman staring out of the second-story window at her. A voice in her head told her to run, but her feet would not move.

Marion had been watching the young girl on the street for several minutes. She had initially been looking across the harbor

— 153 —

at the city of Charleston. Just a half hour before, her husband Greg had been unexpectedly called into work and she feared something major was happening in town.

In all the years her husband had been in the National Guard, this was the first time he had been called to active duty. She had been at the window since he left, scanning the horizon for signs of smoke or unexpected activity of any kind. She could hear sirens in the distance, which only served to heighten her anxiety.

Her eyes darted back and forth across the harbor in front of her. To her right, Patriots Point was visible. The USS Yorktown rose from the harbor at that spot, permanently moored as a floating museum. Scanning left across Charleston harbor, the two massive concrete supports, cabling, and a roadway deck which constituted the Ravenel Bridge sprang from the ocean below. That structure connected Charleston to the city of Mount Pleasant.

Continuing left, she could see the tail of a cruise ship that was currently docked in port, waiting to take on passengers. Massive cargo cranes from the shipping port itself could be seen, motionless, waiting for another of the hulking, ocean crossing cargo ships to arrive. Even further to the left was the city itself. The marina was in the foreground and behind it were hospitals, office buildings and a surprising number of church steeples.

Farthest to the left was the cylindrical structure of the Charleston Holiday Inn. Nowhere on the horizon could she see any signs of distress.

The only thing seemingly out of place was the young girl who had, just five minutes prior, walked down the street and stopped in front of her house. The girl just stood there, staring at the house and surrounding property. Just as she turned to walk back down the street, Marion tapped on the window and motioned for the girl to approach the house.

Madison saw the woman motion for her to come to the door, and then vanish from the window. Seconds later the front door opened and a nicely dressed blonde-haired woman called out to her. "Hello there, young lady, can I help you?" she said in a welcoming voice.

"I'm looking for a friend's house. She said she lived on this street, but I can't remember the house number," Madison lied. She was not sure who this woman was or how she might be related to her aunt. She was having a hard time figuring out how to navigate this strange situation she found herself in.

"Well, come on up, I have a phone you can use to call your friend and get her address. You drink coffee? I just made a fresh pot," Marion said to the girl.

"Thank you, ma'am, that would be very helpful," Madison called back, working her way to the nearest driveway and approaching the house. She figured once she was inside, if this was meant to be, things would just sort themselves out one way or another. She was not going to force the issue. She would just go with the flow, and see where it took her. Madison made her way up the stairs and into the house, Marion closing the large mahogany door behind her.

"You can put your things here in the hallway while we have that coffee. There is a phone in the kitchen that you can use," Marion said as she led the girl to the kitchen area. She handed the girl a cordless phone. "Here you go. You take cream and sugar?"

"Thanks, yes, cream and sugar would be great," Madison replied. She had no idea who she was going to call. She didn't know anyone in the area and certainly didn't have anyone's phone number memorized that she could actually call. She pretended to punch in some numbers on the phone and held it up to her ear. *Please don't let anyone call the house right now,* she thought, knowing that if the phone rang, the blonde woman would quickly realize she had not actually made a call. After thirty seconds, she put the phone back down and said, "No answer."

"That's OK. You can try again in a few minutes. In the meantime, here is your Joe. I didn't catch your name," Marion replied.

"Dixie," Madison replied. "Thank you for the coffee and the use of your phone. I don't want to be a burden; if you have somewhere you need to go, I can be out of your hair real quick."

"Don't you worry about that. I am housebound for the next few hours, so we are in no rush. I'm glad I saw you out there. It gives me someone to talk to while I worry away the morning."

"Is there something the matter? Anything I can help you

with?" Madison asked, just now noticing the stress the woman seemed to be under.

"No, no dear. My husband Greg is in the National Guard and he was called into work unexpectedly just a half hour ago. It was not a scheduled exercise, and it has me concerned – that's all. Nothing seems to be out of the ordinary in town, and the local news is not reporting anything urgent. It is probably just an exercise of some kind, but something about it doesn't feel right. I'm probably overreacting, but it certainly is nice to have someone to keep me company just the same," Marion said.

Madison shivered. She wondered if her experience from the previous night had anything to do with this. Probably best not to mention anything to this woman as it would only cause her more worry. She was about to ask the woman's name and how she came to live in this big house when a door opened on the far side of the kitchen, and a group of teens piled into the room.

## *All In The Family*

"Morning, Miss M," Mako said, as he led the group into the kitchen, opened the refrigerator door and grabbed a container of OJ. Brooke, who was right behind Mako, stopped suddenly, causing CJ, Riley and Tanner to pile up behind her.

"Dixie?" Brooke said, puzzled. "You tracked us down that quickly?"

Mako pulled his head out of the refrigerator and joined his friends in staring at Madison standing there in CJ's kitchen.

"Brooke, what do you mean, tracked you down? Do you know this girl?" Marion asked, understanding now that it was probably not a coincidence that this girl was standing in front of her house.

Madison was frozen. Why was the band from last night standing in the kitchen of her supposed aunt's house? Did she have the right house? Thoughts spun around in her head, none of them making much sense.

"You must be here for your hundred dollars," CJ said. "You left in such a hurry, I didn't even realize you knew you won."

"I won?" Madison said in surprise.

"That's putting it mildly," Mako replied, beaming. "You blew the doors off that place! That was a thing of beauty." The young man was clearly enamored with this unknown girl and it showed in the way he was fawning over her.

"Wait a minute, if you didn't know you won, why are you here?" CJ said, trying to figure out how this girl had twice now shown up out of nowhere.

Marion took control of the conversation at this point, clearly not understanding what was going on in her own kitchen. "Dixie, what really brings you here? You are obviously not here by accident. You know my nephew and his band, yet you seem surprised to see him here."

"Yeah girl, spill the beans. You're among friends here," Brooke added.

Madison stood in frozen silence, not knowing what to say next. Her cover story was clearly blown at this point, but how should she go from that to "I'm looking for my aunt and brother, who I never met, whose house I may or may not currently be standing in."

"Connor, did you tell Dixie where you lived last night?" Marion asked her nephew.

"No, we didn't really talk much actually," CJ replied.

"Not much talking, but they sang their butt's off," Riley added. "Those were two voices made to be sung in harmony."

"Connor?" Madison said, looking at CJ. "Your name is Connor?" It was then she knew she was in the right house. Mako had called this woman "Miss M'. Marion, her aunt, was the woman standing before her.

The gears in Marion's head also began to turn. Was it possible? They looked very much alike, the eyes, the smile. They appeared to be the same age.

"Yea, CJ is my nickname. John is my middle name. In fifth grade there was three other Connors in my class so my friends took to calling me CJ," Connor replied.

Marion continued to study the young girl. Her brain was working overtime, trying to figure this mystery out. Her heart skipped several beats as the realization hit her. "Madison?" Marion said to the young girl. The young girl looked at her speechless, but not denying the name. "You're Madison, aren't you? You are! You're Madison!" she cried. Marion had closed the gap between them. She threw her arms around her niece.

Madison closed her eyes and it felt like the floor had fallen out from under her. She had worked through every possible variation of how her reunion with her parents might go. When she found out that they were gone, and that it was an aunt and brother that were looking for her, she had very little time to work through these new scenarios. Standing here now, she realized she could have had a lifetime to contemplate them and never would have been prepared for the actual moment. She realized that all that time, she was focused on the wrong thing. In the actual moment, it wasn't about what she felt. It was about what she didn't feel. Alone.

Her aunt was shaking slightly as she cried into Madison's shoulder. In this unplanned and unexpected moment, Madison hugged her back. It was not the light, polite hug that she had had a lifetime of. It was firm and heartfelt. This was the way she hugged Jeremiah and her Nana Jean. Madison didn't care that she couldn't feel the floor.

When Madison opened her eyes, she could see Connor's stunned face. All he could manage was a slight, confused smile.

Riley was the first to speak. She flung her arms around Conner and began to cry. "I can't believe this. After all this time. You have your sister back. I told you God would bring her back to you. I prayed so hard for this," she said to her boyfriend.

"Wait, wait, wait," Brooke said. "You're telling me this is your sister, CJ? Get outta town. The one you haven't seen since you were both little kids?"

"Karma, baby. Good Karma," Mako added. "That explains the simpatico on the stage last night."

Marion released her bear hug on the young girl, and instead took her by the hand. Tears were flowing freely down her cheeks. "We have so much to catch up on. Are you hungry? Do you need anything?" she babbled, overwhelmed at the situation.

"No, I'm good." Madison smiled as she turned to her now-confirmed brother. "So, you got my hundred bucks," she joked.

Connor laughed. He had a sister again. He had felt a connection with Madison last night. It was no wonder they paired so well musically. He now realized he had read the situation all backwards.

"Hey guys, let's get out of here and give these guys some space," Riley said to her band mates.

"No, please, I don't want you out driving on the roads right now." Marion said, wiping her cheeks and collecting herself slightly. In the emotion of the moment she had almost forgot that her husband was responding to an unknown event downtown and she was not about to let the kids drive off until she knew what was going on. "Just hang out in the garage and have your normal band rehearsal, at least until I know it's safe. Connor will be out with you shortly."

"OK, Miss M. Dixie, er Madison, if you feel up to it later, it would be awesome to get some of those skills of yours on tape. It is really cool to see you again," Tanner added as he and the rest of the band headed out to the garage.

"Madison, we have so much to talk about and a lifetime to do it. I'm going to do whatever I can to make sure this is a place you can call home. We don't know anything about each other, but that is all going to change. Know this. You are with family now and wherever we go from here, we go together." Marion said to Madison. The tears on her cheeks had started to dry, but when she stopped talking, a new group had begun making their way to her chin and she was again hugging her niece.

"Auntie M, you're going to smother her before she even has a chance to see her room." Connor said to his aunt.

"You already have a room for me?" Madison said in a puzzled tone.

"Auntie M has kept a room ready for you in every house we've ever lived in. Want to see it?" Connor asked.

"That is a great idea, Connor." Marion said, again releasing Madison from her grasp. "Why don't we get your stuff and get you set up in your room. When you have had a minute to shower and settle in, we can... well... catch up, I guess you can call it.

I don't even know what I am saying right now." Marion gushed.

Madison realized she had not bathed since she was in the hospital and it was probably obvious. She was in such a rush to get away from the hostel, and whatever it was that was in the alley the night before, that she had skipped the shower.

"That sounds great. Thanks." Madison replied. She was thankful to have some time to collect herself before any big conversations started.

Together they went back to the front hall to gather Madison's belongings. Marion picked up Madison's knapsack and Connor grabbed the Reaper. Madison fell in line behind Marion as they walked down the long hall leading to the bedrooms. Connor was lagging slightly behind them holding his cell phone to his ear. At the end of the hall, they entered a door on the left that opened up into a large, well-furnished bedroom.

Madison could not believe that she was going to be staying in a room this nice. She had seen bedrooms like this in magazines, but never in person. As they placed Madison's things on the queen-size bed they couldn't help but notice the look of awe that she had on her face.

"My room is across the hall if you need anything. Auntie M, I'm going to go check on the band and get them going. I tried to call Riley on my cell but my call isn't going through. I think it's time for me to upgrade my service. I'll be back in a few," Connor said as he backed his way out of the room.

"I'm going to leave you to it as well. I'll be back shortly with clean linens. You have your own bathroom over there," Marion said, pointing to the entrance to a small bathroom. "You should have everything for a shower, if you want. If there is anything you need, all you have to do is ask. You are home now and I could not be happier." Marion started crying again as she hugged her niece again and left the room, closing the door behind her.

## *Days Gone By*

Madison looked at her reflection in the mirror that protruded from the back of a large chest of drawers. Her hair was wet from her shower and needed a good brushing. The bump on her head was barely visible now and the pain was all but gone. Although she was not ready to accept what it meant, she did notice that the face staring back at her looked happy.

She turned away from the mirror and walked over to the queen-size bed where her knapsack was sitting unopened. She changed into her new jeans, shirt and jacket that Wilfred had purchased for her. She sat on the edge of her bed and began wondering if she had been just a bit too harsh on the man. Did she get him in any trouble by running away? She needed to find a way to tell him that she had arrived, unharmed, and to thank him for his help in getting here. That and she just plain liked the old guy. And what of Jeremiah? Why didn't he make an attempt to see her when she was in the hospital? Surely he had to have heard she was in there. She was deep in thought when a quiet knock came from the bedroom door.

"Come in," Madison said, as her mind returned to the present.

The door opened and her aunt entered the room, arms full of fresh bedding. "Wow, nice threads, young lady. Here I thought I was going to have my work cut out for me in the fashion department." Marion put the bedding on a chair in the corner of the room and sat down beside her niece.

"These are the best of the lot," Madison replied. "I'm afraid I don't have many choices when it comes to getting dressed."

"Well, you have come to the right place then. I am always looking for a reason to go shopping. Whaddya say we hit the mall later and splurge a little?" Marion said.

"A couple of new outfits would be nice, but I can pay for my stuff. Well, I can pay you back I mean, once I get a regular gig set up," Madison replied.

"Nonsense. I owe you how many years of birthday and Christmas presents? I think I am getting out of this easy. Now, let's not talk about that any more, it's decided. You must have a million questions, I know I have. Mind if I go first?" her aunt asked.

"Shoot," Madison said.

"What brought you here today? I mean, not everything, but

how long have you been in Charleston and what made you leave wherever it was you were before that?" Marion asked.

"I want to hear this too," Connor said as he popped his head in the open door. "I was walking to my room and couldn't help but hear you guys talking. Mind if I join you?"

"Not at all," Madison said. "Park it over here and let's catch up on some things." Connor sat next to Marion on the bed and Madison began describing her life in Boston, her boiler room pad, Jeremiah and his magic harmonica, the building implosion, and finally Wilfred and her train ride down to Charleston.

When her story was done, Marion was in tears again, amazed at the strength of the young girl. She had seen a similar strength in Connor over the years; always protecting those he felt needed it, never giving in to peer pressure or caring much about what people thought of him. He led by example and was true to his nature. Marion now knew it was a quality that ran in the family. She thought of her sister and how proud she would have been of her children.

"My turn," Madison said. "What happened to my parents? How did our family fall apart so badly?" She paused for a second and then added "why didn't you try harder to find me?"

Since walking into the house, she could see the kind of life her brother had led, sheltered, protected, loved, fed, and kept warm on the coldest of days. She had had none of that and, as much as she prided herself on her self-sufficiency, she could not shake the fact that nobody had bothered to find her in all those years. She needed to clear the air. If things were going to go south, they might as well go right now and save everyone a lot of grief later.

"Madison, we never stopped looking for you. Ever," her aunt explained. We tried everything, hired everyone I could think of who might know something about what happened to you. They were all dead ends. I'm still not sure how the Boston police department figured all this out, but I am so glad they did," she said, hugging her niece again.

"As for your parents, let's start with your mom. Willow, your mother, was my sister. She was my only sibling and was a year younger than me. We grew up in Hansen, Massachusetts with our parents. We lived a pretty unstructured lifestyle as our parents were what you could call hippies. They home schooled us, which mostly consisted of teaching us to play musical instruments. I was never very good at it, but your mother was a natural. She leaned to play the guitar like she came out of the womb with it - and her singing voice was second to none."

Marion paused for a minute, lost in a memory of her childhood days. After a pause, she continued. "Anyway, soon after my 19th birthday, I found myself in a Mexican jail after following my boyfriend to Mexico to mule drugs over the border. I lost track of Willow at that time. Seven years later, June of 2003, I was released, made my way back to the US and started hitchhiking my way back across the country. Lucky for me I was picked up in Texas by a Navy airman named Greg, my now husband. He was headed here to Charleston, so I tagged along. After a short stay, I continued back up to Hansen, but Willow, and my parents, were gone. I finally tracked her down to Wilton, NH only to find she had died of cancer in 2002."

"What about my... our dad." Madison asked, giving Connor a look to acknowledge their shared past.

"From what I could gather, he was a free spirit himself. His name was Levi Wolfe. Apparently he and your mother never formally married, but by all accounts they loved each other very much. Nobody I asked knew what he did for a living, but they all said that he would often take off for long periods of time. Evidently, in 2000, he left on one of his trips and never returned." Marion replied. "When your mother died, the authorities could not find a next of kin, so you and Connor were brought into the foster care system."

"But if we were both in the system, how were you able to find Connor and not me?" Madison asked.

"You and Connor were placed with two different foster families. We quickly found that Connor was living with a family in Durham, NH. I had the foster care system release him into my custody as soon as I could. You, however, seemed to be lost. The last record the foster care system had of you was from earlier that year, living with the Dorman family in Nashua, NH. Unfortunately, the Dorman's were killed on New Year's Eve and you seemingly vanished from the face of the earth. I hired a local private detective to try and track you down, but he had no luck. I had no choice but to bring Connor back to Charleston with me and to continue my search from here. We put out a missing persons alert on you and I made sure it was renewed every year. When DNA technology became available, we provided a sample of Connor's blood on the off-chance that if you were ever tested, we could find you that way. It seems like the combination of good police work and DNA technology is what finally brought you to us."

"Well, that and you almost being crushed by a building," Connor added, still having a hard time grasping just how lucky his sister was to still be alive.

"I grew up thinking my last name was Jaques, not Wolfe." Madison said. "Wilfred mentioned something about a clerical error on some paperwork when I was placed with the Jaques family,"

"Oh my," Marion said in a quiet voice. "You were in the foster care system the whole time, just under a different name? No wonder we couldn't find you. I am so sorry, sweetheart." *All that time lost due to a clerical error* Marion thought. "We can't get that time back, but we can make the most of what we have now."

"That sounds good to me, Aunt Marion," Madison said. She hugged her aunt.

"Me too," said Connor. "Now, if I can borrow my sister for a while, I want to go formally introduce her to my friends and maybe get in a quick jam session. You have to teach me some of those sick chords you were playing last night."

"You guys have fun. I am going to go back to the living room and check the news again. I still haven't heard from Greg," Marion said.

"Auntie M, I'm sure everything is OK. Stop worrying so much. We got Madison back today. Nothing bad could possibly happen to ruin this day for us. We'll be in the garage. Let me know when you hear from Uncle Greg, OK?" Connor said.

"Sure thing. I'm going to go through our bug out bags just in case. You can never be too prepared. Is your 10mm cleaned?" she asked Connor.

"Jeez, I'll clean it before we go to the range. I always get it done," Connor replied.

"Connor, you know the rules. That gun is to be cleaned as soon as we get back from the range and not a second later. A dirty gun is an unreliable gun. I want it done before you go to bed tonight, understand? Now, go back to your friends, and tell Mako I saw him drinking directly from the OJ container this morning. If I catch him again, he's going to be mowing our lawn this summer for free."

Madison grabbed the Reaper and followed Connor out of the room and back toward the kitchen and the garage beyond.

"I know all of this must be weird. It is for me. I feel like I need to apologize for the way my life turned out after hearing about how tough you've had it." Connor said as they proceeded down the hallway.

"Not at all. I am happy that you've had the life you have. I can't help but think how my life would have been different if we had been found at the same time, but none of that matters now. I have had a pretty good life and, with a few exceptions, wouldn't have changed it for the world. I certainly would never want either of you to feel uncomfortable around me. I would rather leave now than ever think that my being here would come between you and your family." Madison said.

"Our family." Connor corrected her.

Madison gave him a playful nudge with her shoulder that made him stumble slightly as they walked.

"On a different note, what's with the guns and bug out bags?" Madison asked. She had heard folks in the south liked their guns, but this was the first time she had heard such a casual conversation about them.

"Uncle Greg grew up in a military family, and served in the Navy as an airman for many years. I was taught to shoot a handgun when I was twelve. His philosophy is that it is better to know how to use one and not need it than to need it and not know how to use it. Auntie M and Uncle Greg keep the ammunition locked away, but I am responsible for the cleaning and maintenance of my weapon," Connor said.

"Well, my Nana Jean told me once that any fight can be avoided with a few well-chosen words and the clarity of mind to walk away. To each his own, I suppose. I agree that if it came down to it, and I had to use a weapon, it wouldn't hurt to know how. Maybe you could teach me sometime?" Madison asked.

"For sure. We have a family trip to the range every Sunday. We usually head out around 2pm, just a few hours from now actually. I can give you a lesson if you want," Connor replied.

"Awesome. And what about the bug out bags?" Madison continued. "Why would you need a bug out bag here in this sleepy town?"

"Don't ask," Connor laughed. "Auntie M's a bit of a zombie freak. She is constantly talking about the impending zombie uprising. She insists upon watching every low-grade zombie movie ever made. Trust me - some of the worst movies ever made have zombie themes. Uncle Greg and I race to get to the remote first out of fear of being subjected to yet another flesh eating masterpiece. I swear she is a bit tapped. We both know it is a harmless obsession, but she really does have several ready-to-go emergency bags. She insists that they are actually for hurricane preparedness, but I know it is just a weird extension of her zombie obsession."

"That is too funny. I love it. Until just recently, I was queen of the Boston rats. Nothing wrong with a little harmless fantasy,"

Madison chuckled.

"Speaking of fantasy, I still can't believe my sister is standing here in front of me. It seems very unreal, but at the same time, it kinda feels normal. You know what I mean?" Connor asked.

"I do. And hey - let's not let this brother/sister dynamic get weird. Don't feel like you have to act any certain way around me. Let's just hang out and be friends and take it from there. No pressure, if that makes any sense at all."

"Man, that is good to hear. I have been struggling for the last half hour with what to call you and whether I should hug you or whatever. Waddya say I call you Madison and maybe mix in a sister here and there when it feels right?"

"Sounds like a solid plan to me. And on that note, what do I call you - CJ or Connor?" Madison asked her brother.

"My friends all call me CJ. Auntie M and Uncle Greg have even taken to calling me CJ on occasion. But you want to know a secret, I sort of like Connor better," Connor replied.

"Connor it is then, bro" Madison said as they reached the garage door. "And let's get this out of the way now..." She turned and gave her brother a big bear hug.

"Right, nothing weird about this?" Connor joked as he hugged his sister back. They separated and Connor opened the garage door. "After you, sis."

# CHAPTER 11

# A Job Well Done

❖

*T*he market district in Daka, the capital city of Kre Norta, was not for the weak of mind or body. It was notorious for its trade in illegal commodities. Unlike Domi, where you purchased out of a storefront, in Daka, you purchased out of an alley. It attracted the most nefarious, brazen, violent humans on the planet. Where there is demand, Daka would provide the supply.

Neam Leache stood at his second floor window overlooking the open air market below. He ran several of the tables down on the street, displaying a wide variety of fruits and vegetables. To the uninitiated, his wares seemed to be ridiculously overpriced. A pound of radishes cost the equivalent of a luxury automobile. A potato was much as a mid-sized home.

To the initiated, the radishes equated to a crate of twenty automatic assault rifles with exploding ammunition. A potato translated into an un-manned assault tank with ten-mile range. Both were illegal to own or possess in every country in the world.

The buyer would purchase the fruit or vegetable from the stand. Inside, a microchip had directions to a rendezvous point. Often the first rendezvous point would just be another table with a fruit or vegetable on it. A microchip in that object would direct the buyer to the next rendezvous location.

This would continue until Neam was satisfied that the purchaser was *not part of any law enforcement agency. Only then would he actually direct the purchaser to a location where he would deliver the goods. To an outsider, it would seem crazy to hand over the money without getting the product immediately in return, but Neam had a reputation of never going back on a deal. Once he accepted payment, delivery was guaranteed.*

*His small marketplace office was sparse of furniture and comforts, very much unlike the luxurious and ornate compounds he owned in various corners of the world. He had amassed a small fortune, but like most alpha males, it would never be enough.*

*A small alarm sounded from the compact laptop sitting on his comically small wooden desk. The words "Human Liver" stood out at the top of a communication from his most trusted and skilled operative.*

*I still can't believe I pulled this one off. I am going to be the richest man on the planet, Neam thought to himself. He never had an issue with self-confidence, but his ego had now reached an all-time high.*

*For years Neam had been trying to infiltrate the Domi and mine its vast databases of scientific and manufacturing technologies. Just over a year ago he managed to get the plans for the new programming pods and two vials of unprogrammed nanobots, from the health lab high up in the government floors of the Domi building. His inside operatives managed to use the supply tunnels under the building to smuggle them out. It wasn't until the next morning that the Domi building security noticed the unauthorized access to the pod design, and missing vials of nanobots.*

*Domi officials had no real concern over what was stolen. The Ministry of Health knew what Neam was soon to discover. Without the programming needed to run the pod, and subsequently the nanobots, these devices and schematics were completely useless.*

*Getting to that programming was all but impossible. It was among the most highly secure pieces of code in the world. The data never left the confines of the Ministry of Health's central computer. That computer had no external connections to any other computer, inside or outside the lab. Internal security measures did not allow the program to be downloaded in any way. The program could only be transferred from the central workstation directly to the nanobot programming pod sitting twenty feet away in the same lab. Access to the code was strictly managed and restricted to only individuals with the highest level of security clearance. Currently, that consisted of four people.*

*Neam had almost given up on the project until a few months ago when he received some very welcome information. The Ministry of Health was building a new, state-of-the-art lab to better process the increasing demand for health treatments. He had an operative working on the team that had been hired to do the cabling for the new lab.*

*His inside resource split the fiber optic cable running from the central workstation to the programming pod. This new cable was then routed to an office on the thirtieth floor that conveniently had been rented by Neam under the name of one of his many dummy corporations.*

*Neam was now able to intercept every programming request that was made between the lab's workstation and the programing pod. At this point his library of nanobot programs was nearly as large as the Ministry of Health's.*

*Neam's operation was nearly complete, but did have one last obstacle. Although he could intercept the programming, there was no way to identify the target organ or tissue that the programming was supposed to treat. He came up with a brute force approach. When a program was intercepted, his team compared it, bit by bit, with the programs he already had on file. When a new program was identified, his team would abduct some poor soul off of the street and lock them in a room. The individual would be held without food or water for two days. At the end of the second day, they were offered a small glass of water. Unbeknownst to the victim, the water contained nano-bots programmed with the unknown code.*

*Over the next fifteen minutes or so the captive would undergo the nano-bot treatment. Sometimes this was painless, if the victim did not suffer from the ailment the nanobots were programmed to treat. However, when the na-nobots found the target disease, the pain inflicted ranged from mild discomfort to excruciating. Neam did not see the need to waste money on sedating his test subjects given their subsequent fate.*

*Once the treatment was complete, the captive would be led to a small room, set up with surgical equipment. There, the nanobots would be retrieved from their mouths and they would be injected with a combination of a strong benzodiazepine and potassium, the result of which was death that would occur in minutes.*

*The cadaver would then be autopsied and, using high-powered micro-scopes, the organ or tissue containing nanobots would be discovered. This process could take weeks and require multiple test subjects if the treatment was for one of the more obscure diseases. When a target disease was finally identified, the program would be catalogued and treatments would begin being sold.*

*This process was painstaking and the drastic rise in the number of missing person cases had begun attracting unwanted attention. To solve this,*

*Neam opened up testing and treatment centers complete with their own nanobots and programming pods, in each of the three continents of the world. Each hub immediately received unidentified programs as they were intercepted from the Domi facility. Sharing the workload in this manner had the dual benefit of both decreasing the time it took to identify what a given program was, and also diminishing the number of people who went missing in any given area.*

*Customers bought treatments from Neam by purchasing a banana from the fruit stands. One banana, one treatment. Unlike the government of Sapientia, Neam allowed the purchaser to bundle several treatments together. Buy two bananas, get the third one free. His prices were also far more reasonable, at one tenth of the cost of a treatment at the Domi. After all, if someone could afford the original, they wouldn't be purchasing his bananas in the center of a city like Daka.*

*Neam stared down at his latest communication, brimming with renewed pride. His plan was working to perfection. Best of all, he had incurred none of the research and design expense associated with such a revolutionary breakthrough yet would be reaping all of the profits. The cat was out of the bag - and there was nothing the good folks of Sapientia could do about it. There was no limit to the amount of money he would make from this technology. The world was his for the buying - or taking, if need be.*

# CHAPTER 12

# Outbreak

❖

## *Mobilize*

Greg Quinn pressed aggressively down on the accelerator of his Ford F350 as he exited the on ramp and began the uphill leg of the bridge connecting James Island to the city of Charleston. As he weaved his way through the sparse Sunday traffic, his two-way military radio crackled to life.

"Command to Captain Quinn."

"This is Captain Quinn. Hello, Colonel. Over," Greg responded, recognizing the voice of his commanding officer.

"Captain, there has been a change in strategy. You are to proceed directly to the Custom House downtown. The Charleston police have set up a command post there and need immediate assistance in dealing with an unknown threat, possibly terrorist and biological in nature. We have disabled the cell towers in the downtown area to prevent remote detonation of explosive devices, if this is indeed terrorist in nature. You will rendezvous with the rest of your advanced tactical team and provide assistance to the local police as needed. The remainder of the unit is mustering at the Joint Air Base in North Charleston and will roll out within the half hour. Make a threat assessment upon arrival, and radio me for further instructions. I have two choppers being fueled and on standby. If air support is needed, I can have them over the threat area in a matter of minutes. This operation is classified. Are we clear? Over."

"Affirmative, Colonel. ETA in ten minutes. Will assess the threat and make radio contact, ASAP. Over," Greg responded. He placed the radio back on the passenger seat.

This was certainly no exercise. He fought every instinct he had to turn his vehicle around, pile his family into the truck and drive them far away from the city. Had cell service not been interrupted, he certainly would have broken protocol, called Marion and insisted she get Connor and as many of his friends as she could out of the city.

His best chance at protecting them now was to terminate this threat as quickly as possible. Besides, he had married a strong woman who was more than capable of handling adversity. They will be fine, he told himself, as he pushed down harder on the accelerator and gripped down harder on the steering wheel.

Greg took a route to his destination that would avoid traveling along or past Market Street. Instead, he chose to take Lockwood Drive along the water, down Broad and then finally East Bay Street, which ran directly in front of the Custom House.

This route had him approaching the Custom House from the south, with the City Market and North and South Market Street directly beyond that to the North.

Seven minutes later, he found himself a few hundred feet from the front of the Custom House. He could see many police officers hunkered down behind their cruisers, facing the market area beyond. He took a quick right and then a left onto the road that ran along the back side of the Custom House.

If the market was chaotic, he would need the ability to assess the situation before he found himself square in the middle of it. He rolled past several dozen additional police cruisers, parked at various angles on the street and in the adjacent parking lot behind the Custom House. Many had the rooftop bubble lights still flashing, their doors and trunks open. This was a sure sign the officers had been in a serious rush to get to where they needed to be.

No sooner had his own truck door opened than he heard the sounds of gunfire. He grabbed the radio from his passenger seat, clipped it to the belt on his fatigues and raced toward the back entrance of the Custom House. More gunfire erupted as he climbed the back stairs, passing several officers talking frantically into their two-way radios.

Greg reached a hand down to his holster and gripped the handle of his sidearm, but did not un-holster it. As he approached the top of the stairs and crossed the landing leading to the building's entrance, he noticed that the large wooden door was propped open. Rather than enter immediately, he took a position with his back against the building to the side of the open door.

Greg un-holstered his weapon, and in a swift motion, turned his body so he could take a quick peek inside. There were many officers and men in camouflaged clothing moving about the room, but he could see no apparent threat. He pointed his weapon toward the floor, entering the building cautiously.

Inside he could see the chief of police and four of his fellow team members leaning over a table, apparently reviewing a map of the Market Street area. He re-holstered his weapon and made his way over to the table.

"Chief, I am Captain Quinn. I see you have met several members of my unit already. My orders are to assist your efforts in any way possible. You will have the full support of the National Guard, but I have to make an assessment of this threat to direct our forces most efficiently. What are we dealing with?"

"I hope you wore your Superman jockey's, because we are up against something superhuman. Some sort of illness is spreading rapidly through the civilian population. The afflicted are exhibiting extreme aggression and seem to have reverted to animalistic behavior. They are attacking any and every living thing in their area. And by attacking, I mean eviscerating. The victims of these attacks, if not killed immediately, appear to contract the disease and then become threats themselves – all within moments."

Greg's calm exterior did not betray the myriad of thoughts racing through his head. It was all he could do to process this information and formulate a strategy.

"What resources do you have in place to contain the current threat?" Greg asked the chief.

"The initial call came in from the City Market. What appeared to be a homeless man on methamphetamine was attacking and biting shoppers. By the time my officers arrived, there were a dozen or so individuals exhibiting this aggressive behavior. They attempted to arrest these individuals, but they themselves became victims. I am currently using my force to set up a perimeter surrounding the entire market, but there are reports of several breaches on the south and west sides. These officers are under shoot-to-kill orders, and even then, unless the afflicted are struck in the head, our service weapons are proving completely inadequate at stopping these assailants."

"You're telling me that a shot to the center of mass is not neutralizing these targets?" Greg asked in amazement.

"As hard as that is to believe, that is the current situation we find ourselves in," the chief responded.

"OK, we need to move command and control to a more remote area and establish a new perimeter. Chief, tell your men to fall back two blocks and reestablish the perimeter. Let me call the colonel and get our resources deployed to those locations. I'll check back with you once this is in motion." Greg turned, pulled his two-way radio from its belt clip, and raced back out the way he had come in. When he reached the landing, he keyed the mic on his radio and called his commander.

"Captain Quinn to Command. Over."

"This is Colonel Stanton. Over."

"We have a major outbreak of an unknown contagion. Transmission appears to be through biting of victims. Afflicted individuals are extremely hostile and aggressively violent. Threat is not contained. Repeat, threat is not contained. Engagement orders are shoot-to-kill. Shots to the head are the only effective termination of the infected individuals. We need to set up a containment perimeter five blocks surrounding the Market Street area of downtown. Command and control is not secure. Request evacuation to a more secure location and reestablish command and control. Over."

"Guard units are on route. ETA in fifteen minutes. I'll send a copter to rendezvous with your unit and the police chief at Waterfront Park in five minutes. New command and control location will be determined in flight. Over," the colonel replied.

"Affirmative, Waterfront Park in five minutes. Over and out," Greg replied.

Greg entered the building again, but as he did, he noticed a commotion at the front door. Two of the members of his team were engaged in hand to hand combat with two individuals who had apparently entered through the doors at the front of the building. One assailant was dressed in a police uniform, and the other appeared to be a boy no more than ten years old. The young boy had his jaw locked on the arm of one of the soldiers while the police officer's face was buried in the neck of the other soldier. All four individuals toppled to the floor.

Greg drew his weapon and raced toward the front entrance. The crazed police officer gazed up and saw Greg approaching fast, now no more than forty feet away. The officer, covered in blood, pulled his feet underneath him and leapt high into the air in Greg's direction. Greg halted, initially stunned at the height the officer achieved in his leap. The officer's leap was going to leave him only ten feet short of his new mark. In a split second, Greg realized that his best chance at stopping this threat was to shoot the individual before they landed and had a chance to maneuver to avoid his aim.

Greg aimed for the head and fired just before the officer's feet hit the hard stone floor. His round found its mark, but rather than the body landing with a thump, it disintegrated into a black, roiling ball that continued in his direction. Greg took two quick steps to his left and the mass passed by him, shrinking as it went until it was completely gone.

Without warning, the teenage boy left his victim and sprinted toward Greg. The speed and agility the boy possessed was unlike anything he had ever seen. He did not hesitate in dispatching this new threat, and like the first assailant, Greg had to avoid the resulting black mass. The two soldiers lay on the floor at the front of the building, writhing on the floor as if in pain.

"Do we have a medic in the building?" Greg shouted.

Before anyone could answer, both soldiers jumped to their feet and lunged in opposite directions at other officers who were still in the building. Greg took aim at the soldier on the left and fired. His shot hit the soldier in the side of the chest, but it had no effect. The soldier turned in Greg's direction and, as he did, Greg's next round found its mark. Greg heard a gunshot to his right and saw the police chief just barely succeeding in avoiding the black mass that was all that remained of the other soldier.

"Sir," Greg yelled. "We are evacuating this post. There are helicopters inbound to move us to a new command and control center. Our rendezvous is Waterfront Park, in three minutes. We must leave now."

"Right behind you," the chief said.

Greg addressed the two remaining soldiers from his unit, along with the half dozen officers that remained in the building.

"Everyone: as you can see, our current position is untenable. We are evac'ing immediately to Waterfront Park. We have barely over three minutes to travel three blocks, so let's hustle. Keep your weapons hot. Call out the threats as you see them. The infected move swiftly, and we will need multiple assets on each target. Remember these threats are human beings, so only shoot when you are certain they are infected. Let's not make this worse than it is. We are travelling by foot and will escort any unaffected civilians we encounter along the way to the park with us. Chief, get your men to move back five blocks and reestablish a perimeter. Have them instruct civilians to get to the nearest safe location, even if it's a shop or restaurant and hunker down in place until further notice. Make sure everyone knows to get off the street."

The police chief pressed the mic on his two-way radio and addressed his officers. "This is the chief to all officers. Fall back five blocks from the City Market area. Block all intersections and reestablish a perimeter. Instruct all civilians to enter the nearest safe location and hunker down in place. There is an immediate curfew in effect. No one is to be on the streets, or they risk being shot. National Guardsmen are en route and will provide assistance upon arrival. Stay safe and do your jobs, people. This city needs you today," he said and un-keyed the mic.

"Let's move," Greg said. He led the group out the back door and down the steps, heading to the street beyond.

## *Bridge Over Trouble*

Zachary cursed his luck. He had already polished off three cups of coffee this morning, and his 360-pound frame was pushing hard on his bladder. It was almost 8:30am. On most mornings, he would only be ten minutes from his last stop by now. But this was turning into anything but an ordinary morning. Not only had they closed the Wappoo Bridge for repairs, rerouting him an extra five minutes over the James Island Connector, but the police seemed to be out in force. Every time he got his bus rolling, he would quickly have to pull over to let yet another blaring cruiser pass by.

Zachary wove the large diesel bus through morning traffic, winding his way down Courtenay Drive and approaching Calhoun Street and the on-ramp to the James Island Connector. As he passed the Medical University of South Carolina, he noticed two ambulances approaching at high speed. He slowed down briefly, allowing them to take a left in front of him into the hospital parking lot.

As his bus passed the hospital entrance, he noticed that neither ambulance made it all the way to the hospital entrance. No sooner had the ambulances taken the left into the parking lot, they both came to an abnormally quick stop. Zachary kept one eye on the road, but craned his neck to try and see if he could catch a glimpse of what was happening in the parking lot, still just twenty feet from his bus. He saw the back doors of the ambulances fly open and several people spilled forth, apparently in a great hurry. The bus had now progressed to a point where he could no longer see what was happening and assumed they were making a run for the hospital. *Must be something wrong with the vehicles,* he thought.

By now, he was approaching the Calhoun Street intersection. The light was red, and he slowed his bus to a stop. It was only a few seconds before the light turned back to green. Zachary made a right hand turn and accelerated toward the bridge on-ramp.

A passenger at the back of the bus yelled, "I think this guy wants on," motioning toward the back right side of the bus. Zachary ignored the man as there was no way he was going to make an unscheduled stop this morning. A few seconds later he heard a noise come from the back of the bus. It sounded like he had hit a low hanging tree limb with the top of his bus.

Zachary checked his outside mirrors and saw nothing out of the ordinary. In his rearview mirror he saw the passengers looking up toward the roof of the vehicle. He listened for any more noises, but heard none. He turned back to the bridge ahead and accelerated up to fifty-five miles an hour, climbing the uphill leg.

A black Ford pickup truck travelling in the opposite direction caught his attention. It was driving way too fast and aggressively as it passed the slower moving traffic. *Where are the police when you need them?* he thought.

As the bus reached the crest of the bridge and began its descent down the other side, Zachary heard the noise on the roof once again. It sounded as though someone was walking around up there. He considered pulling over. By now, however, he was nearing the end of the bridge and figured it made more sense to pull over where there would be more room on the shoulder.

The thumping was getting louder now and Zachary checked his rearview mirror again. No sooner had he looked into the mirror than the emergency escape bubble on top of the bus came shattering inward. In a flash, the shower of Plexiglas was followed by the form of what appeared to be an elderly woman in her seventies.

The creature immediately began tearing at the nearest passenger. The rest of the passengers began to panic, and several of them rushed toward the front of the bus, screaming as they ran. In this rush of people, a heavy-set man seated toward the front of the bus lost his footing and landed in Zachary's lap.

Zachary lost control of the bus. It lurched to the right and barreled directly towards the large concrete divider that separated the bridge from the Harborview Road off ramp. The bus struck the concrete barrier head on, causing most of the passengers to hurtle forward. Many ended up in a heap to the bus driver's right, but several flew past him and were thrown from the bus through the front windshield.

The elderly woman / creature was one of those who flew past. Unlike the other two airborne passengers, she was flying horizontally, and exited the bus in two pieces: her mid-section had caught the vertical pole that supported the handrail lining the entry stairs. The pole had sliced her cleanly in half. For a split second, Zachery had made eye contact with the woman as her upper torso flew past him. It appeared to Zachery that even as she flew by, she was reaching with her arms at him in an attempt to rip at his flesh.

Thank god for seatbelts. He was dazed but not seriously hurt. He sat silently for several seconds in his seat, trying to gather himself before attempting to help the injured passengers. Out of the opening where his windshield used to be, he saw the bodies of the two passengers that had exited the bus first. Their bodies were twisted in unnatural angles. They were not moving. In a strange coincidence, the upper and lower torso of the elderly woman had landed in such a way that they almost appeared to be a whole body again. The two halves sat mere inches from each other.

As he said a silent prayer for the injured, he noticed something strange was happening to the elderly lady's corpse. It appeared that black tendrils were extending from the woman's upper torso in the direction of her lower body. He wiped his eyes, sure that he was suffering from a concussion. His vision cleared, but the scene did not change: more and more tendons of black made connections between the two halves of the woman's body.

In a sudden jerk, the lower torso was pulled toward the upper torso, making the corpse whole again. A split second later, the old woman was back on her feet. She swiveled to face the bus and began sprinting back in its direction. Zachary realized he had survived the crash, but not the incident. He quickly unbuckled his seat belt and fell to his right down the short set of stairs that led to the pavement below. His large girth made it a tight fit, but Zachary managed to roll out onto the pavement just as the elderly lady leapt back through the front opening and onto the bus.

As the overweight bus driver struggled to reach his feet, he could hear the screams coming from his bus. His passengers were being slaughtered and he could do nothing to help. Those that were ambulatory were being taken out first. The rest, suffering from various broken bones and life threatening injuries, got to watch the horror unfold in front of them as they awaited their turn at death.

The last thing Zachary heard as he spun and began running down the Harborview off-ramp was blood spattering in almost comic volumes against the remaining windows. Zachary made it only thirty yards before he could run no further. The years of sitting in that driver's seat, eating donuts and other high calorie foods, had bloated his body to a degree that made even the least strenuous exercise insurmountable. He turned to face the bus again, his hands at his hips and his lungs gasping for air.

The screaming had stopped and the elderly woman was now outside of the bus staring directly at him. Zachary could not get enough air in his lungs and bent at the waist and brought his hands to his knees. He hoped that the woman's aggression was based on movement, sort of like a T-Rex. He had no option other than to stand there and let fate take its course.

The elderly woman mimicked the bus driver's stance, only

she was bracing for a leap and a run. In his head, Zachary began reciting the Lord's Prayer. He thought about his wife at home and how much he loved her. Did he even say goodbye this morning? Had he remembered to kiss her cheek as he did most every morning before heading off to work? As the passengers on the bus discovered only moments before, motion had nothing to do with the attack. The elderly woman crossed the hundred feet in a flash and was upon Zachary before he could finish the first line of his prayer.

Luckily for him, death came quickly. His last gasp of air came not through his mouth, but directly through his trachea, due to the gaping hole created as the assailant's teeth ripped through his neck. The old woman spent the next thirty seconds dismembering the heavyset man's body. Small pieces of flesh and bone showered the area in a forty foot radius.

The octogenarian only stopped the assault when her attention was drawn to the traffic moving along Harborview road just a few hundred feet down the off ramp. She rose from the sea of red and sprinted down the off ramp to the unsuspecting travelers below.

## *Disturbing Images*

"So - you got a boyfriend back in Boston?" Brooke asked Madison before she even had a chance to take a seat in the garage. The band was still there, waiting for the "All Clear" from Miss M, but they weren't getting much practicing done.

"No. No boyfriend. The only real friend I had was Jeremiah and he had to have been in his sixties. You guys would have liked him. He played a mean harmonica," Madison answered. Mako seemed very pleased with that response.

"Did you really have a building land on you?" Riley asked.

"Well, not technically. It missed for the most part." Madison laughed.

"The Lord does work in mysterious ways," Riley said, shaking her head.

"Really, the Lord? I don't think any superior being had much to do with a building nearly crushing a teenage girl. I would hope he had something better to do with his time," Mako said, knowing this would get a rise out of Riley.

"Not this again, Mako. Give Riley and the rest of us a break. I think we have enough to talk about without rehashing your thoughts on God," Connor groaned. "Let's just agree that it's awesome Madison is here with us and let's get down to playing some music. I want to hear that Martin get strummed a bit."

"Amen to that," said Tanner.

"Whoa guys, check this out. For some reason my calls aren't going through, but I can still get to the internet. Check out this video. Some Whiskey Tango chick just destroyed the Hardee's on the Crosstown," Brooke said.

The kids all crowded around Brooke's phone as she replayed the video. They strained to see the video on her small screen. It appeared to be shot from one of the patrons inside the fast food restaurant. What had apparently begun as some type of video blog on cheeseburgers had instead captured a scene of horrific bloodshed.

In the video, a clean-cut man in his early twenties was enthusiastically sharing his expert opinion on the tastiness of his burger. Over his shoulder, a teenage girl could be seen entering the building dressed in beat up jeans and an Army jacket. Within seconds, she launched onto the nearest table and propelled herself toward a group of what appeared to be cable company employees. She could clearly be seen biting and ripping at the men with a savage ferocity. The other patrons began screaming and running for the exit.

The girl shooting the video with her cell phone dropped the device, apparently scrambling toward the door. The image was now turned ninety degrees, as the phone landed on its side on the floor. You could still see the interior of the restaurant although the lens was now pointing toward the service counter. The carnage taking place could be heard in the background. Within moments, the girl in the Army coat could be seen jumping the service counter and attacking the workers hiding in the kitchen beyond.

Marion suddenly burst through the garage door. "Everyone

get in here. Shut and lock this door behind you. They are broadcasting an emergency message on the TV. We all need to see this."

One by one, the kids scrambled through the garage door and rushed into the living room. Marion turned up the volume on the wide-screen TV mounted above the fireplace. Dirk Mannington, the Channel 2 anchorman, was visibly shaken as he faced the camera and described the situation that was unfolding in downtown Charleston.

"The local police are requesting that everyone stay in your homes and lock your doors. Do not venture outside under any circumstances whatsoever. What we do know at this hour is that there is some type of outbreak happening in the downtown Market Street area. The exact nature of the contagion is not yet known, but what is known is that persons afflicted with this ailment become incredibly violent and must be avoided at all cost. The National Guard has been called in and is attempting to quarantine this area of the city, but at this time, every attempt to contain this threat has been unsuccessful. Once again, remain inside with your doors locked and secured until further notice."

"Auntie M, we just saw a video of a girl attacking people in a restaurant on the cross town. This isn't just in the Market Street area," Connor said. "It is also really strange that we have all tried to use our cell phones and none of our calls are going through. It isn't just my service."

"I don't like this at all. OK, here's what we are going to do.

Connor, go get your pistol from your room. I'm going to get the two handguns from my safe. Mako and Tanner, send your parents a text and let them know you are staying here with us until this is over. Riley, send your parents a text and tell them if they are not already on their way to stay at home and lock the doors. I know they don't watch a lot of television and they may not know what is going on. If they are already on their way, tell them to hurry!" Marion said. She turned and headed down the hall toward the master bedroom. Connor leapt up and ran to his room to retrieve his weapon. Riley pulled out her iPhone and sent a text to her mother.

"Where do you live?" Madison asked Riley.

"Just a mile or so from here. My parents walk here after church on Sunday mornings for brunch. If they have already left, they should be here within a half hour at the most," Riley replied.

Riley had barely finished her sentence when a text from her mother popped up on her phone "Left 10 minutes ago, be there shortly."

The news was now showing an aerial shot of the downtown Charleston area. A military helicopter was taking off from the Waterfront park area.

"This just in. The following video is graphic in nature. If you have small children, or are sensitive to this type of material, you may not want to watch this," the anchorman said as the video that Brooke had just shown in the garage began to roll across the big screen.

Connor returned from his room, gun case in hand. He joined the others watching the screen. Riley, whom he had sat down beside on the couch, buried her head in his shoulder, turning away from the television.

Marion also returned with two gun cases of her own and looked on in silence. On the other couch in the room, Brooke had taken up a seat on the arm of a couch upon which Madison and Mako were sitting. Unfortunately for Madison every time the crazed attacker was shown on the screen, Brooke involuntarily smacked her on the shoulder. With every smack, Madison leaned further away from Brooke and closer to Mako, which did not seem to bother the boy in the least.

"This is where she disappears into the kitchen. I wonder if she is on drugs or something," Tanner said.

The video was now showing parts that they hadn't seen in the garage. Thirty seconds after the girl had hurdled the counter and attacked the workers in the kitchen, the backs of two police officers were seen entering the frame with guns drawn.

"Come out with your hands up. Police department, come out with your hands up or we will open fire," the officer closest to the camera shouted.

A young girl could be seen rising up from behind a stainless steel kitchen appliance. Her hair was matted and her face was dripping with red liquid. The image quality was not ideal, but the viewer could clearly make out that this was the same girl who had entered the building and attacked the cable workers. The girl bolted from the back of the kitchen directly toward the officer closest to her.

The officer was now clearly threatened by her approach and opened fire. Two rounds hit the girl directly in the chest in what appeared to be a shot through her heart. A black spray exited the back of the girl as each bullet passed through her. The bullets did not have the intended effect. The girl kept coming, reacting only for the split second it took the bullet to pass through her. The other officer then fired and struck the girl in the head, which brought her down instantly. She dropped behind the counter, out of sight of the camera.

"OMG," Brooke said, now falling off the arm of the loveseat onto Madison's lap.

"Ms. M, my parents are out there in this. They had already left the house when I texted them. I hope they are alright" Riley said, tears welling up in her eyes.

"I'm sure they are OK. They should be here any minute." Marion replied trying her best to sound confident.

"Connor, we need to load," was all Marion could get out before they were all once again glued to the scene on the TV. As the officers approached the counter, two more people appeared in the kitchen. They wore the uniforms of restaurant employees, only these were soaked with blood. The officers didn't have time to take aim before they were overwhelmed by their assailants. The officer closest to the camera was hit with such force that his hat was dislodged from his head and came directly toward the camera, blocking the view. The officer's screams were quickly silenced, leaving the audience to imagine the horror taking place only a few feet away.

"Auntie M," Connor said. "What spreads by biting people and can only be killed by a headshot?"

"Zombies," she replied. "But they aren't real. Right? It has to be something else." Marion was still unable to parse the images she had just seen on TV.

"Whatever we call it, we need a plan to defend ourselves," Madison said, barely managing to get up from under Brooke's weight and stand. Madison had been responsible for her own safety long enough to know her Nana Jean's advice was spot on. "It takes much less energy, and is much more effective, to run your brain than run your legs."

"That's what these are for," Marion said. She opened her gun cases and produced two 45 caliber pistols. "Who here besides Connor knows how to shoot one of these?" she asked the group in the room. Tanner immediately responded with "I do," but no one else spoke.

"Never had the inclination, or the need, to shoot a gun. I use my big boy words to avoid confrontation," Mako replied.

"Maybe the police should have asked that girl nicely to stop chewing on them," Tanner replied, clearly irritated. "If they show up here, you can answer the door and negotiate."

"Enough of that, guys," Marion interrupted. "Tanner, you take the Sig. I'll keep the Glock and Connor, you have your Kimber 10mm. Let's get them loaded. Madison, stay with me. I need you to learn how to load these guns. The rest of you, go and make sure all the doors and windows are locked. Riley, keep an eye out front for your parents. Go everyone, now."

"Mako, looks like you won't have to use your negotiating skills. Turns out they won't make the front door after all," Tanner said. He held the Sig Sauer 45 caliber pistol in his right hand.

## *Uninvited Guests*

Madison watched Connor as he field stripped and cleaned his handgun.

"I hope there isn't going to be a quiz on this, because I didn't get half of that," she said, staring at her brother.

"Don't worry, you won't need to know how to do all that. Let's keep it really simple. Come over here and take this," Marion said to Madison, handing her a 9mm pistol. "This is the safety. It stays on always, until you're ready to shoot. No exceptions. This button drops the magazine out the bottom of the gun. When the gun is empty, click this and put a loaded magazine in its place. Pull back on the slide and you are ready to fire."

"That seems doable, but I really hope I don't have to shoot this," she told him. She practiced loading and unloading the magazine clip from the pistol.

"Run Mom! Run faster," Riley Lee screamed from the front window. Marion took the pistol from Madison and slid a loaded magazine into the weapon as they all ran into the front room where Riley was staring out the window.

Outside, they saw Riley's mother and father were running down the road toward the house. Mr. Lee was twenty feet behind his wife and slowing down considerably. The man had two bad knees and it was a wonder he was running at all. Behind the two, an even older woman was chasing them at an incredible pace. It was obvious to the observers that Riley's parents were not going to make the house. Without warning, Tanner bolted out the front door and was running quickly down the driveway.

As Tanner reached the halfway point down the driveway, he began firing at the Lee's pursuer. He hit the woman in the chest, but to his dismay, it had no effect. Mrs. Lee ran past Tanner and headed up the driveway toward the house as he fired at the attacker again. He missed. The elderly woman made one final leap and tackled Mr. Lee thirty feet from the end of the driveway. Marion was now standing shoulder to shoulder with Tanner and both began firing at the old woman. Riley exited the house and met her mother at the bottom of the entryway stairs. Both were watching the horror unfold in front of them.

Mr. Lee was now face down on the pavement, his attacker sitting on his back, pinning him to the ground. She leaned forward in an attempt to sink her teeth into the elderly man's shoulder. The woman jerked as each round entered her body, but it wasn't until a round found the base of her skull that the attack ended. To everyone's shock and amazement, the woman dissolved into a black, undulating mass.

Mr. Lee, now free of the weight of his attacker, pulled his knees up under him, leaned back into a kneeling position and tried to get up, all the while attempting to wipe the black, slimy, quivering mass from his body. A small amount of the black substance entered his mouth just as the remainder fell away to the ground.

For several moments, the man struggled to get to his feet. And then it began. His entire body convulsed and shivered. Riley was now screaming at the top of her lungs for her father. Marion began to move toward the man to help him get to his feet, but Tanner held out his arm and stopped her.

"Remember the video? We may be too late. There's nothing we can do to help him. We don't want to be too close if he turns," he said.

After fifteen seconds of watching her father writhing at the end of the driveway, Riley could not take it any longer. She sprinted down the drive toward the street where her father continued to kneel. She was halfway down the driveway, just reaching the spot where Marion and Tanner stood, when her father leapt to his feet in one fluid motion.

The expression on the man's face was of pure rage. His posture changed into that of an aggressor. He crouched and let out an animalistic growl. Tanner knew he was infected and did not wait for the man to begin his assault before he opened fire. Marion followed suit and both unloaded the remaining rounds in their pistols into the man. They could hear Riley screaming behind them. Just as the last round left Marion's gun, Riley's hand swung down hard on Marion's right arm in an attempt to stop her from firing at her father. It was too late.

One of the rounds had struck the man in the head and he fell to the ground. Half of the man's body dissolved into the same black substance as the elderly woman. The other half remained flesh. Some areas of the man's body were completely missing, while others gave the appearance of being severely burnt. Skin and tissue dissolved right down to the bone. The black mass was rolling in their direction and Marion grabbed Tanner by the arm and pulled him toward the house as they both pushed Riley in front of them.

The black mass that had emerged from Mr. Lee's body dissolved before it reached the driveway. Riley ran into her mother's arms, sobbing uncontrollably.

Mrs. Lee was shouting at Marion and Tanner. "You killed my husband. Why? Why did you shoot him? He was fine. The old woman was dead. He was getting to his feet. I don't understand," she said, choking out the words through her tears.

"Come inside, everyone. Mrs. Lee, I will explain when we get in the house, but we have to move now. It is not safe out here," Marion said, insisting they all start moving back to the relative safety of the house.

When they were all locked back inside, it was Riley who began filling her mother in on what was happening. "That old woman, she was infected with something that made her violent. It can be passed from one person to the next. I don't know what that black stuff is, but it makes the infection spread," Riley said to her mother.

"Here, watch this," Brooke added, replaying the restaurant video to Mrs. Lee.

"Oh my God," she said as the video rolled across the small phone.

"Let's all get back to the television and see if there are any instructions on what we should be doing," Marion said, walking back down the hall into the living room and motioning everyone to follow. Riley and her mother walked arm in arm down the hall behind Marion, unable to take their eyes from the small cell phone screen.

"It must be the apocalypse. God is punishing us. It was only a matter of time," Mrs. Lee said as they all reached the living room and sat down to watch the coverage on the news.

## *Regroup*

Greg led the heavily armed group south on Concord Street toward Waterfront Park. In the summer, Waterfront Park was a popular tourist location in the city, but this was early December. They expected the park to be relatively empty, making a helicopter landing safe.

As the group passed the Cumberland Street intersection and made their way past the Port Authority on the left, a man dressed in chef's whites appeared in the street behind them. He saw the group and immediately began running in their direction. The officer in the rear of the group leveled his weapon but held his fire. He was unsure if this individual was infected or just in need of assistance.

The man was running very fast and when he got to within fifty feet of the group he leapt onto the roof of an SUV parked on the side of the road and continued airborne in their direction. By now, the man was close enough that the officer could make out the SNOB embroidered on the man's chef coat. He fired three shots. The final one found its mark. The black mass rolled underneath a car twenty feet from the group.

"Looks like the chef got served for a change. No one is eating at Slightly North of Broad tonight." the officer said, chuckling at his own joke and looking around at his comrades.

"Less chatter, gentlemen," Greg said, visibly annoyed. "And

call out those targets. We don't need anyone playing hero here."

To the right, a young girl barely in her teens was half running, half stumbling toward the group. The soldier to Greg's right said "I got this one." and raised his rifle to his shoulder.

"Hold your fire soldier." Greg said. The girl stumbled and fell onto the road just fifty feet from the group. A feeble "Help" came from her as she struggled to regain her feet.

Greg left the group and rushed to the young girl lying in the street. Her head was wrapped in a gauze bandage and she was wearing light blue pajamas.

"We're here to help you. Let's get you on your feet now." Greg said as he helped the girl to a standing position. She was weak and could barely stand. He signaled for another of the soldiers to come and help.

"My name is Greg, and me and these other fellas are going to get on a helicopter to reach some place a bit safer. You want to come with us? Maybe we can get you back to your family?" he said to the girl. She began sobbing at the word family but was able to speak a quiet "yes."

"This gentleman is going to carry you as we have to hurry and you are in no condition to run." Greg said as the soldier picked up the girl. Together the group began hustling toward the park.

They reached the far end without incident and made their way to the open field just north of the central fountain. A large green military helicopter was approaching from the east, over the water. When it slowed to a hover over the field and began descending to land, Greg saw movement in the street back in the direction they had just come from.

Several small groups of infected had entered the grassy field and were sprinting in their direction. The men opened fire as the helicopter landed behind them. One by one, they entered the wide helicopter door, spinning to continue firing as their comrades followed suit. The young girl was crying and buried her head against the man carrying her as they entered through the door.

Greg was the last to enter, and the aircraft lifted just as several larger groups of infected entered the field. Within seconds, the area directly below them was completely filled with infected.

The pilot handed headsets to Greg and the police chief so the men could communicate over the roaring helicopter engine.

"We've been airlifting civilians to Fort Sumter. There's a makeshift medical tent there. They should be able to help her." The pilot motioned to the young girl as he spoke.

"OK. Let's head over there to drop her off. In the meantime, patch me in to the colonel," Greg replied.

The helicopter made its way over Charleston harbor toward Fort Sumter as Greg hailed the colonel on the radio.

"Captain Quinn to base, over,"

"This is the colonel. What is your status? Over."

"The entire City Market and surrounding area is untenable. Infected have overrun the area. Police have pulled back five blocks but are in serious need of reinforcements. I suggest we relocate the hard outer perimeter to two miles and work our way back in from there. We should implement the emergency broadcast system and instruct civilians in the infected zone to find a safe location and stay indoors. Over."

"Understood, Captain. Base camp is now Summerall Field at the Citadel. Over."

"Confirm, Summerall Field. We are dropping a civilian off at Fort Sumter and will rendezvous to your position after that. ETA fifteen minutes. Over and out."

Greg motioned to the police chief to give his headset to the young girl seated beside him. He did and the girl placed the headphones over her head.

"Do you like the helicopter ride?" he asked the young girl.

"It's loud."

"I know. We won't be on it long - just a few more minutes. What's your name?"

"Morgan," she said.

"Well Morgan, have you ever been to Fort Sumter?" he asked.

"Once, on a school field trip."

"Well we're headed that way right now. You'll be safe there. They have doctors and people to help you get back to your family." Greg said to the young girl.

"My family died last night." the girl replied. "My head hurts so I want to stop talking now."

Greg was shocked at the abruptness and lack of emotion in her voice. They sat in silence until the helicopter landed in the field at Fort Sumter.

Back on the ground, Greg rushed the girl to the medical tent and then hustled back. They were soon airborne, now heading toward Summerall Field at the Citadel, Charleston's Military College.

The skids of the helicopter had barely hit the grass when Greg leapt off. A young cadet in his late teens was there to greet him.

"Are you Captain Quinn?" he asked.

"Yes," Greg replied.

"Follow me. The colonel wants to see you immediately," the boy said. He led the captain towards the building where the colonel had set up shop. They entered the pristine stone building, headed down a long hallway and turned into a classroom turned base camp. Greg saluted the colonel as he entered. The colonel saluted back and said, "at ease, Captain."

The colonel dismissed the cadet. The boy quickly exited the room.

"They're a little young for such responsibility," Greg said to his commander.

"Hard times, hard measures," the colonel replied. "I've enlisted the help of the senior cadets at this fine establishment to protect our own perimeter. They have been well trained in the use of most small firearms and assault rifles. They have taken up positions in the buildings on the outer edge of campus and are instructed to shoot anyone attacking civilians on the street, or attempting to gain access to these buildings. The younger cadets are positioned on higher floors and have bullhorns pointed out the windows. They are instructing civilians not to attempt to enter the Citadel or risk being shot, that they should instead find a safe location indoors and stay there."

"In order to contain this threat, I suggest we create a hard outer perimeter that we can guarantee has not yet been breached. From there, we can begin to shrink the border until we have all of the infected in one area," Greg said.

"I agree. Plans are already in motion. I have closed all bridges leading out of the city. We are closing roads starting from two miles out of ground zero. I have the National Guard from Georgia and North Carolina en route to aid us in the blockade," the colonel replied.

"How do we know if that is far enough out? I think we need some surveillance flights to see if we can establish how far this has spread," Greg added.

"My thoughts exactly. I need you to take one of the small surveillance choppers and head south over James Island. Let me know what you find. I have Apaches from the Army air base performing these duties to the North and West."

"Yes sir," Greg said. He turned and left the room.

## *Local Armory*

On the big screen TV, the reality of the situation became all too clear to the small group gathered in Marion Quinn's living room. Riley and her mother were huddled on the loveseat. Mako and Tanner were sitting on the arms of the couch watching the emergency broadcast that was being shown on the TV.

The scene was shot from a helicopter flying over the market street area. It showed mayhem in the streets. From the helicopter's height, it was difficult to make out the fine details, but the overall picture was unmistakable. Several people were seen running in the streets and being overtaken by other, wilder, more aggressive figures. It was the exact scene that had just taken place outside their house, but with many more people involved. The announcer was reading an emergency statement issued by the police chief just moments before.

"Find a safe place and stay indoors until further notice. If you see someone acting strangely or aggressively, do not attempt to help them. If you are caught out in the open or find yourself under attack by an infected individual, a shot to the head is the only defense."

As she listened to this final statement, Marion could only shake her head at the ammunition laid out in front of her on the dining room table. Connor and Madison were on each side of her, helping in any way they could. "Only seventy rounds for the 45s," Marion said to Connor as they counted and recounted the rounds. That was not nearly enough. The 10mm situation was not nearly that good.

"Only thirty for the 10mm," Connor replied. They both knew the ammunition would go fast. It was no easy feat to hit a moving target with the kind of accuracy it would take to stop their assailants.

"Madison, how are you holding up, honey? It's been quite a day for you," Marion said to Madison. She placed her hand on her niece's shoulder.

"It has been quite a day for everyone. And it's going to get worse. I probably played this day out a thousand times in my head over the years. Pretty much dreamt of every possible angle and outcome. I gotta say I missed the zombie apocalypse somehow," Madison replied.

"You and me both," Marion replied. The young girl had an amazing inner strength, which shined through in her demeanor. Marion's heart sank for an instant as she imagined what the girl must have survived to be so calm and collected right now. But letting her mind wander was a luxury Marion couldn't afford at the moment. It was time for a plan.

"Everyone, gather around. We need to come up with a plan that can keep us all safe and alive until this thing passes or help arrives. My husband will move heaven and earth to get back here and help us, but he has responsibilities that will keep him away indefinitely. Our immediate need is self-defense and security, but eventually we will need to consider food and water. We only have three handguns. If the time comes and we need to defend ourselves, Connor, Tanner and I are going to be using these. Madison, Mako, and Riley, your job will be to make sure these magazines are full at all times. If you have any questions about how to do that, now is the time to ask. I know this has all come up on us very fast, but it's here and we have to deal with it," Marion said.

She wished she could give each of them a crash course in shooting the pistols, but knew she could not risk the noise - and certainly couldn't spare the ammunition. She had everyone watch carefully as she loaded the magazines with bullets. When she was done, she unloaded them and had Madison, Mako and Riley practice reloading them. When she was satisfied, she handed Connor and Tanner several loaded magazines each. She placed the remaining loose ammunition into her range bag and gave that to Madison to hold.

"Stay by my side at all times. I need you to be my re-loader in case we need to use these," Marion said to Madison. This was true. But what was truer was that she did not want to risk losing this girl so soon after she had come into their lives. She would do whatever it took to keep her and everyone in her house alive that day.

"The news said to stay indoors, but I have serious concerns about the defensibility of this house. There are too many full-size windows that are easily accessible from the outdoors. For a normal burglar situation, the security system and firearms are fine – but these aren't burglars. A house alarm would only attract unwanted attention and we do not have enough ammunition to defend against any significant attack," Marion said to the group.

Mrs. Lee disagreed. "The news said to stay inside. You saw what was out there. They killed my husband. We need to stay indoors until help arrives. God has a plan for all of us and I believe we need to stay put. He will provide for us. Trust in him and you will be rewarded. We just need to stay here, keep quiet and we will survive," she said.

"Mrs. Lee, I agree that we need wait this out. I just don't believe the place to do that is here. By all appearances, this thing is going to get worse before it gets better. We need to find a house that is better suited for survival," Marion told the woman. It might be a day or more before her husband could return from his duties.

"What about Matt Marine's house?" Connor said. Matt Brown, aka Matt Marine, was a neighbor who lived twelve houses down the street. His house was one of the large mansions that lined the oceanfront side of White Point Boulevard. Mr. Brown would routinely walk his German Shepherd past the Quinn residence and, on more than one occasion, would stop in and listen while the band was rehearsing.

"He was listening to practice one day an overheard me talking to Mako about my 10mm. He said he had a shooting range in his house. Completely soundproof. He said I should take you and Uncle Greg over there sometime to shoot. He even gave me the code to his garage in case he wasn't home. I thought it was strange that he would give me the code to his house, but I think he is just a lonely guy and doesn't have a lot of friends. I left it on a shelf in the garage. If he has a shooting range, chances are he has guns."

Marion and Greg had spoken to the man on several occasions as the kids practiced in the garage. She knew he had had a family of his own at one time. A wife, two teenage boys, and a seven year old daughter. They had been killed during a home invasion while the man was overseas serving his second tour in Iraq. His home security system failed that night. He received a very large sum of money from the subsequent lawsuit.

"That does sound promising," Marion said. She remembered that Mr. Brown's house had security bars on all the windows. She had always thought it looked more like a prison than a home.

"I vote for the neighbor's house. Too much glass in here," Madison added. The short trip up the street was more than worth the risk.

"I'm in," said Tanner.

"Absolutely not," Mrs. Lee jumped in. "This is a bad idea. We have what we need right here. If we are quiet, there is no reason we can't stay right here until help arrives."

"And I am staying with my mom. God will see us through this," Riley added, looking at Connor with tears in her eyes.

"Come with us Riley. Please. Mrs. Lee, we need to stick together," Connor begged the girl's mother, reaching out and taking Riley's hand.

"We are far safer if we stay together, Mrs. Lee. The safest place for all of us is at Mr. Brown's house," Marion added.

"You can do what you feel you must. We will pray you make it safely. Riley and I are going to stay put right here," Mrs. Lee stated in a tone that left no room for further discussion.

"At least let us give you one of these pistols. It sounds like we will have all we need once we get to Mr. Brown's house," Marion said to Mrs. Lee.

"I'm sure that won't be necessary. You may need those out on the street. We will be safe here. We will keep quiet and pray. No need for guns. You go ahead. God has a plan for everyone and I will put my faith in his plan," Mrs. Lee continued.

Mako, after hearing this last statement, groaned and shook his head. It did not go unnoticed by the rest of the group.

Mrs. Lee glared at Mako and gave her daughter a hug.

"OK then. Riley, Mrs. Lee, I think your best chance is to stay upstairs and use whatever you can to block the staircase. Everyone, go into the garage and get anything you can carry that Riley and her mom could use to survive the next few days."

The group descended upon the garage and collected bottled water, canned food, can openers, flashlights and anything else they thought might be useful. They carried these items up to a bedroom on the second floor. Connor grabbed the paper with the code Mr. Brown's house on his way back into the house.

Among other things, Marion carried a can of white spray paint with her as she ascended the stairs to the second floor of the house. The second floor consisted of two bedrooms, a study, and a common bathroom. The study had books and a computer set up with internet access. The bedrooms each had a television to keep the Lee's occupied.

Marion had the group collect all but one of the mattresses, and anything else they could find that could be used to make a barricade. They brought them to the hallway and began building a barricade at the top of the stairs. While they were busy with their task, Marion walked down the hall, spray paint in hand, and climbed out a bedroom window onto the roof. She returned a minute later and told everyone but Riley and her mother that it was time to go.

One by one, each member of the group squeezed through the small opening in the barricade and made their way down the stairs. Marion was the last to go. Before descending, she turned to talk to the Lee's one last time.

"When we get down, use the last of these pieces of furniture to block this hole. This should be enough to keep you safe if anyone manages to get into the house. Just stay quiet. If we find help, we will be back for you."

"Good luck. God be with you," Mrs. Lee responded. With that, Marion made her way down to the main entrance hallway. She bumped the black guitar case that was firmly in the grasp of her niece. "That won't be of much use to us where we are going. You can leave that, and we will be back for it later," Marion explained, knowing the large, bulky case may just be the difference between life and death for the young girl.

"If this stays, I stay," Madison replied. Marion did not know the young girl well at all yet, but it was clear that the girl meant what she said.

"OK, but promise me you will let it go if the time comes and it is life or death. Agreed?" Marion replied.

"Agreed," Madison said, nodding. It was clearly a waste of time to have this argument with her aunt. She appreciated that the woman wanted her to be safe, but knew her aunt didn't yet understand that the Reaper was as part of her as her right hand. She would never leave it behind.

"We are going to need to take the band van. Not only won't we fit in my Jeep, but Greg was not done changing the oil this morning when he got called in. My oil pan is still sitting in the driveway." Marion said the group.

"The van is still full of band gear from last night." Tanner replied. "I barely had room for Mako and Brooke this morning on the way over, and even then, Brooke had to sit on Mako's lap."

Marion weighed her options. She certainly did not want to risk the noise that would accompany unlading a van full of band gear. She also did not want to have to take three trips back and forth between Mr. Brown's house. She opened the door, walked out onto her porch and surveyed the neighborhood, straining to hear any signs of distress. It was quite. She motioned to the group to follow her and whispered "we're walking, let's be quick and quite."

"Be safe," Connor whispered loudly up the stairs to Riley before locking the door behind them.

# CHAPTER 13

# An Answer To A Prayer

*E*taf *finally finished with the last of her scheduled patients. As her nurse assistant escorted the Vice Director of Tourism out of the lab, the second dinner cart announced its presence at the lab door. It had already been a very long day and Etaf realized she was starving. She had eaten first breakfast at 0600 hours and rushed straight to work. She had just a small salad for lunch at 1600 hours and now, at 2600 hours, she was famished. These twenty hour work days, coupled with the stress and worry at home, were taking their toll on her, both mentally and physically.*

*Etaf scolded herself for not being more diligent with her eating schedule. She needed to eat all of her meals if she expected to keep up this frantic pace and keep her wits about her. She still had a lot to do tonight and would need to be sharp. She pulled one of the prepared dinners from the cart and sent it on its way.*

*Etaf sat at her workstation and browsed through her recent communications as she ate her supper. Time to put her plan in motion. She sent out one message to Opeh. It read simply, "time."*

*Opeh had been waiting all day for a message back from Etaf. When her incoming communication screen flashed, she opened it immediately. It was the message she had been hoping for.*

*She collected baby Roez from the small crib in her office and headed down to the one hundred and thirtieth floor. Her presence at this late hour raised no concern from the various security checkpoints at the end of the secure hallways. As security director, she had unlimited access to the building. All areas, that is, except those deemed top secret. The lab of the Ministry of Health was one such location. The security guard manning the desk at the end of the one hundred and thirtieth hall recognized Opeh immediately.*

*"Ma'am, you know I can't let you in here without authorization," he said, looking down at the small child in the woman's arms.*

*He had heard that the director and her life partner had a child, but this was the first time anyone had seen the baby in the building.*

*"Call Etaf, she is expecting me," Opeh replied. After a quick call to the lab, the security guard stood down and allowed Opeh access to the hallway. Etaf was waiting at the door and together they entered the lab. Etaf turned and locked the door behind them. The action was highly unusual; this section of the building was accessible only to individuals with top secret clearance. As a result, the maneuver set off an alarm at the security guard's station. Etaf's phone began to ring. It was the security guard asking if everything was OK.*

*"Yes, we are fine. We are having a sensitive, private conversation and do not want anyone walking by to eavesdrop," Etaf said into the receiver.*

*"OK, ma'am. Please unlock the door and open it when you are done. Regulations state that an occupied, high security room can only remain locked for a twenty-minute period without an armed guard present. We need to be sure you are not being forced to do something against your will," the guard*

*explained.*

"Could you just give us a couple of hours?" Etaf asked. "It is me, my life partner, and our child in here. Come on in and look around if you want. We have a lot to talk about and there will undoubtedly be a lot of crying going on. Surely you do not want to listen to that all night?" Etaf responded.

The guard hesitated. He had heard about the trouble Etaf and Opeh were having with their baby. A very sad thing indeed. His compassion overtook his need to follow the rules and, against his better judgment, he replied, "take all the time you need. Let me know if there is anything I can do."

"Thank you. You are very kind," Etaf replied as she hung up the phone.

"Well, that is it. We have all the time we need. Give me half an hour to get the program ready," Etaf said to Opeh, who was now openly weeping. Opeh took Roez from her arms and laid her on the hospital bed. She turned and held Opeh for several minutes without speaking. Their moment was broken by the fast, jerking motions coming from the bed. Opeh rushed to Roez and picked up her child, doing her best to comfort her through yet another seizure.

"Hurry," she said to Etaf. "I don't think she can make it through many more of these."

Etaf sat at her workstation and pulled up the nanobot programming library. She began programming a new master set of code. She used the existing code as a template, building her updates from that. Her changes were relatively simple, expanding the list of target cells to include all cells. This would surely fix whatever little Roez's ailment was.

*Etaf also completely removed the step that governed the collection of unknown cells. There was no way she could catalog these results without revealing her highly illegal activity. She would retrieve the nanobots at the end of the procedure and use the reset program to wipe their memory.*

*She sat staring at her new code, looking for obvious design flaws. This entire coding process had only taken her twenty minutes. It would only take another ten minutes of computing time to run a simulation of the new program, to ensure it would have the intended effect on the patient - and no unwanted side effects.*

*She was about to start the simulation when the phone rang again.*

*Etaf picked up the receiver and said, "Hello."*

*"This is the security officer on duty. Sorry to disturb you but my supervisor is on his way down to inspect the room. The security measures operating in your lab have set off an alarm in his office. Your door has been locked for more than twenty minutes and that violates protocol. Please unlock the door and make the room ready for examination. Store any and all classified materials in their appropriate receptacles."*

*Etaf hung up the phone abruptly. "Opeh, an alarm has been set off. They are coming to inspect the room," she cried.*

*Opeh responded quickly. "I was not aware that these protocols were in place. I don't have high security clearance so I was not privy to these processes. How much time before they get here?" she asked.*

*"Two minutes, three at the most," Etaf replied.*

*"Is your program ready? We have to do this now. Roez won't make it through another day," Opeh pleaded.*

*"I haven't run the simulation. What if I missed something? I could kill our child,"* Etaf responded. For the first time in many years she was uncertain of herself.

*"We have nothing to lose. We are going to use the program as is,"* Opeh responded sharply. Etaf keyed in the command to send her new program to the nanobot programming pod. She jumped up, grabbed a nanobot vial from the refrigerator and pulled a syringe from the drawer underneath. She quickly crossed the room to the programming pod and placed the vial inside. The pod closed agonizingly slowly. It seemed as if the next five seconds took an hour. When the programming was done, Etaf did not wait for the pod to completely open before grabbing the vial from within. She quickly opened the syringe, pushed the needle into the vial, and drew up the clear liquid.

There was a knock at the door. No time to lose now.

*"Last chance to stop,"* Etaf said as she positioned the needle against Roez's thigh.

*"Do it. And pray!"* Opeh responded.

Etaf pushed the needle into her child's thigh and dispensed the liquid. Roez began to cry uncontrollably. Etaf could not risk using anesthesia as she had no idea what it would have done to the child, given the unknown nature of her illness. Opeh picked up the child and held her up close to her chest. She rubbed the baby's back as her body shook uncontrollably.

Open knew in that instant that this would be her child's last convulsion. She would either make it through and be cured, or she would perish in the struggle. Etaf held them both loosely, the child sandwiched and engulfed in pure, unconditional love.

*The knock at the door became more insistent.*

*Etaf yelled over the wailing of her child, "I'll be right there."*

*"You must open this door now," the voice on the other side insisted. "You have ten seconds to comply before we will be required to use force to gain entry."*

*Etaf looked toward the door, ready to let go of Roez and Opeh and open it when Roez became suddenly quiet. Opeh, who had been holding Roez with one arm and Etaf with the other, suddenly tightened her grip on Etaf.*

*Opeh let out a slight cry and Etaf felt a warm fluid running down the front of her shirt. Roez began thrashing violently again against her mothers. Etaf pulled out of Opeh's embrace and realized the warm fluid she felt was blood. Roez was now gripping Opeh's shirt with both hands. Her baby teeth were sunk deep into her mother's neck and she was thrashing and tearing at her.*

*Etaf turned from the horrific sight unfolding before her eyes and ran toward the door. She knew her program must have had a fatal flaw and her hubris had killed her child and her beloved Opeh. In that instant, as she raced away, she realized her error. She failed to update a critical piece of code in the cell status logic. Every cell the nanobots were inspecting was coming back as abnormal. The base brain function cells were still be being ignored, but the higher level brain cells, and every other cell in Roez's body, was being consumed and replicated. In the case of the higher level brain cells, that replication was failing. Her nanobots literally ate her child's brain. That had to be what was going on inside her child, she thought, as she reached for the locking mechanism on the door.*

*As Etaf turned the lock, she felt a weight land on her upper torso. The sharp pain tore through her right shoulder and brought her to her knees. Before she could react, Roez jumped off her back and landed on the floor in front of her. Roez looked directly into Etaf's eyes, but any recognition of her mother was not evident in that glare. In the next fraction of a second, Roez leapt for Etaf's face. Etaf's last conscious thought was how pretty the young girl's eyes were. They look just like Opeh's.*

*The two security guards managed to burst their way through the lab door. With guns drawn they rushed into the room. Their first sight was that of a blood soaked eighteen-month-old child tearing at the now lifeless body of Etaf Fiel. This small, vicious child lunged for the nearest guard. As unfathomable as it was to have to fire at such a young attacker, the man's survival instinct took over and he did just that. It had the desired result and the room now fell quiet and motionless.*

*Before the horror could register, both women rose to their feet and lurched forward toward the grief-stricken men. Two gunshots later and the room again fell silent.*

*It only took the forensic crew a few hours to discover exactly what had taken place in the room. A quick simulation of Etaf's program indicated the exact scenario that had played itself out in that room only hours earlier. The fact that this incident ever occurred needed to be erased from history. The negative press would be irreparable. Unfortunately for the Ministry of Defense, the Domi residence, the country of Sapientia and the entire world, their cover up efforts would ultimately be of no consequence.*

# CHAPTER 14

# On The Move

## *Exposed*

"We need to move quickly. Form a circle and stay in a tight group. Call out anything you think is suspicious," Marion said to the group as they made their way down the street toward Mr. Brown's house. The distant thumping of helicopter engines drifted over the harbor from downtown Charleston.

Marion and the group hugged the side of the road, trying their best to stay hidden. They made their way past the first few houses without incident, but soon began to hear muffled screams. They were coming from somewhere close by.

The group quickened their pace, tightening the circle that they formed as they walked. They had instinctively ordered themselves such that a person with a firearm was next to a person without one. Eyes faced in a full 360-degree view of the roadway.

Tanner was the first to spot motion at the far end of the street. Several people were running from one house across the street and attempting to enter the house on the other side. Before they made it ten feet across the front lawn, they were overcome by other, much faster figures. Tanner looked at Brooke, who had witnessed the same scene. Neither said a word.

Up to this point, their small group had been much more fortunate than that one currently being disemboweled on the lawn down the street. They were now just a short distance from Mr. Brown's front door when their luck changed.

From the doorway of a small ranch style brick house, one hundred yards back in the direction they had just come, the first infected individual spotted them. That was the same doorway the muffled screams had emanated from just a few minutes ago. There stood a heavy-set man, in his late thirties, wearing a suit and tie. On an ordinary morning, one would have assumed he was just leaving the house for a normal day at work. Not today.

No sooner had he exited the house and spotted the group on the street, he began charging at them. The portly fellow had taken only three strides when two more individuals emerged from the same house. The first was an young girl and the second a woman in her early thirties, apparently the wife and daughter of the man now rocketing in their direction. These two quickly joined the hunt.

"Incoming," Marion yelled to the group as the heavy-set man came running, still too far away to begin shooting.

"Incoming! My direction," Tanner said as a different group emerged from a house on the opposite side of the street. This new group was seven people strong and all of them were headed directly at them.

Madison wrapped her arms around the Reaper as Connor stepped in front of her, weapon raised and pointed in the direction of the larger group of attackers. Marion knew there was no way the group was going to make Matt Marine's house before being overcome. Better to make a stand here, in the road, where they could stay steady and take better aim than be dragged down from behind on Mr. Brown's front lawn.

"Tanner, Connor, in the front with me. Everyone else, get behind us. Nobody shoots until they are within range. It won't do any good to miss and we can't afford to waste ammunition." Marion knew that with ten attackers and only three guns, they would not make it through this assault. If body shots would have done them any good, then maybe, but head shots, no way.

The nearest attacker was now one hundred feet away and Marion was about to begin shooting when a helicopter appeared, seemingly out of nowhere, and passed directly overhead. It was moving in the direction of the Quinn's residence.

The assailants were instantly drawn to the loud noise overhead. The zombie's assault halted abruptly. Surprisingly, each and every one of them turned and chased down the road after the helicopter. *Greg,* Marion thought to herself, as she watched the helicopter now hovering over her house.

"Everyone run! Now!" Marion said as she got the group

heading toward Matt Brown's house. As they ran across the front lawn, Marion grew concerned when she spotted the front door was open wide. The group reached the large concrete patio surrounding the ornate wooden front door. Marion signaled for them to stop behind her. She cautiously peered into the open doorway. Two figures were in plain sight and they noticed her immediately. Each hurled themselves in her direction, racing across the open foyer. Marion slammed the door closed with such force that it almost blew out the gas-fed porch lanterns that adorned each side of the entrance.

"Connor, open the garage door. It's our only chance."

The helicopter was once again approaching in their direction. Behind it, a group of infected, now numbering in the twenties, was in frenzied pursuit. Connor sprinted to the garage door and entered the code on the paper that Mr. Brown had given him.

The door creaked, opening at an agonizing pace. Marion dropped to the ground, her handgun pointed under the heavy garage door as it slowly ascended. Now directly overhead, the helicopter hovered for a brief instant and then quickly banked and headed back toward the Quinn residence. The scourge of infected that were running behind the thundering craft now splintered, most of them turning again and following the helicopter back down the road. However, a much smaller group of five continued toward Mr. Brown's garage.

The door had now opened enough for Marion to get a clear

view of the interior of the garage. It was not empty, but she could not see any movement coming from inside. When the door was just three feet off the ground, she entered and motioned everyone else to follow her inside.

Brooke was the last through the door and as soon as the young girl ducked under it and cleared the protective beam that ran along the door's bottom edge, Marion hit the button on the wall unit to close the door once again.

The door began descending at its lumbering pace. Marion and Tanner hit the floor in a prone position pointing their fire-arms down the driveway, and waited for the door to close completely. The door still had two feet to go when the first small group of infected reached the end of the driveway. Marion and Tanner began firing in an attempt to slow the marauders down enough for the garage door to close completely. It slammed shut just as the first assailant bounced off of it.

The garage windows of this upscale house had security bars on the outside, and the doors themselves were very heavy duty. Marion's initial assessment was that the room was secure, at least for the moment.

She could hear the zombies outside banging on the door, looking for a way in. Tanner returned to his feet and joined the others as they gazed in awe at a vast assortment of musical equipment that was sprawled out before him. Banks of speakers, several amplifiers, microphones, guitars, a full drum kit and all sorts of recording equipment was sitting in Mr. Brown's garage. All of it appeared to be brand new.

Along with the band equipment, a pristine 1993 black on black Porsche 928 GTS was parked in the last bay of the garage. Connor was the first to notice a note taped to the front of the kick drum. He bent over, picked it up and read it aloud. "CJ and gang, I thought you might be able to use a proper rehearsal space. It's good to see young kids have such a productive, positive hobby. Hope you like the gear. Come by and use it whenever you want. Your #1 fan, Matt Marine."

"Right now, I'm Matt's number one fan!" Brooke said, admiring the dual Bag End speaker cabinets and Ampeg amplifier that were situated to the right of the drum set on the back wall of the garage. On a stand in front of the gear sat a Gibson Thunderbird bass guitar. Brooke walked over to the bass guitar setup and turned on the Ampeg amplifier, cranking the volume to ten. As she did, the speakers let out a loud pop and then went quiet.

"Brooke!" Marion yelled in a loud whisper.

"Sorry, the pots must be dirty," she whispered back. Connor looked at her as if to say, "Now is not the time to be a smart ass."

"Get over here. We have to work together if we want to survive. Do we understand each other?" Madison said.

"Yes, ma'am," Brooke replied. Mako and Brooke joined the rest of the group as they discussed their options.

"Auntie M, did you see the size of that group of infected

outside of our house? I'm worried about Riley," Connor said.

"There is nothing we can do about that now. They are going to be fine as long as they keep quiet and don't do anything stupid. Now, we need to focus on getting inside to those guns. I saw two infected inside the house when the door was open. We have to assume they are still in there," Marion said.

Just then, there was a loud crashing noise against the door that led from the garage into the house. The group jumped backwards, away from the door. Marion, Connor and Tanner pointed their weapons in the direction of the noise. Thump, thump, thump. Again and again the door was struck from the inside.

"They don't know how to use the doorknob," Mako said. "If they did, they would be in here by now."

"Good point, Mako. They may be fast and strong, but they don't appear to be very smart. We need to find a way to get them out of that house. Any ideas?" Marion said.

"We could bait them into the garage and shut them in here," Madison said.

"How do you propose we do that?" said Mako. "I'm up for most any experience in life, but I'm very sure being bait is not on that list."

"No, someone who knows how to shoot will need to be the bait," Madison continued. "The shooter can lock themselves in the car and draw the infected people that way. When they get to the car, the person inside can knock them off in relative safety.

Everyone else can hide behind something here at the doorway and run into the house once the infected run by to get to the car."

"That just might work, Madison," Marion responded. "I can't think of any other way to get into the house. My only fear is the windows of the car will be no match for one of those things, but it's a chance we are going to have to take. Let's get those speakers lined up perpendicular to the wall nearest the door. Leave just enough room between the speaker cabinets and the wall that someone can reach around them and turn the door knob. Hopefully it is unlocked. That should give you time enough to pull your hand back in before they spot you."

"Auntie M, I am not comfortable with this. What if the windows break?" Connor replied.

"I'll be in the car with her," Tanner said. "Two shooters will increase the odds of surviving considerably."

Marion could not argue with him. If she only had to concentrate on one attacker, she would stand a much better chance of hitting them in the head.

"OK, Tanner. You and I will be in the car. Thanks," she added, gratefully.

Mako and Brooke went to work moving the Bag End speaker stack, which was already very close to the garage door, into a position that provided an ample hiding place. Marion entered the passenger side front of the car and Tanner took up residence in the rear seat, as small as it was. When everyone was in position,

Marion and Tanner pointed their 45s in the direction of the garage door that led into the house.

"Tanner, those kids are right in our line of fire, so be sure you are going to hit your target before you pull that trigger," Marion said to her counterpart.

"No worries, Miss M. I got this," he replied, trying to sound like he meant it.

Marion nodded to Connor and he reached through the gap between the speakers and the wall and turned the knob. It turned freely and he gave the door a quick, awkward push inward before retracting his arm back behind the speaker cabinet.

The door swung slowly, but the push was sufficient to open it completely. From her vantage point within the car, Marion could now see into the house. A long, well-lit hallway extended out before her. The end appeared to open up into a large foyer.

Nobody was in the hallway that she could see. Connor, Brooke, Madison and Mako could not see inside the house. They were huddled behind the speaker cabinets staring at Marion and Tanner in the car, awaiting some type of signal that they should enter the house.

After ten seconds or so, there was still no motion coming from the hallway. Madison waved and got Marion's attention. She made a pushing motion with her hand, palm facing outward at a 45 degree angle. "Honk the horn," she mouthed to her aunt. Marion understood and with her free hand, reached over to the steering wheel and gave the center a quick but firm push. The horn blared and echoed through the garage. The strings of the bass picked up the noise and vibrated, causing the speakers to emit a low, mishmash of notes.

Instantly three figures appeared in the hallway and rocketed toward the garage. Marion put up her hand, palm outward, indicating to Madison and the rest to stay put and get ready. The three infected exploded through the doorway and quickly surrounded the car. Luckily, the windows in the car had withstood the initial impact of the assault. Marion and Tanner held off firing to give the kids a chance to get into the house.

Connor, Madison and Mako rounded the end of the speakers and ran into the open garage door. Connor had his 10mm out and pointed down the hallway. Brooke, in her haste, stumbled getting up from her crouched position and accidentally kicked the Gibson Thunderbird hard in the process. The garage erupted in a very low, deafening growl.

Brooke froze beside the wall of speakers and pressed her hands to her ears. She was facing the Porsche and was screaming at the top of her lungs. The effect of the low, thundering noise was immediate. Not on Brooke, but on the zombies. They stopped moving and dropped to the ground, vibrating as if being electrocuted.

Marion wasted no time in exiting the vehicle, closing the door and dispatching the three assailants. She ran toward Brooke as the resulting black masses enveloped the vehicle. The substance covered the car windows to the extent that Tanner was no longer visible inside.

When she reached Brooke, Marion turned off the amplifier and the garage was once again bathed in silence. The black mass stopped moving on the car and dripped harmlessly to the floor, like used motor oil. The passenger door once again swung open and Marion took aim at the vehicle. Tanner exited and looked around.

"Now I know how ol' Jeb felt in the Beverly Hillbillies," he joked. Marion laughed and ran to give Tanner a hug.

"You're a good man, Tanner."

## *False Hope*

From his position one hundred feet over his house, Greg could not tell if anyone was home. He could see a small crowd of people below him running in his direction. They were moving incredibly fast and he fought back his instinct to land and give them assistance. He was sure he made the correct choice when he realized one of people running at a sprinter's speed was a gentleman well into his eighties.

As he looked back down at his house, he noticed a white arrow painted on his roof. It pointed him back down the neighborhood the way he had just come. He spun his chopper and headed back in that direction.

Outside of Mr. Brown's house he could see a group of six people trying to access the garage. He recognized his wife and nephew as two of the people and the rest looked like friends of Connor's, all but one long-haired blonde girl they must have picked up along the way.

He remembered the crowd of infected and realized they were following the sound of his chopper. He turned to look back up the street and, to his horror, he saw that he was indeed leading them directly toward his family. Quickly he reversed course back down toward his house to give his family the time they needed to access the neighbor's garage. In short order, his chopper was again hovering over his home and once again, a crowd of the infected was collecting under his location.

His plan was to wait for a full minute before heading back to a vantage point where he could see the house his family was attempting to enter without actually drawing the threat in their direction.

After thirty seconds, with a crowd of at least thirty infected below him, he noticed the back door of his house open and two women exit and run toward him. Before he could warn them in any way, they were engulfed by the violent crowd. He knew the only thing he could do was try to lure the crowd away again, and proceeded further down the road away from his family. The crowd once again followed, but he knew it was too late for whoever had come out the back door.

After another thirty seconds the low fuel indicator on his control panel began blinking and gave a warning buzz. All at once he realized he was jeopardizing countless people, desperate for help, by hovering over the neighborhood in his helicopter. Survivors may assume he was there to help when, in reality, there was very little he could do for them.

He had no weapons on his small, Hughes OH-6 Cayuse helicopter and certainly could not risk landing to pick anyone up. He circled back toward Mr. Brown's house, this time keeping several hundred yards away so as to not attract any unwanted attention in his family's direction.

The garage door was shut and several infected were milling around outside. Just before he banked to head back toward Summerall Field, he noticed all of the infected outside the garage drop to the ground in unison. They stayed there for a short period of time and then once again regained their feet.

*What was that?* he thought to himself, as the low fuel buzzer again went off in his cockpit. He was confident that his family was now safe inside the house. Reluctantly he made his way back toward base camp.

## Show Me The Cache

Connor was the first one down the hallway, walking cautiously and deliberately as he listened intently for the sounds of movement ahead of him. There were three doors in the hallway and all of them were open. Connor briefly looked in each one as he passed, searching for the gun room. Unfortunately, none of the rooms fit the bill. Madison and the Reaper were right behind, quietly shutting any open doors along the way. When they reached the end of the hall, they stopped, crouched down, and waited for the others.

"This is all just a little too bizarre for words," Connor said to his sister, in a voice no louder than a whisper.

"True that," Madison said. She placed her hand on her brother's shoulder.

Behind them, Marion had closed the garage door behind her as she and the rest of the group began making their way down the hallway. She hesitated momentarily and then turned to lock the door. *Can't be too careful,* she thought to herself.

"Tanner, protect the rear. I'm going to head up front and see if there is anyone left in the house." Marion made her way up to where Connor and Madison were crouched. As she passed Mako and Brooke, she gave them a reassuring smile and a quick touch on the head.

"Any signs of life in here?" she asked as she reached Madison and Connor and looked out into the large foyer.

"No," Connor replied. "The first one to enter the garage and attack the car was Matt Marine. I'm not sure who the other two were, but he lived alone - so there's a good chance that no one else is here."

"We are going to be cautious, all the same," Marion replied as she turned and motioned for the rest of the group to gather. When everyone was close enough to hear her whispering, she put a plan in motion.

"Connor and I are going to go out first. Stay here until we give the all clear. When we do, wait for my signal - and only then come out and join us. Any sign of movement, run for the garage. Understand?" She said.

Everyone nodded in agreement. Marion and Connor exited the hallway and together walked slowly and quietly out into the foyer. There was no sign of movement. They motioned for the rest of the group to enter the foyer.

There were two other hallways that branched off the foyer in opposite directions, and like the one they had just exited, neither had doors.

"We need to find the gun room. Let's start with the hallway on the left," Marion said to her nephew. She motioned to the group to follow them. They fell back in line and proceeded across the foyer and down the hall. They passed an open family room on the left, and an office on the right before coming upon a closed doorway.

Marion signaled for the group to stop. She put her index finger to her lips to indicate that they should be quiet. She placed her hand on the knob and turned it without resistance. As she opened the door, a light went on automatically startling her and causing her to jerk backwards slightly. Tanner and Connor pointed their weapons at the door, but there was no motion inside. Marion opened the door wide and they all beheld a storage room full of provisions.

"Looks like he was prepared for anything." Brooke said. They gazed at shelf after shelf of MRE's, bottled water and a wide variety of canned and dry goods.

"And I bet that is the gun room," Mako said, pointing at the only other door in the hallway. That door looked heavier than the rest and it had a small, head level port hole in it. Marion walked to it and, again, turned the knob. It took a bit of force, but the knob twisted and the heavy door swung inward. Marion raised her handgun and peered into the room. Again, the lights inside went on automatically and gave her an excellent view of the shooting range beyond. The entire ceiling was lined with florescent lighting, throwing a blanket of cool light in a manner that left no corner of the room in shadow. Cautiously, she opened the door wide and scanned the room. It was clear. She motioned for the group to enter.

One by one the kids filed past her into the large room that was set up just like any standard indoor shooting range. Marion marveled that anyone would have such a room in their house.

Marion turned to shut the door when Madison spoke. "Shouldn't we get the food and supplies from the pantry and pile it in here? That way we don't need to go back out into the hallway once we hunker down."

"Excellent idea, Madison. Everyone, let's get that done as quick as we can. Tanner, guard the hallway behind us. We don't want any surprises."

Several minutes later, Mako carried the last of the water from the pantry into the large shooting range as Tanner followed behind. Marion closed and locked the door once they were safely inside.

They all breathed a bit easier now that they were safely in the room together. The shooting range itself consisted of six lanes, each with an overhead pulley system for sending paper targets to the far end of the room. The wall at the far end was lined with what appeared to be mattresses of some kind, placed there to stop the bullets from leaving the building as they traveled down the range.

The walls were lined with a cloth-type material designed to deaden the sound of gunfire. Facing down the gun range, the wall on the left contained a square outline with a cord hanging from its left side. Connor walked over to it and pulled on the rope. A panel swung open from hinges along its right side exposing a large window that faced the front of the property. Natural sunlight spilled in through the opening.

Connor took a quick peek out the window and noticed that it was protected with security bars on the outside, as were all of the windows on the lower floor of this house. He shut the panel almost immediately after that and held up four fingers to the rest of the group. They all knew that meant that he had seen four infected at the front of the house.

On the wall opposite the one containing the window was a similar outline, although this one was the size of a door. Marion approached this panel and swung it open slowly. It was indeed a door that led to a small sunroom that faced the rear of the property and overlooked Charleston Harbor and the Ravenel Bridge. The door itself had security bars on it, but the sunroom beyond appeared to be completely unprotected. As with all of the houses on the waterfront side of the street, there was a long dock with a boat moored at the end. She shut the door and whispered, "Nobody back there."

"I don't think we need to whisper anymore, guys. This room was made to silence gunfire, so I don't think us talking in our normal voices will stir up any trouble," Madison said. Marion laughed, realizing that she had been whispering for no good reason. She walked over to the two doors in the room that they had not yet checked out.

Marion cautiously opened the first and lighter of the two doors. It was a bathroom, fully tiled with some type of off-white marble. *Beautiful*, Marion thought. Besides a toilet, it had a large vanity and even a shower. *This place is getting better and better.* Most importantly, the room was unoccupied.

Marion made her way to the other door, which was much heavier than the bathroom door. When she tried the knob, it did not turn. "It's locked," she said to the group. "Look around and see if we can find a key.

The group fanned out and began searching the room. Madison walked up to the door and gave it a second look. Around the frame, she saw several small nails sticking out of the fabric to the right of the door. *Strange*, she thought. As she turned to help the other search the room, her foot hit the floor and it made a hollow thump sound. Bending down, she knocked on the floor and noticed one board made a hollow sound and it had a small hole drilled into it.

She reached up and grabbed one of the nails from the fabric and inserted it, head first, into the hole in the board. The head of the nail caught on the underside of the board and she lifted up. The two foot long, four inch wide board lifted, exposing a small space under. Hidden in the cavity underneath was a set of keys.

"Got it," Madison said to the group as she rose up with the keys.

"Yes, chica, way to go," Brooke said. She ran up to Madison and smacked her on the shoulder.

"I never would have seen that, Madison. Good set of eyes on you," Marion said as she reached the young girl, gave her a peck on the top of her head, and took the keys from her hand.

Marion put the key into the door knob and turned. A heavy

clank came from the locking mechanism as it disengaged. The door was surprisingly heavy and required a bit of force for Marion to pull it open. Tanner was the first to peer inside. The light in the room went on as soon as the door was opened and gave him a clear view of the entire room.

It did not contain any infected, but something that on a normal day that would be considered equally deadly. The entire length of the ten by twenty foot room was lined with weapons of all kinds. Closed drawer cabinets lined each wall up to waist height. Each one had a white label describing its contents. Above those cabinets hung more cabinets with wire mesh doors. Each cabinet was dedicated to a particular style of weapon, from swords and knives, pistols in every caliber ever made all the way up to automatic assault weapons. Behind one mesh door several hand grenades were visible.

*Wow, this guy has an arsenal.* Marion thought. She knew that many of these weapons were not legal by any stretch of the imagination. "Tanner and I are going to take an inventory of the room to get an idea of the ammunition situation. Everyone else stay back for now."

"Way ahead of you Miss M," Tanner said pointing to a clipboard that was hanging on the back of the door. Attached to it was a complete inventory of every drawer and cabinet. Tanner took the clipboard down and began reading the ledger of the contents of the room.

"Drawer L1, 1000 rounds of 9mm, 3000 rounds of hollow point 45 caliber, 1000 rounds of 10mm 200 grain full metal jacket," Tanner read aloud. He flipped to the last page. "Cabinet U20 - three M16A4 assault rifles, four AK-47 assault rifles. Man, this guy could outfit a small army."

"OK guys, we don't know how long we're going to be safe here and we need to make the most of this place as we can while we are here. Mako, Madison, Brooke, this is a perfect time for you to learn how to handle one of these handguns. Are you up for that?" Marion asked.

They all nodded in agreement.

"I promised Madison I'd show her to shoot back at the house. Can I teach her?" Connor asked his aunt.

"Sure, Connor. That sounds great. Tanner, you teach Brooke. I'll teach Mako. Stress the safety aspect first and continuously. If you are not comfortable at the end that they can be trusted, we will not be giving them a weapon. The 1911 style 9mm's will be the easiest to shoot. Tanner, pull out three of those and the ammunition to go with them. You and Connor can take whatever handguns you want and fill the backpacks with as much as you can carry. Tanner, Connor and I have shot the AK's many times at the range. Can you handle one of those?"

"I can live with an AK," Tanner replied.

"OK, let's get to it."

## *Throw Out The Playbook*

Greg landed his helicopter back at Summerall Field. Activity at base camp had picked up considerably in the last hour. Several Apache and other attack helicopters were scattered across the field, busily being prepped for service. Greg had a brief discussion with the grounds crew regarding the state of the aircraft he had just landed and then quickly made his way towards the colonel's command center.

"We need as much as you can spare. We need to stop this here in South Carolina, or you will be fighting this war much closer to home," the colonel said into his military command phone. "The governor is declaring a state of emergency. They are clearing interstate 95 of civilian traffic as of 1200 hours. You should have a clear shot to up to highway 17. Local law enforcement will have that road ready for your arrival at 1300 hours. Rendezvous at the air field at 1345. We will do our best to keep this in check until you get here. God be with us, Colonel. This is a nightmare scenario."

Greg waited silently as the colonel put down the phone.

"Captain Quinn, the situation here is escalating rapidly. The initial forces of the Georgia and North Carolina Guard troops will be here within the hour, but the size of those forces will not be enough. We have requested a full-scale participation of all available military personnel within a three hundred mile radius of our position. Command and control will be shifting to Virginia where active military will take over this operation. Until that time, we need to throw everything we have at this to stop it here in Charleston. I believe the fate of this country and even the world rests on our ability to keep this in check until help arrives. What did you see out there? I could certainly use some good news this morning, Captain."

"I hate to disappoint you, Colonel, but I'm afraid our containment efforts have thus far failed. Infected are moving unchecked through the neighborhoods on the other side of the James Island Connector. There is a Carta bus at the end of the bridge with many civilian casualties. It's chaos out there. Whatever this virus or infection is, it is not showing any signs of abating."

"I have the best infectious disease minds in the country on their way here. Full participation from the CDC and WHO. Unfortunately, we lost one of the leading scientists on infectious disease just this week down in Mexico. She was one of those who perished in the Holbox accident. I'm starting to think that was not an accident, after all."

"What instructions are we giving civilians? I noticed a lot of people out of their houses. They need to be barricaded in right now, not out on the street," Greg told the colonel.

"We have the emergency broadcast system running continuously, instructing civilians on just that fact. Curiosity is a strong motivator, but we all know what it did to the cat. Luckily, at least in this case, our great state has some of the least restrictive gun laws. Our civilian population has a fighting chance if it comes down to it. As you are aware, those at sea, or with quick access to watercraft, are using Fort Sumter as a safe haven. We are directing several larger helo's out to that location to airlift survivors to a place further out of the infected zone."

"I'm not sure that using helicopters is the safest form of evacuation. The noise from my helicopter seemed to attract the attention of the infected and uninfected alike. We may just be calling the wolves to the slaughter."

"The fort is surrounded by water. That should provide sufficient protection for the evacuation. We will continue with that approach until a more suitable solution can be implemented. Right now, I need you back in the air. Did you see the Apaches out on the field?"

"I did, sir," Greg replied.

"I need you behind the stick, weapons hot, over in Mount Pleasant. Infected have begun traversing the Ravenel Bridge. Stop them using every means necessary. Understood, Captain?"

"Understood," Greg said. He saluted the colonel and turned to leave the room.

As he made his way back out onto the field he found himself struggling with the reality of the situation. His orders were to fire on people who, though infected with an unknown virus, had nonetheless been fellow Americans. Many of whom he would likely have known or met at some point in his many years of living in the Charleston area. He knew he could not hesitate, or back down from the task in front of him. The colonel was not exaggerating that the fate of the entire world may depend on his and his fellow serviceman to do the job that was necessary. With a heavy heart he took his position behind the stick of the waiting helicopter.

## *No Rest For The Weary*

Marion looked at the young, worried faces gathered around her in the shooting range.

"It's been a morning unlike anything we've ever been through. Each and every one of you has risen to the occasion and together we are surviving this. We will continue to survive, as long as we stick together and use our heads and our abilities," Marion said. "This house appears to be well-suited to protect us from whatever it is happening outside."

She looked at Brooke and saw that tears were forming in the girl's eyes.

"Brooke, if at the end of this you are not comfortable with firing the handgun, you don't need to carry one. But it's important right now that you at least know how. Do you understand?"

"I do. I'll be OK," Brooke replied.

"Tanner, Mako and Brooke: try to reach your families to let them know where you are and that you are OK. I'm sure they are worried sick. The phones appear to still be down, but the internet is working. Text, tweet or email. Do whatever you can to make contact while we still can." Marion said "I am going to turn on the TV and see if there is any new information that may be useful. We can pick up the guns and do some shooting when you are finished."

"If anyone needs to use my phone, I have a connection," Brooke announced.

"I'll take you up on that," Tanner said. "I left mine back at CJ's house. My family lives out on John's Island and they should be OK, but my brother Michael is working at the shipyard. I want to check on him." He and Brooke moved to the corner of the room.

"I have a message from my parents," Mako said. "They were both at work up at the Boeing plant and are safe. I'll let them know I'm OK."

Marion, Connor and Madison watched the television as the rest made contact with their families. The news was full of horror stories related to the events currently unfolding. Panic had set in, and the police and military did not seem to have a handle on the situation. A continuous banner scrolled along the bottom of the screen, reminding people to stay inside with windows and doors locked and to avoid any unnecessary noise. People should draw shades and blinds and not allow motion of any kind to be seen from the street. Infected individuals should be avoided at all costs. Anyone caught walking in the street risked being shot and even killed.

The anchorman was indicating that these orders could be in place for several days as the authorities developed a plan to deal with the outbreak. The screen showed an aerial view of Fort Sumter, where several hundred people were gathered. Boats could be seen bringing more survivors and supplies.

Within ten minutes, everyone had gathered again in front of the wall-mounted television.

Marion addressed them again. "It looks like some people are gathering at Fort Sumter. That is just a quick boat ride from here. There is a boat at the end of the dock at the back of this property. My guess is the set of keys that Madison found has one that starts that boat. We won't know for sure until we get out there, but it may be our only option. Even if it doesn't start, it is better to be floating out on the water than running through this neighborhood again. That is our fallback plan if we are forced out of this house. Now, we could sit and watch this TV all day and get more and more afraid of what is happening outside, but that is not going to improve our situation. Let's be productive and get started with the shooting lessons. We can talk more about the fallback plan when we finish. Let's get to it."

They broke into groups of two. Soon, the sound of gunfire filled the room.

\*\*\*

After an hour, Marion gathered everyone back together again.

"Madison, how did that go? Are you comfortable with your firearm?" she asked.

"Well, I don't know that I'm necessarily comfortable, but I don't think I'm a liability. Knowing what is out there, I think I am more of an asset with a gun than without one," she said.

"I agree, Auntie M. She did really well. I trust her completely," Connor said.

"Well, I am going to spend some time reviewing gun safety with each of you before entrusting you with a loaded weapon, but it sounds like you made great progress today. How about you, Brooke?"

"Piece of cake," she replied.

"Well, not so fast," Tanner interrupted. "You have great enthusiasm, but I'm not convinced you have a healthy enough respect for the firearm yet. You need to learn to keep your finger off the trigger unless you're ready to shoot something."

Brooke gave Tanner a well-practiced eye roll.

"I don't expect anyone is going to be an expert after one session of range shooting, but the purpose here is to get you comfortable enough that you can defend yourself without being a danger to the rest of us. Brooke, let's you and I spend a bit more time working on the safety aspects of handling a firearm. Mako, you did very well. Now, let's review our plan. We are going to stay in this room as long as possible. In the event that is not possible, for whatever reason, we will use the boat out back to get to Fort Sumter. I am open to suggestions if anyone has a better idea?" she asked.

"My brother Michael is at Fort Sumter right now. He and his friend Sarah hopped on a small john boat and got there half an hour ago," Tanner said. "Maybe we should just go there now?" he added.

"I don't think we should risk going outside again unless absolutely necessary. My husband knows we are here and will move heaven and earth to get to us. We have food for weeks and access to fresh water, not to mention a place to go to the bathroom and shower," Marion replied.

"OK, Miss M. I trust you. I'll let my brother know we are here," Tanner replied.

"That settles it. Now, it seems we are going to be here a while. Let's settle in."

There were army surplus blankets in the gun room. Tanner handed them out to his friends. Madison put her blanket down in between her aunt and Mako along the wall on the left side of the room. A smile quickly formed on the boy's face.

"I hope Riley and her mom are OK," Madison said to Mako.

"Me too. They should be here with us right now. They are not safe there," he replied.

"I take it you don't believe that God will protect them then," she said.

"No, I don't. I think they put themselves in a dangerous situation because they refused to think the situation through logically. I just don't understand that thinking. If there is a higher power, I doubt it will single them out to save."

"Well, if there is a higher power, what makes you think it would be incapable of saving them? They both found comfort in their faith during a very stressful time. I happen to agree with you and I think the smart move was to come here. But there were also no guarantees that we would be any safer than them after everything was said and done. Was that helicopter passing overhead fate, luck, or the hand of God? Surely without it we would not be sitting here right now. I know Riley and her mom would see that as God's intervention and would have taken great comfort in it. Personally I think it was dumb luck, but that thought certainly doesn't comfort me. I guess my point is this: as long as we are alive, we will never know whose view of the world is the right one. That leaves us free to choose the one that makes the most sense for us individually," Madison said to her new friend.

She looked up and saw that Connor was facing them, having overheard their conversation. He nodded at his sister, thinking about his girlfriend and her mother holed up, alone and scared, back at his house.

"It sure wouldn't hurt for each of us to pray, or send some good vibes or whatever in their direction. If our yard back at home looks anything like the one out front of this house, they could use it."

Mako reached over and wrapped his hand around Madison's. She did not pull her hand back right away, trying to determine if this was a sign of sympathy or affection, or if it even mattered. Before things got complicated, she pulled her hand back and moved her blanket over to where her brother was sitting.

"I'll say a prayer for them," she said as she sat down. She closed her eyes, and for the first time in her life, said a prayer on the off chance it would have any positive effect on the women back at her aunt's house.

The group fell silent. The only noise in the room was a few of the MREs being opened and the continuous din of voices coming from the TV screen.

Marion stood up and checked the back yard again. She could see a military attack helicopter flying over the harbor. It was headed toward Fort Sumter. Shortly afterwards the sound of heavy gunfire could be heard. She suddenly longed for another adult in the room to help share the load. She shut the cover of the back door and walked back over to her blanket.

After half an hour, Brooke got restless and walked to the front window, opening the soundproof portal just wide enough to take a look outside. There was a group of twenty or so zombies milling around the front lawn.

Seeing a unique opportunity, the young girl turned her back to the window and positioned her phone at arm's length in front of her. As she had done a thousand times before, she clicked a selfie, the view of the front lawn showing prominently in the background. Little did she know as she posted the picture to the internet, that it would become one of the iconic photos of the zombie uprising.

She captioned the photo, "Me and my Z peeps. Dropped only by a shot to the head or a head-banging, drop D played loud and proud on a Gibson Thunderbird and a Bag End stack turned up to 11. My parents were wrong - they thought playing bass in a band would ruin my life, but turns out it saved it. Once again, Brooke: One Parents: Zero."

Satisfied her post had captured the moment, she put her phone back in her pocket and slipped, unnoticed, into the gun room. A few minutes later, a male voice echoed in the room with her.

"You should not be in here," Tanner said, interrupting the young girl as she rummaged through various drawers and cabinets. "Lots of stuff in this room can ruin your day."

"More than it is already?" she shot back as she walked past him out of the room. "Hey, let me show you something," she added and led Tanner over to the window at the front of the house. She slowly opened it to show him the growing horde outside.

Tanner gulped as he saw the thirty or so infected individuals milling around the front yard. Suddenly the garage door of the house across the street began to open. Brooke and Tanner watched as a white sedan quickly backed down the driveway. An elderly man was behind the wheel and jammed on the brakes as he reached the street. The zombies in the front yard lunged toward the vehicle before it had a chance to get moving again. Several reached the vehicle and jumped on the hood and roof. As the car lurched forward, its tires squealed as they lost traction.

No sooner had the vehicle left their sight, and the front yard appeared to be clear of zombies, a younger couple bolted from the front door and sprinted in the direction of Mr. Brown's house.

"I think they want to get in here. They must know about this gun room as well," Brooke said. Marion joined them at the window, having heard the screeching of the car.

The couple had just reached the front lawn when the first infected re-appeared on the street, heading directly for them.

"We cannot risk opening the door," she said quietly.

The couple ran out of view as they approached the front of the house. Several zombies were now running closely behind them. A look of horror fell upon Marion's face. "We didn't lock the front door!" she cried.

Marion sprinted to the door that lead out into the hallway and opened the small portal window. She listened for activity at the front door. To her horror, she heard the front door open accompanied by blood curdling screams. It left little doubt that the couple did not make it, and that this house was no longer devoid of infected.

Brooke, hearing the screams coming from the other end of the house, let out a quick, startled shout of her own. Marion quickly turned and covered the girl's mouth and they all stood in silence for several seconds. They stared motionless through the small opening in the door.

Their worst fear was realized within seconds. Not only were there zombies in the house, but two of them were on fire. During the confrontation at the front door, the flailing arms of the attackers had broken the glass globes that contained the gas-fed flames of the porch lights.

More and more infected began pouring into the house. The zombies that were on fire began running erratically through the house, bumping into and landing on top of other infected. The flames spread to from one to the next, faster than the virus itself. Soon the various parts of the house began catching fire and smoke began filling the hallway.

Marion reached up to shut the portal door just as a zombie darted through the haze, landing with a thud against the door. Its face and teeth pressed terrifyingly up against the bars of the small window. Marion slammed the portal door shut and faced the silent teenagers. "Time for Plan B."

## Boat People

"I count eight in the back yard," Connor said as he peered out the back door.

"If we are going to go to the boat, we need to do it quickly," Tanner said, as he looked out the front window. The group of zombies on the front lawn had grown dramatically in size. As he watched, he noticed several times that a small group would take off sprinting toward some unknown prey, only to return again and with more friends.

"Hey, I got an idea," Mako said. "I couldn't help but notice a case of firecrackers in the gun room. This guy's appetite for things that go boom isn't limited to guns. We could use them to create a distraction in the front yard as we bolt for the dock."

The thuds coming from the hallway door were growing heavier and more frequent and the smell of smoke was now very apparent in the room.

"Whatever we are going to do, I agree with Tanner - we need to do it now."

"I agree," Marion said. "Mako, get the firecrackers and see if you can find a longer piece of fuse. We can link several bricks of firecrackers together. The longer fuse will give us time after we light it to gather at the back before they go off. With any luck, anyone in the back yard will hear the commotion and run to the front. Sound like a plan?" The group nodded in agreement and began readying themselves for their escape.

Mako pulled several bricks of firecrackers from the gun room and connected them together with a twenty foot fuse. As quietly as possible, Tanner tied the end of the fuse to the window bars. He figured the zombies would notice the movement when he tossed them out the window and did not want to risk dropping the fuse before it was lit.

"Does anyone have a lighter or matches?" he said. He realized that he had no way to light his payload.

Mako pulled a lighter from his pocket and tossed it to his friend.

"I am not going to ask why you have that, but don't think that went unnoticed," Marion said. She loaded one of several camouflage backpacks they had found in the gun room with various weapons and ammunition.

"Let me know when," Tanner said to Marion. He prepared himself to toss the bundle out the window.

She looked at the group of kids around her. They were scared but surprisingly composed.

"Connor, I'm going out first, but you need to be right behind me. I want two skilled shooters in front. Madison, Mako, and Brooke in that order. Tanner, you have the rear again. Keep an eye out for anyone coming around the end of the house. Call out threats as you see them. We are going to move fast across the back yard to the dock, but don't run. Fast, controlled and quiet. When we get to the dock, move as quickly as you can to the boat. If we are under attack, we need to get in the boat and push off from the dock as quickly as possible," Marion told them. "You three," she continued, looking at Brooke, Mako and Madison. "Be sure your guns are cocked and loaded, but safeties on. Just remember to click them off if the time comes when you need to fire. NOT before," she added, looking directly at Brooke.

"Madison, your guitar is going to be a real problem," she said to her young niece. "Is there any chance I can talk you into leaving that here, just for now?"

"I get it. It doesn't make sense to bring this with me. But please understand, leaving it is not an option," she said as she gripped the Reaper tighter.

"Madison, let me carry it. I'm no good with this pistol and I really don't think I have it in me to shoot anyone," Mako said to her. "You seem to be a much better shot anyway. I carry, you shoot. Deal?"

Madison couldn't argue with his logic. She knew she would use her weapon if need be - and was actually surprised by how accurate she was with her pistol. If he was not going to fire his weapon in self-defense, it made sense that he be the one to carry the guitar.

"Deal," she said. "But know this, if anything happens to it, I will squash you like a bug." He knew she meant every word of it.

"Understood," he smiled, taking the Reaper from Madison and giving her a nod.

They lined up in order at the back door. Marion turned to Tanner and shouted, "Now!"

He lit the long fuse. As it began to hiss, he hurled the fire-crackers out the window. The bundle hit the ground with very little noise, but its motion stirred the attention of the zombies in front of the house. He quickly fell in line behind Brooke on the opposite side of the room. They waited for the firecrackers to do their job.

Marion had her eyes on the zombies in the back yard when the firecrackers began to explode. The creatures initially hunched down, trying to determine where the sound was coming from, then took off for the front of the house. Once they disappeared from sight, she waited for five seconds and then led the group out through the sunroom and into back yard beyond.

They moved quickly, but did not run. Their heads swiveled backwards as each of them scanned the sides of the house for movement. They crossed the back yard quickly and approached the dock beyond. The noise from the firecrackers stopped just as Marion reached the first plank of the dock.

"Quickly," she whispered. She motioned the others to pass her and continue down the wooden structure to the boat. Madison and Mako both made the dock and started running for the boat. As Brooke turned her head from looking back at the house to looking forward toward the dock, she tripped over one of the small garden gnomes lining the ocean bank at the rear of the property. Tanner, still looking towards the house, fell over her in a heap. He quickly regained his feet and began helping Brooke up when he noticed a round metal object protruding from the young girls back pocket. He instantly recognized the object as a hand grenade and grabbed it from her.

"No way you should be carrying this in your back pocket. You could kill us all with this thing," he said, helping her to her feet.

"Incoming," Marion yelled and motioned Tanner and Brooke to start running. Three fast moving zombies had rounded the house on the right side and were rocketing in their direction. Marion began moving backwards down the dock at a fast pace. As she moved, she swung the AK from her shoulder and readied it to fire.

Brooke was in full sprint by now and quickly caught up to Marion, passing her on the dock. Tanner had managed to get ten feet down the dock when he realized the assailants were going to overtake him. He turned and began firing at the nearest of the three. Marion paused briefly, waiting for Brooke to clear her line of fire. When the young girl had passed, she raised her weapon, her finger already on the trigger. The realization of what she saw caused her to hesitate for a brief moment.

Two of the assailants were Riley and her mother. They had not made it. The house was not safe after all. She gulped down that emotion and opened up on the attackers. The noise was deafening.

Riley's mother and the other assailant went down rather quickly, but Riley had evaded the initial volley of bullets. If Riley recognized her friends at all, it never showed on her face as she bore down on Tanner. When she was within arm's reach of him, a round from Tanner's AK found its mark.

Riley was so close to him when she was dispatched that the resulting black residue engulfed the young man's face. In an instant he knew he was done for. In that same instant, he knew what he had to do. He recalled what had happened to Riley's father earlier that day. He pulled the pin from the grenade, fell to the dock and yelled back to his friends, "RUN!"

Many more zombies were now spilling from around the side of the house. They were attracted by the sound of gunfire and were now running full speed toward the dock. Marion realized she had no chance of defending herself from the horde of zombies heading directly at her, so she turned and began sprinting toward the boat. She was grieving the loss of Tanner before the grenade even exploded.

When it did, it threw her forward with such force that she landed face first on the dock, twenty feet from where she had been and closer to the boat. Dazed but functional, she quickly returned to her feet and ran the rest of the way to the boat. When she got there, she turned back toward the house, and saw that the explosion had taken out a large section of the dock. The zombies closest to Tanner at the time were thrown back toward the house. Several of them had also been thrown into the water, and were now attempting to walk out to where Marion and the kids were. They were moving very slowly, obviously having a difficult time walking in the waist deep Pluff mud that lined the South

Carolina shores.

"Was that Riley?" Connor asked his aunt, choking back tears.

"I think so, but there is no time for that, Connor. Everyone in the boat, NOW!" The events left no room for emotion. Mako and Madison jumped into the Boston Whaler, followed quickly by Connor.

Marion tossed Connor the boat key and shouted, "get it running, I am going to undo the ropes."

He took the key and jumped into the caption's chair behind the controls. He reached down to the ignition, but to his horror, the key did not fit.

"It doesn't fit!" he yelled.

"Everyone, look in the boat for a key." Marion yelled as she struggled with the mooring ropes. At the shore, where the dock used to be, a crowd of zombies was gathering. More and more were taking to the water, but none were having success at walking. At their current pace, Marion figured it would take them five minutes or more to reach the part of the dock that remained intact.

She finished untying the front rope and was moving to the rear when she noticed, from the back of the pack, one zombie sprinted from the house toward the shore. As it reached the water's edge, it leapt, landing just four feet from the intact end of the dock. Other zombies began sprinting and leaping toward the dock.

Marion realized they were now just a few seconds or so from having to defend themselves again. "We're pushing off. Connor, Mako, take the oars and row with all your might!" Marion quickly finished with the last rope. As she prepared to shove the boat from the pier, she noticed the Reaper sitting on the dock beside her. She lunged for the guitar, grabbed it by the handle, and hoisted it with her onto the boat. She quickly turned and using the guitar case and its extra couple of feet of length, thrust their boat off of the dock. Madison saw Marion place the Reaper onto the boat's bench seat and turned to gave Mako a menacing stare. Madison jumped up and gave her aunt big hug. "Thank you!" she said, squeezing her tight.

"Looks like your guitar came in handy after all." she replied.

Soon, a new problem revealed itself. "There are no oars!" Connor yelled. He and Mako frantically searched each compartment and cubby hole on the vessel. Marion's shove had only moved the boat a dozen or so feet from the end of the dock. Marion turned to look back toward the house and saw that a pack of five zombies were now sprinting down the dock in their direction. She opened fire on them.

Madison, Connor and Brooke followed her lead. The last of the assailants went down only a few feet from the end of the dock, the black roiling mass dropping into the ocean harmlessly in front of them.

More and more zombies were now leaping from the shore

onto the end of the dock. Marion knew there was no way they could fight them all. Surely one of them would make it into the boat and then it would all be over. Tears welled in her eyes as she released the spent magazine from her weapon and pushed home a fresh one. "Reload," she instructed the kids as she readied herself for another salvo.

As the last glimmer of hope faded from Marion's mind, a deep, thundering noise erupted from the opposite side of their small vessel. The zombies on the dock stopped running and lost all coordination. Several dropped from the dock into the water.

Everyone turned their backs to the dock and looked out toward open water. There, a large sightseeing charter boat was just fifty feet from their location. "Wilfred!" Madison yelled as she saw a familiar face behind the wheel of the vessel. The old, grizzled man who had escorted her from Boston to Charleston waved at his young travelling companion.

"Looks like you could use a hand, little lady. Take this rope and tie off to your boat. I'll pull you out where it is a bit safer," Wilfred said as he tossed a rope to the smaller boat.

Mako caught the rope and tied it to the bow cleat. Wilfred pulled the smaller vessel until they were a safe distance off shore.

The weary group was very grateful as they began boarding the larger vessel. Madison and the Reaper were the last to board and Wilfred greeted her with a smile. "Welcome aboard. I see you found your family after all."

# CHAPTER 15

## The Final Bow

Neam sat poolside at his opulent villa just a few miles outside of Daka. His cold drink and fine cigar were doing little to improve his spirits. Just that morning, he had lost touch with two of his treatment labs. His central server showed that their equipment was still active, so it was not an issue with power or the ability to communicate. They just went silent.

Every operative he had on the ground within one hundred miles of either facility had been sent to investigate and correct the situation, but none had reported back. As the hours passed, more and more of his facilities became unresponsive. He was becoming increasingly nervous and jumpy, expecting the world police to be conducting an organized assault on his compound any minute. He could not take the waiting any longer. Ten hours had been far too long to remain this passive. It was time to act.

As he rose from his chair, Neam caught sight of his bodyguard running towards him at breakneck speed from the villa. Assuming the worst, he spun around in a complete circle, looking again for the authorities that he was sure had begun their assault. Not seeing anything out of the ordinary, he spun back toward the villa just in time to see his bodyguard, six feet away and in mid-leap.

The man's arms stretched in front of him and quickly made impact with

*Neam's chest. Their momentum launched them into the swimming pool. As the men sank below the surface, Neam began to lose skin, blood, and muscle at an alarming rate. His assailant was raking; gnashing and gnawing at him with such ferocity that, to a casual observer, would make it appear as if the water were boiling. Neam's last breath was not of air, but of water. Before he could choke the liquid from his lungs, they were ripped from his chest and set adrift in the magnificent pool.*

*This first day of the worldwide epidemic was complete pandemonium. Firsthand news accounts were almost nonexistent. Any news crew that managed to get close enough to capture video of one of the assailants in action, were quickly overtaken themselves. From what the scientists could gather on that first day, any victim that did not sustain sufficient injury after the initial assault to die immediately were themselves infected and became assailants.*

*On the second day, the Government of Sapientia issued a worldwide press statement that their top-notch scientists had worked diligently through the night and determined what this disease was. Unfortunately, there was no cure at this time and the people of the world should seek safe shelter until their scientists could come up with a treatment. Unfortunately for the people of planet Mundi Primus, this information was not the least bit helpful.*

*From deep space, a single beam of unfathomable intensity was let loose on the planet known as Sapientia. Its impact was instantaneous and absolute. Every last human on the planet expired along with the planet itself on that fateful day. Pulverized remnants of the massive globe shot out into space in every direction, no portion larger than a ping pong ball.*

# CHAPTER 16

# Fort Sumter

## *Blame Game*

"Wilfred, this is my aunt Marion and my brother Connor," Madison said, introducing her old travelling companion to her new-found family. "Over there is Mako, Brooke and Tan..." She cut herself short, the sharp, painful vision of Tanner's demise replaying in her mind. "Mako and Brooke," she said again. Brooke was sitting on one of the benches of the lower deck crying uncontrollably.

"Nice to meet you all. I only wish it were under better circumstances." Wilfred said, his heart heavy for the young girl with the pink streak in her hair. "I'm heading over to Fort Sumter. I have been bringing folks over there all morning. You're lucky I came by when I did. I am running on fumes and this is my last trip."

"Thank you. Thank you for coming when you did. I don't know what we would have done if you had not been there," Madison said to Wilfred.

"We should all be safe at the Fort until a rescue effort can be mounted. The National Guard has already begun airlifting survivors from that location to areas further beyond the city. You should sit until we reach the Fort. It is only a ten minute trip from here, but the ocean can get rocky. Your friend looks like she could use a shoulder right about now," Wilfred said, motioning to Brooke.

Wilfred returned to the boat's controls. He eased the vessel back in the direction of Fort Sumter and leaned forward on the throttle.

Madison sat down on the bench between Brooke and Mako just as the boat began to pick up speed. She put her arm around her new friend and tried to console her. Brooke was reading a text on her phone from Tanner's brother Michael. The text read, "What's up, bro? A friend and I are at the Fort. Helicopters have been landing and picking people up. This is awesome!"

"This is all my fault. Tanner's dead and it's my fault," Brooke said, choking as she struggled to get air amidst her sobbing. "If I didn't try to take that hand grenade, he would still be here. I'm so stupid." She stumbled over the words. Tears rolled down her face.

"That's not true, Brooke. If you didn't have the hand grenade, none of us would be here right now. Those zombies would have run right down the dock and killed us all. You saved us. Tanner saved us." Madison said, as Brooke cried into her shoulder. Though it was little consolation for the loss of her longtime friend, Brooke saw there was some truth in what her new friend had said.

"Poor Riley," Mako said, slowly shaking his head from side to side. "She and her mom didn't make it. That was them back near the dock. I'm sure Tanner realized it. You OK, Connor?"

Connor just sat on the bench by his aunt, his elbows on his knees and his face buried in his hands. His aunt sat next to him with her hand on his back, rubbing slowly.

"He'll be OK," Marion said. "We will all be better when we get to the fort. There will be other survivors there and the military will be there to keep us safe. We'll be OK." She sounded like she was trying to convince herself as well as them. They fell silent as the boat gently rocked through the waves on its way to safety.

The day had been sunny up to that point, but clouds began to roll in. The weather hadn't called for rain, but these clouds certainly looked like the precursor to a storm.

Wilfred was making adjustments to the speed and direction of the boat as he neared the dock at Fort Sumter. The fact that the tide was nearly full made this a bit easier, as he did not have to worry about the many sand bars that surrounded the fort. He had made the maneuver countless times over the years, but today was a bit more difficult due to the fact that another large sight-seeing vessel was already moored at the dock.

On a normal day, the various charter boats had a schedule they kept so there was only one boat at the dock at any one time. Today was obviously an exception to this. The sea captain's vast expertise soon had his vessel alongside the dock. There were several people already standing on the dock, waiting for him to finish his maneuvering so they could tie off his boat. He gave them the OK and they secured the vessel.

"Let's go, guys," Marion said, rising to her feet. "Let's stick together until we know what is going on here. OK?" she said to her weary charges.

"OK," Madison said. Mako held out his hand to help her to her feet. She took his help and when she was standing, she helped Brooke up as well. They all disembarked the boat, and walked down the long dock toward the old fort.

Wilfred was the last one off the boat. He followed Madison and her company as they entered the fort, staying behind them but not letting them out of his sight. Having so many scared, desperate people in such a small area had the potential for danger. His responsibility was to not let anything happen to Madison while she was under his watch.

## *Safe Landing*

Madison walked behind her aunt, her hand tightly gripping the Reaper, as the group passed through an opening in the walls of the old civil war fort. Once inside, the ground opened up into a large field. Several hundred people sat in smaller groups scattered around the grassy field. Past them, in the center of the fort, stood a more modern concrete building. The building was

Battery Isaac Huger. It was built around 1900 as part of the Harbor Defense of Charleston during the Spanish American war. Its black facade stood in sharp contrast to the old brick and mortar walls of Fort Sumter surrounding it.

They found a patch of grassy lawn that looked particularly comfortable and sat down. In the distance, approaching fast, was the thumping sound of a helicopter and the swishing of the rotor as it churned through the air. A large green, double-rotored behemoth passed over their heads, slowed to a hover above the other side of Battery Huger, and descended onto the field beyond. It stayed on the ground for only a minute and then took off again, heading back in the direction it came. When it was sufficiently far enough away that conversation was again possible, Mako spoke up.

"That must be the military taking survivors off to a safer place, away from the city."

"It is," a voice said. The group looked up to see Tanner's brother Michael approaching. He had recognized Connor, Mako and Brooke from the band his brother ran sound for. "I just came from where the helicopter took off. My friend Sarah got on board, but space was limited so I volunteered to stay behind. The pilot said that was the last flight coming out here. We are all going to have to stay here until they can come up with another plan to get us off the island."

He turned to Connor and said, "what's up? Hey Mako, hey Brooke.

"Hi Michael, I am Connor's aunt, Marion. This is Madison, Connor's sister," Marion replied.

"Connor's sister? I didn't know you had a sister, CJ. Where have you been hiding her? Did Tanner know this? If not, he's going to freak. Where is he anyway? He sent a text saying he was with you guys back at your house," Michael asked, looking around the lawn for his brother.

The look on the faces staring back at him told him everything. His legs buckled. He dropped to the ground, just getting his arm down in time to keep himself in a near sitting position. Brooke began crying again. She leaned into Madison.

The group sat for a few minutes without speaking.

Marion began taking a good look at their surroundings. There were no military personnel to be found anywhere. She saw a medical tent, but no medical personnel were inside.

"Michael, how long have you been at the fort here?" Marion asked.

"I've been out here a couple of hours now."

"Where are all the military and medical people?" she asked.

"They all left a half an hour ago. The wounded had all been treated and the most seriously injured have been evacuated already. The military said we would be OK here and there was really no need for them to stay. They were needed elsewhere in the city, so they left," he said.

This concerned Marion deeply. One infected person could wipe out everyone on the island.

As Marion and Michael were speaking, Madison caught sight of Wilfred on the stairs near the roof of the Battery. He motioned for her to join him. She turned to her aunt and said, "I'm going up there to talk to Wilfred for a bit, if that's OK with you." She pointed to the place where Wilfred was standing. "I'll only be a few minutes."

"That's fine. Just meet us back here when you are done. We won't leave this spot until you return," she said to her niece.

Madison rose to her feet, turned to her brother and handed him the Reaper. "Would you mind holding onto this for a bit? You can play it if you want."

"Well, if you insist," he said, taking the instrument and eagerly pulling it from its case.

Madison turned and made her way across the field to the Battery. As she neared the stairs, she could hear her brother playing the Reaper. He was good. A smile crossed her face as she realized he was the only other person, other than her Nana Jean, who had ever played that instrument. Long ago, she had vowed to be the last person to lay hands on the strings of the perfection that was the Reaper. As she grabbed the staircase railing and began to climb the steps, she realized the rules were changing all around her in every way imaginable.

# *Fort Rescue*

Greg pressed firmly on the firing button on top of the cyclic of his Apache helicopter. This was his third sortie over the Ravenel Bridge. He was becoming numb to the reality of what those bullets were striking. This entire day had become surreal. He felt like a bystander in a movie playing out before his eyes. The only thing keeping him going was the hope of seeing his family again when this was all over. As he released the firing button, the bridge was once again cleared of infected. His fuel situation was low but not critical. As he circled around to make another pass over the length of the bridge, his radio came to life.

"Base to Captain Quinn. Over," the voice in his headset rang out.

"This is Captain Quinn. Over," he replied.

"The rescue at Fort Sumter has been halted. The last pilot indicated an alarming number of infected lining the shore opposite the Fort. We need you to take a pass over the fort and assess the threat. Over."

"Understood. En route to Fort Sumter, ETA two minutes. Over." Greg banked the helicopter and headed out over Charleston harbor in the direction of Fort Sumter. He knew the noise of a helicopter-based rescue was going to attract the infected to the one spot they did not want them attracted to. There were upwards of five hundred survivors on that island and it was going to take time to get them all off. The last thing they needed was to draw more attention to them. In very short order he was hovering over the sandbar that loosely connected the fort to the mainland. It was now just past high tide, so the sandbar was still too deep to be used to cross the expanse. That would only be true for another couple of hours. Once low tide hit, the hundreds of infected that now lined the mainland shores would pour onto the island.

Out of pure frustration Greg once again depressed the red firing button. He cut down a dozen of the nearest infected, but many more seemed to take their place. He knew he could not stay there as the noise from his aircraft was drawing more zombies to the shore. He turned and hovered briefly over the fort.

As he looked down, he spotted someone waving their arms at him frantically. He spun the helicopter slightly to get a better view and realized it was Marion, his wife, waving at him from the field below. Right beside her, Connor was waving his arms over his head frantically. He waved back, keeping his chopper in a hover just above their position.

An idea crossed his mind. He grabbed a spare two-way radio from the passenger seat, changed the channel to a frequency seldom used by the military, and dropped the radio to an open spot near where his wife and nephew stood. He saw her run to it and pick it up. He hoped the fall had not ruined it as he tuned his headset to the same frequency.

"Thank God you made it. I can't believe it's you. Is everyone OK?" he asked his wife over the radio.

"We are. We are good. I've never been happier to see you," she answered back.

"I can't stay here long. The noise of this thing is attracting the infected. We will have help here as soon as possible to get you off this island. Stay safe. I love you," he said to his wife.

"Before you go, Greg, I have some news. Look on the roof of the Battery," she said. Greg spun the helicopter so he had a clear view of the rooftop. "The girl with the blonde hair, standing with the older gentleman. That's Madison. Our Madison." Greg stared at the girl for several seconds and gave her a wave. The girl waved back, looking puzzled at the helicopter.

"I'm not sure she knows who I am, but I can't wait to introduce myself. Keep the radio tuned to this channel. I'll call back when I can," he said. With renewed hope, he banked the helicopter back in the direction of Summerall Field.

The last thing he heard in his headset before turning back over to the active military frequency was his wife saying, "I love you. Be safe."

## *True Calling*

"I think that was my uncle," Madison said to Wilfred as the roar of the helicopter subsided as it made its way back across

Charleston Harbor in the direction of the city.

"Is your family everything you had hoped it would be?" he asked.

"It's hard to answer that. I had considered so many versions of them over the years that I'm not sure I knew what to expect. I do know that I feel as close to them as I have anyone in my life and I've only known them for a short while. It's pretty weird, but a good weird," she said.

"Well, what I am about to tell you is going to be weirder still, trust me. There is no easy way to start this except to say that I am not who you think I am. At least not entirely," the southern gentleman said to Madison.

"What do you mean?" she said, taking a step back toward the staircase. Just then, a lightning bolt shot out of the sky and struck just a few feet from where Wilfred stood. Madison instinctively dropped to the ground, covering her face with her arms. Adrenaline coursed through her body as she waited for the thunderclap. To her surprise, there was none. Instead, a familiar voice greeted her.

"Hello Rain, it has been a while. How's the Reaper?"

It was a voice she never thought she would hear again. She jumped to her feet, turned and spun to face the man who spoke the words. Before her stood Jeremiah. She ran to her old friend and gave him a bear hug.

"Well, well. It is good to see you too," Jeremiah said, hugging his young friend back.

"I don't understand. Where did you come from? How did you get here? I couldn't find you in Boston before I left and now you just show up here? What was with that lightning? Are you guys OK?" she said, blurting out every question that was in her head all at once.

"One thing at a time, my young friend," he said. "Wilfred, you old goat, I see you are still kicking around down here in the south," he said to Wilfred.

"Beats those cold New England winters, J. I've got it made down here," Wilfred said back to his old friend.

"You two know each other?" Madison asked in astonishment. "Wait a minute. Jeremiah, where are your glasses. Can you see me? For real?"

"Yes, I can see. I always could. You'd be surprised how people will act when they think you can't see them. I was able to see the world the way it really was and not how people wanted me to see it. That's how I got to see you so well. As for Wilfred and I, we go way back. Way longer than you can imagine. He and I have a lot to talk to you about and not much time to do it. Most of this is going to come as quite a shock to you at first, but hear us out. It will all become clear in the end," Jeremiah said to her. Madison stepped back from her old friend and shifted her gaze from one of them to the other as Jeremiah began explaining things to Madison.

"Wilfred and I belong to the same group or organization, if

you will. It is called the Raye. The Raye are made up individuals from almost every intelligent species in the universe," he said, pausing to let that last statement sink into the girl's head.

"The universe? Are you saying you're not human?" she said, staring at them. If this were anyone but Jeremiah, she would have left right then. But it WAS Jeremiah. The one person she had complete faith in. That, and the fact that he just now seemed to have ridden a lightning bolt down from the heavens, gave her enough evidence that what he was saying may have some truth to it. Still, her practical side would not let her accept this.

"We are not alien. We are as human as you are." Jeremiah said.

"Look, I'm not sure what is going on here, but you are not really asking me to believe that aliens exist in the middle of a zombie outbreak are you? Really?" Madison laughed, completely overwhelmed.

"I know it is a lot to take in Maddie," Wilfred added. "But this may just be the magic you were hoping existed in the world."

"Right. I'm still going to need proof." She said to the older gentleman. "A sleight of hand trick won't work here."

"OK, this should do it. Look to your right." Jeremiah said.

Another lightning bolt shot from the sky and struck the roof just a few feet to Madison's right. When the bright flash dissipated, Jack, the boy she met at the hostel, stood right where the lightning bolt had hit.

"Hey Dixie, or should I say Madison." Jack said to her. "Good to see you are still with us."

Madison was in shock. She had to accept that what she just saw was no magic trick. Whatever that lightning was, it was certainly not anything she could explain. It was like magic. Maybe they were not lying to her after all.

"It was Jack here that saved your life last night. When you left me at the train station, it was his turn to keep an eye on you. One of the very first infected had a bead on you in the alley and he dispatched the threat." Wilfred said to the young girl.

Madison remembered the bright light that had struck her assailant. Seemed to be the same light that she had seen strike the roof just a minute earlier.

"The fact that you haven't left tells me we were not wrong in choosing you," Wilfred added. He glanced at Jeremiah and then back at Madison. Jack went over and stood next to Wilfred. "Chosen? You chose me for what?" Madison said.

"To be one of us," Jeremiah explained. "To be Raye. We are guardians of the human race. Here to help humankind evolve into its full potential. You see, we have been watching you for quite some time now."

"Why me? I'm not so special." Madison said.

"Quite the contrary, young lady. You and your brother have been special since birth. See, your father, Levi Wolfe, was Raye. His given name was Running Wolf. He was a pure-blooded Paiute Indian. We lost Levi back in 2002 during a MAR uprising in Central America at the ripe old age of one hundred and sixty-seven."

"One hundred and sixty-seven? How does a human being live to be one hundred and sixty-seven?" Madison asked.

"Using the same technology that you see in these infected people, these zombies if you will," Jack added.

"Is this some alien technology?" she asked.

"Well, if by alien you mean it didn't come from this planet, then yes, it is alien. However, we humans invented it a long, long time ago," Wilfred replied.

"I don't get it, how did humans invent it but it not come from this planet?" she asked, puzzled by this logic.

"This is not the first world that humans have lived on," Jeremiah explained. "Our species initially evolved on a planet known as Mundi Primus. It was many, many thousands of light years from here. On that planet, our technology had advanced to the point where we were using nanobots, tiny microscopic machines, to treat human diseases and ailments. It is the application of that technology that keeps the human Raye population alive for so long. It was known as MAR. Mechanical Autonomous Replication. The technology was well on its way to curing every known human ailment. However, due to misguided act of pure love, that technology was altered in a most destructive way. The result was that the technology developed to save mankind ended up dooming it. Mundi Primus was destroyed by the Raye in an attempt to obliterate this insidious technology. It worked, for the most part. There was no sign of MAR activity in the universe until just over sixty million years ago, right here on planet Earth. Once again, the Raye attempted to wipe out the uprising using an asteroid strike. Unlike Mundi Primus, the Raye hoped to spare this planet as it was a prime candidate into which the human species could be reintroduced. Once the MAR uprising was subdued, the Raye spliced human genes with those of the indigenous ape population. This new branch of the ape species quickly evolved into us, the modern day human. This quick, drastic introduction of new genes into the indigenousness ape population is why scientists have never been able to find the missing link in human evolution on this planet."

"Wow. My head is spinning," Madison said, trying desperately to keep up with all of this information she was being given. She took a few seconds to organize her thoughts.

"OK, so if the Raye are so powerful, why don't they just squash this MAR uprising again? Why are you sitting back while so many people are dying? It doesn't seem too guardian like to me," she said, thinking of Tanner back at the dock.

"To understand why we can't intervene here, you need to understand why the Raye exist at all," Jeremiah continued. "Diversity in the universe is shrinking. The technologically advanced races in the universe began colonizing the inhabitable planets, interfering with evolution of the native populations, or worse, eliminating them altogether. Evolution is the key to growth - and growth is the key to everything. It is how the impossible becomes possible."

Wilfred added on, "it's how the unknown becomes known. Without it, all life will stagnate and eventually cease to exist. The Raye were formed with one purpose: to protect new, evolving worlds so that, one day, the life on those planets could contribute and expand the collective knowledge of the universe. For natural evolution to take place there can be no overt guidance or interference from an outside intelligence. Even if that means a species or a planet does not survive."

"Let me give you an example from your own family's history," Wilfred continued. "Your father befriended a bounty hunter named Samuel Losman back in the 1850s. Samuel had inadvertently been placed smack in the middle of a minor MAR outbreak. Your father helped Samuel eliminate the MAR threat, although Samuel simply thought they were hunting a murderous villain. In turn, Samuel spent the rest of his days protecting a nice couple by the names of Boone and Annie. Annie went on to start an orphanage that fed, taught and protected many of the less fortunate children of the old west. Several of those children grew up to be great leaders, both morally and politically. The Raye protected and guided Boone, who in turn made Annie's accomplishments possible. Levi, your father, did this without ever revealing his true identity. Do you understand?"

"I think so," Madison said. "I think if most people saw Jeremiah or Jack ride down a lightning bolt, they would think they were angels. By proving angels exist, it would prove God existed and would essentially bring scientific research to a grinding halt. We have to get to where we are going organically if we are going to evolve and grow into our true potential."

"You pretty much have it all correct," Wilfred answered. "And you mentioned God as well. Whether or not there is one master architect of the entire universe is still very much an open question. It remains a mystery to us all. Many species have falsely worshiped beings from a different world under the mistaken belief they are deities. It is always the less evolved and less technically advanced species that succumb to this thinking. It is very easy to jump to the conclusion that, just because something can't be explained, it actually has no explanation, and therefore must be the work of a divine being. In time, all things will become apparent. It is exactly why life in the universe must continue to evolve."

"You said the Raye use the MAR technology to live so long. Do you have those things inside you? How old are you?" Madison asked Jeremiah.

"I am just over two hundred years old. Wilfred here has me beat by fifty or so years. Not much of the original equipment remains, I'm afraid. Pretty much just the grey matter up here," he said, tapping his head with the index finger of his right hand. "I have seen this great nation grow from infancy. The Civil War was by far the most disheartening point. Wilfred here was actually a magician in a travelling sideshow in the early 1930s. I believe you went by Billy the Amazing, didn't you?" Jeremiah said to his friend.

"I did indeed. I had to give that life up, unfortunately. Let's just say I used some of the company's technology to enhance my show. I was kindly asked not to do that any longer," Wilfred answered.

"Well, thankfully you held on to some of that technology," Jeremiah said to his old friend, placing his hand on the man's shoulder. "Madison, we actually have Billy the Amazing here to thank for not having a building land on our heads," Jeremiah said.

"Our heads? You were there too?" Madison asked, surprised by Jeremiah's statement.

"Indeed I was. I reached in to pull you from the window, but I was too late. The building was coming down all around us. That is when Wilfred here intervened with one of his technological gadgets, given to him by his Raye superiors. He used the device to instantaneously move us from the alley to the sidewalk and out of harm's way."

"That's the same device that got me into so much trouble with my magic show," Wilfred said. "I had worked out a bit where Billy the Amazing was locked in a trunk on stage in front of the entire audience. I activated my device and was instantly transported to a position behind the audience. I would then reappear, walking down the aisle with the key to the trunk in hand. I blew many an audience members' mind that day, and almost lost my association with the Raye. That is the one and only time I abused this great gift I have been given."

"Well, that was then; this is now. And right now, I owe you my life. I can't begin to thank you enough for that," Madison said to him.

"So, my dear, you have a decision to make. This is a great honor and a great burden at the same time," Jeremiah said.

"Do I really have a choice, now that I know the Raye exist?" she asked.

"You do. Being Raye is a purely volunteer position. You can say no and go on to live whatever life you choose. Many have done so. A few have tried to expose the Raye here on Earth. With no success, I might add. Nobody would believe their story and they could not produce a single bit of proof to back up what they were saying. Crackpots, they're called," Wilfred explained.

"Well, I am going to have to think about this," Madison said.

"There is one more thing you have to consider. If you accept, you cannot stay here with your family. You will be sent to a place where you will learn a great deal more about the Raye, other civilizations throughout the universe, and how to use this advanced technology for travel and protection. Riding a lightning bolt takes some practice," Jeremiah joked. "We don't need an answer right now, but we will need one soon."

"OK. But right now we have a more pressing issue. At least I do. As long as I am still a member of this human race, and not a Raye, I can directly intervene on humankind's behalf. Those zombies are starting to make their way across the sandbar over there," she said, pointing in the direction of the mainland. The tide had begun to recede, and as a result, the depth of the water covering the massive sandbar that connected the island to the mainland was lowering.

"Low tide is three hours away, but I would guess it will only be two hours at most before the water will be shallow enough to allow the crossing. Anyone left on this island at that time will surely not survive the day," Wilfred said.

Already Madison could see that the infected were testing how far out they could go onto the sandbar before their heads went underwater. There was little doubt that they would cross as soon as it was physically possible.

"We have to warn everyone. Wilfred, will you still skipper us in your boat? That is not against your code or anything?" she asked.

"I can and I will. To everyone else, I am still just the captain of the sightseeing charter. I will do whatever I can in that capacity to help," he said.

"I'll have to leave you here I'm afraid." Jack said. "I have to go help Melinda. This is not the only place where help is needed. You are in good hands with Wilfred."

"Will I see you again, Jeremiah?" she asked her old friend.

"Regardless of what you decide, you will see me again. For now, I need to take my leave with Jack. Good luck."

## *Safe Harbor*

Madison raced down the staircase and across the field to where her family was sitting. As she arrived, breathless from the exertion and excitement, Connor was placing the Reaper back into its case.

"That is really quite a guitar, sis. I'm very jealous. This here is Morgan. She is going to hang with us for a while." He said motioning toward a young teenage girl sitting to his right dressed in National Guard camouflage and a bandage around her head.

Madison gave Morgan a quick nod hello and spoke to the entire group.

"Guys, we are not safe here. The zombies on the mainland are collecting at the shoreline. They are testing the depth of the sandbar that connects this island to the shore. We have at most two hours before they are going to be able to cross. Everyone has to be off this island by then," Madison said, still trying to catch her breath.

Marion heard the conversation and, once again, took charge

of the situation. "Looks like we need to get back in the boat. Where is Wilfred?"

"There are a lot of people on this island. We are not all going to fit on that boat. And where will we go now?" Brooke asked.

"There are a few islands in this harbor that are not connected by such shallow waters," Mako said. "I know Shute's Folly Island and Drum Island are two that are very close."

"Great, and then we are stuck on some island with no food or water," Brooke replied. Her spirits had recovered slightly. "Not to mention no bathrooms. I vote negative on that."

"Well, how about that?" Madison said, pointing to a massive cruise ship anchored at the deep water marina next to the ship-yards. "It is basically a floating island, complete with all modern amenities. I bet we could wait this out almost indefinitely on there. On our trip down from Boston, Wilfred said he could pilot anything that floated on water. I say we take him up on that."

"That is an excellent idea," Marion replied just as Wilfred approached with another man who none of them had met before.

"This is Captain Gill. That is his boat tied up next to mine on the dock. His boat is having engine trouble but his fuel tanks are nearly full. His crew is busy siphoning the fuel from his boat into mine. It will take multiple trips, but we can get everyone off the island within two hours. There are no authorities of any kind here, so we're on our own," Wilfred said.

"We think the cruise ship over there would make an excellent place to wait out the zombie apocalypse," Brooke jumped in. Both captains turned to look at the bright red tail of the cruise ship towering above the buildings along the shore where it was moored.

"That is a good idea, but we don't know if that ship is safe. We may be sending people from the pan into the fire. We certainly can't risk trying to board from land. I am sure that dock is crawling with infected," Wilfred said.

"True, but I know for a fact there are three empty garbage scows floating not far from that boat," Captain Gill said. "I passed them on the way over here. The tugs that were pulling them to shore ended up abandoning them when those tugboat captains decided to head for a safer harbor. Luckily they had the presence of mind to anchor them before they left. It is not ideal, but the water is deep enough to keep everyone safe and it will be easy to load and unload people onto them."

"That sounds like a good plan to me," Wilfred added. "It may not be ideal, but we don't have time for perfection right now. Captain Gill and I will go get the boat ready. I need you all to let the other survivors know what we are doing. Tell them we have plenty of time so there is no need to panic. The reward for being on the first boat will be having to smell garbage the longest. I'm sure that will get you some volunteers to be last. By my calculations, it is going to take four full boat trips to get everyone off the island. I estimate the round trip to be thirty minutes, so if everything goes to plan, we should have everyone off the island before the infected breach it."

"Wilfred, how long before we can get the first boat out of here?" Marion asked.

"The first group can board now. The refueling should be nearing completion as we speak," Wilfred responded.

"OK then, we'll get the first boatload of people from this immediate area. Once they are on board, we will split up and let everyone else on the island know what the plan is. Let's go, let's make this happen," Marion said.

The group separated and went about the task of organizing the survivors on the island.

\*\*\*

In very short order, the first boatload was headed across the harbor and the entire group was once again collected on the lawn in front of the dock.

"Morgan, how did you get to be out here alone?" Madison asked the young girl, who had been very quiet up to that point.

"My family is gone." She said. She described the events of the previous night and following morning that brought her to the island.

"Greg, the guy from the helicopter, is my husband." Marion

informed the girl when she was done. "You are a very brave and very lucky girl."

"He seemed nice."

"You don't have to worry any more. I..." Madison paused and glanced at her brother and aunt.

"We are going to take care of you," Marion picked up where her niece had left off. "No one should be without a family. You are going to stay with us until all of this is worked out. Are you OK with that?" she asked.

Morgan nodded and faced the ground.

Madison put an arm around her.

# CHAPTER 17

# Tears

— ❖ —

## *Evacuation*

The evacuation was proceeding without a hitch. It took just under two hours to bring the first three boatloads of survivors to the garbage scows. Although their window for safely evacuating the last of the people at the fort was closing, Wilfred felt confident as he steered his boat back alongside the dock at Fort Sumter.

Madison, her family and friends were among the last of the people lined up on the dock. People began to flood onto the vessel as soon as it bumped the dock and stopped moving.

Connor had moved to the Battery and was perched on top of the roof, watching the shoreline. The infected were now well past the halfway point between the shore and the island and moving fast.

"They're coming!" he yelled toward the dock, waving his arms over his head. Marion and Madison were positioned at the entrance to the dock, helping those who needed assistance to the boat. Marion waved back in Connor's direction, acknowledging him and waving him down in a manner that told him he should join them.

"Everyone, quickly now," Marion yelled to the people still lining the dock, waiting for their chance to board. "The infected have reached the far side of the island." She turned back to see Connor running across the field in her direction. She yelled, "we have no time left. Hurry!" Connor raced to his aunt's side and turned to watch the fort for signs of movement.

"They will be upon us any minute now. I'm not sure we will make it on the boat in time," he said, looking at the line of people still waiting.

"Brooke, Mako, Maddie. You guys ready to use those one more time?" she asked her young charges, pointing to the weapons that were still strapped to their belts.

"Absolutely. We got this," Brooke said. Her demeanor had changed drastically. Her grief had turned to rage. Rage that was about to be taken out on the town librarian, the guy who bagged groceries at the Piggly Wiggly grocery store, the crew from Manny's landscaping, and countless other folks who had the misfortune to be infected with the unknown contagion that morning.

"Here they come," Connor yelled as the first of the infected rounded the far side of the Battery. Very quickly after that, a horde spilled from around and over the building like a tidal wave. There were still twenty souls on the long dock waiting to board the boat.

Marion had her AK assault rifle pointed in the direction of the Battery as she and the rest of the kids walked backwards down the dock, moving in stride with the end of the line of survivors boarding the vessel. Once again, Mako held the Reaper while Madison aimed her 9mm. By the time the first zombie had reached the end of the dock, and anywhere near close enough to begin firing upon, Mako was already climbing onto the boat with the Reaper.

Brooke could no longer contain herself. She opened fire at one of Manny's landscaping crew as he bolted toward them on the dock. Although the effort was cathartic for the young girl, she managed to empty her clip without hitting the man once. Marion was not as unfortunate. She squeezed the trigger and dispatched the zombie with a burst of three bullets.

Brooke, Michael, Morgan, Connor and Madison jumped onto the boat, with Marion just behind them. She stepped backwards onto the deck of the ship as her rifle blasted away at the swarm of infected that were now pouring down the dock. No sooner had Marion's foot left the dock for the safety of the boat deck than Wilfred pushed the throttle full forward. The boat lurched forward, knocking down several of the people who weren't yet seated.

Marion continued her barrage of lead, pausing only once to reload. The boat was twenty feet away from the dock when the first wave of infected reached the end. Their momentum carried them forward as they leapt from the end of the dock toward the boat. They all missed, by varying degrees, landing harmlessly in the ocean behind the boat.

For the second time in three hours, Marion and her young crew took a seat on Wilfred's boat, having fired their weapons at fellow human beings. For all but Brooke, the experience had not become any easier.

## *All Aboard*

Wilfred guided his vessel toward the third and final barge in the string of garbage scows. The scene before him was quite different from the one he left just a half hour ago. Rather than three hundred men, women and children holding their noses and hoping for rescue, he saw eight smaller boats moving away from the barges. Every able-bodied man had left the relative safety of the barges and was now riding on one of the boats moving across the harbor toward the cruise ship, anchored just a thousand yards away. Wilfred noticed Captain Gill on board one of the smaller boats and took note of the name painted on the transom.

"This is Charleston's Water Charter to the captain of the Rebel Yell, do you copy?" he spoke into his handheld mic.

"Yesser, this is the Rebel Yell," a voice with a thick southern drawl answered back.

"May I speak with one of your passengers, a Captain Gill?"

he asked. The radio was silent for fifteen seconds before a familiar voice crackled over the radio.

"Wilfred, I see you made it off the island, but you are late to the party, my friend. You have done your part, now it's my turn. Me and the boys are going to commandeer that fine looking cruise ship and throw one heck of a barbeque on board. Sit tight. We'll swing over in a bit and take you on board," he said to his fellow sea captain.

Hoots and hollers could be heard in the background while Captain Gill was speaking into the radio. To Wilfred, it sounded like the men thought they were actually going to a party rather than a potentially life threatening situation. Testosterone-fueled mob mentality, for sure.

"How exactly do you plan on doing that?" Wilfred answered, concern in his voice. "You know those docks are going to be crawling with infected. Not to mention what you might find on board."

"The docks are clear. Some of the men ran recon while you were taking your last run. No sign of the zombies anywhere. I should have this big sucker out on open water within the hour. I'm kind of glad I got to her before you did. She's going to be quite a dream piloting out of port."

During this conversation, Wilfred managed to pilot his ship up alongside the barge and his passengers began piling out onto the old scow.

"Keep your eyes and ears open, my friend, and good luck to you. Don't get too worked up behind the wheel and forget about us down here," he joked nervously.

Madison walked up beside Wilfred as he hung up the mic alongside the marine radio.

"Hey there, young lady. Feel like joining me for a bit of a sightseeing trip?" Wilfred asked his young friend. "I think the men are in trouble with their plan and I want to get closer in case they need help. If they end up being successful, we can come back here and get everyone ready for a sea rescue. If they aren't, well, we'll need to come up with a new plan ourselves."

"I'm in. I am sure the rest of the gang will want to come too. Who knows, our firepower may come in handy," she said.

Madison hurried off to gather the gang and in short order, she returned with everyone in tow except Michael, who had volunteered to stay behind and look after Morgan.

Wilfred pulled away from the barge and piloted his ship across the harbor in the direction of the cruise ship. Ahead of them, he could see that the boats the men were in had stopped a few hundred feet from the huge dock where the cruise ship was moored. They were obviously discussing the plan. When Wilfred's boat was still several hundred yards away, the boats began to move again, splitting into two smaller groups.

One group headed toward the bow of the ship and one toward the stern. Every hundred feet or so along the facade of the dock there were ladders that extended down to the water line. Each boat made its way to a ladder and tied off to it. From their position some one hundred feet from the bow of the ship, Wilfred and his crew could see the first of the men were reaching the top of the ladders.

At first, things seemed to be going well. The men were making good speed across the dock along the side of the cruise ship and no zombies could be seen. Several began guiding the gang planks back into place so they could board the large ship, but no sooner had they begun moving the metal walkways than infected began pouring from the building alongside the dock.

The building was used for the embarkation process and the dock was now filling with what, until recently, were vacationers awaiting their Bahama cruise. The men did not stand a chance. They were outnumbered three to one.

Marion tried to use the AK to help those closest to her, but she could not shoot with any accuracy from that distance. The boat deck bobbing underneath her did not help matters either. Wilfred backed his boat further away from the dock. At this point, any attempt to help was futile. The intensity of the screams from the dock first rose and then steadily subsided until everything was once again quiet.

"Looks like we need our own plan," Madison said to Wilfred after several minutes of silence and despair.

"I still think this ship is our best chance of survival," Wilfred responded. "Let's take a look around for another way on. The dock is certainly out of the question, but the good news is the gang planks were retracted. There may be infected on the ship, but it appears many of the passengers had not yet boarded and there is no longer any way for them to get access to the ship. The bad news is the ship is still moored to the dock. If there was any-one alive to pilot it, those mooring ropes would be detached and the ship would be long gone by now."

Wilfred eased his boat slowly alongside the large oceango-ing behemoth. To Madison, the boat under her feet had initially seemed like a good-sized ship, but it now felt like a toy next to the vastness of the cruise ship. Faces could be seen in some of the portals that ran along the side of the larger ship. Some were obviously those of infected individuals, but others looked scared and some waved at them as they passed. Mako broke the silence.

"What about that?" he said, pointing to a scaffold hanging from cables at the boat's stern.

"Ah, yes! That might just work," Wilfred said. "These scaf-folds are used by the maintenance crew to repaint sections of the ship while it is in port. They should be able to lift us onto the upper decks."

"But what then?" Marion asked. "Say we make it to the upper deck. What do we do then?"

"These ships are constructed to exacting safety standards," Wilfred explained as he pulled up alongside the scaffold. "The boat is broken up into many segments, each isolated from the next with watertight doors. In the event of an emergency at sea, the captain can automatically shut all of those doors from the bridge. If I can get to the bridge, I can close those doors. That will isolate each deck from the next, and break up each long hallway into smaller, contained sections. Wherever there are infected, they will be trapped in those areas. If there are survivors, they will be protected from the areas of the ship that are overrun."

"But what if we close survivors in with the infected?" Brooke asked, looking back at the face of a child not much younger than herself in a portal window just a few feet from where she stood.

"They will have to stay in their rooms until help arrives. I can make a ship-wide announcement as soon as I reach the bridge," he reassured his young passenger.

"You have my vote," Mako said. The others quickly agreed.

"OK then. Who's going up first?" Wilfred asked.

## *Overboard*

"We can't all go at once," Marion said, pointing to the sticker on the scaffolds control system that indicated a five hundred pound weight limit. "We'll need to make two trips. Wilfred, I think it is a good idea if you and I go in separate groups."

"I agree," he replied. "Usually I would say ladies first, but I must insist on taking the first ride. I am acutely familiar with the layout of this vessel and feel I am best equipped to do recon work. At my weight, I believe only one other person can come with me on this first trip." As he spoke he turned to Madison and made a patting motion toward his jacket pocket. Madison understood what he was telling her. She was aware that the man had unique technology that he could only use if she were the one who accompanied him.

"I'll go with him on the first trip. If we see any trouble, we will come back down immediately. If not, we will send the scaffold back down for you," Madison added.

"I can't say I am comfortable with that, but there is nothing about today that is comfortable," Marion said. "Be careful! If there is any sign of danger, come back to us and we will make another plan." Marion's face showed great concern as she looked at the brave girl in front of her.

"We'll be fine. This is going to work. I feel it," Madison said, as she and the Reaper joined Wilfred on the scaffold. "I promise I will drop this if it comes down to it," she added for Marion's sake. Wilfred pulled the lever and began raising the scaffold. It was surprisingly quiet, and obviously well-maintained. As they ascended, Madison could hear her aunt calling for Greg on the military radio. From what she could tell, there was no reply.

The scaffold slowly made its way up the side of the large vessel toward the veranda deck above. As it did, they passed several cabin windows and what they saw was encouraging. Although only three of the rooms had people in them, they were all alive. In one particular cabin, a family of four had been sitting on a bed, the children crying and their parents trying to console them. The mother noticed Wilfred and Madison passing by and rushed toward the window.

Wilfred yelled to her, "Stay put. Don't leave your room. Help is coming."

The woman nodded, placed her hand to her chest and returned to her children.

Finally they reached the top deck. As it slowed to a stop, Wilfred and Madison scanned the deck for movement. There was none. They quietly swung themselves over the railing and crouched down on the deck.

This section of the ship contained water slides and was set up to cater to the younger passengers. Wilfred reached back over to the control on the scaffold. He used his belt to tie off the control lever to allow it to descend back down the side of the ship. Wilfred knew the maintenance platform was equipped with a safety mechanism to keep it from descending all the way down into the water.

As the platform made its way down the ship, an infected rounded the enclosed staircase and noticed Wilfred. The captain took out a small device from his pocket as the zombie raced towards him. A bright bolt of light shot from Wilfred's hand and struck the zombie. There was no sound as the zombie disintegrated into a black mass, rolling harmlessly off the far side of the boat. Wilfred turned to Madison and winked.

The winch stopped humming, indicating the scaffold had reached the waterline. Madison leaned her head through the railing and watched as the others climbed on. The winch clicked and began to hum as they began their ascent. Madison turned her gaze back onto the deck where Wilfred had again fired at an infected that had noticed them.

The winch, which was emitting a steady hum, suddenly seemed to falter. Madison moved her head back between the railings and looked down. The platform was no more than thirty feet from the top, but to her horror, her family and friends were no longer alone.

An infected had leapt from one of the exposed walkways below the scaffold and was now hanging from its underside. There was no way she, nor anyone on the scaffold, could get a shot at it as the scaffold itself protected it from a clean shot. Madison watched as it swung out with its feet and stomped the side of the boat. The motion made it appear that the zombie was actually walking horizontally up the side of the ship.

In this position, it was going to be able to swing its feet up onto the scaffold without ever exposing its head for a clean shot. Madison only had a second to react before it was too late. She reached down, grabbed the handle of the Reaper, swung it out over the railing, and thrust the guitar downward.

The Reaper caught the assailant in the mid-section, causing it to lose its handhold and begin falling. Madison turned away, not bearing to watch. She heard a loud splash as the Reaper and the zombie entered the water.

## Overwhelmed

Madison sat in silence for the next thirty seconds as her family and friends ascended in safely behind her. Before the platform had come to a complete halt at the top, Connor leapt from it, hurtling over the railing, and hugged her.

"That was quick thinking sis." he said as he gave his sister a hug.

Mako quickly took his place.

"You're awesome," he said and, without warning, kissed her square on the lips. This caught Madison totally off guard. It was her first kiss and it happened so quickly she didn't have time to prepare herself.

When the young man pulled away, she blushed, realizing she was not at all unhappy about the experience. Marion and Brook both stepped up and hugged her at the same time.

"OK. Enough of all of that. We have work to do here," Madison said, again crouching on the deck of the ship. Her heart was heavy at the loss of her longtime friend, but there was no time for grief now.

"She's right," Wilfred added. "We have to get to the bow of this boat and it is a lot farther than it looks. Follow me and keep quiet. Our best chance is not to be noticed at all." Wilfred led them around the water slides and down the narrow walkway along the outer edge of the ship. They walked single file and soon approached the mid-ship area, where their walkway turned into a catwalk overlooking the main pool area on the deck below. Slowly and quietly they began to cross the lengthy expanse.

They were halfway down the catwalk when the poolside speaker system began to blare the Jimmy Buffet song "Margaritaville." The ship's boarding day entertainment program kicked in with the first of many poolside favorites.

Things began to go south in a hurry. Zombies started pouring from every door that faced the pool area. Unfortunately for Madison and the group, one of those adjacent areas was the twenty-four hour buffet, the single most popular place on the massive ship.

In just a few short seconds, the first zombie spotted them on the catwalk overhead. There were four sets of stairs that led from the pool level to the raised catwalk area, two on the port side and two on the starboard side. Madison's group was halfway between each staircase on the port side.

Marion, Connor and Mako concentrated their fire on the aft staircase and Madison, Brooke and Wilfred concentrated on the staircase closer to the bow. For thirty seconds they managed to keep the zombies from getting to the top of the stairs, but that was it. They each ran out of bullets at nearly the same time and when they stopped shooting to reload, the infected quickly reached the catwalk level. As they feverishly worked to reload their weapons, each in their heart knew this was the end.

From out of nowhere, a thunderous noise rose from behind them. Gunfire and tracer rounds erupted from a position just above them. The zombies on the stairs exploded with the impact from the high powered rounds. Madison covered her ears and looked up at a dark green military helicopter rotating back and forth as it sprayed a continuous stream of bullets at their assailants. It was Greg! He had heard Marion's call.

"Run!" Marion yelled and grabbed Brooke by the arm. Everyone followed her as she raced along the catwalk toward a doorway closer to the bow of the ship.

Greg continued his assault, leveling every moving thing around the pool. Marion reached the doorways and they all poured into the door, which led into a hallway. The end of the hall nearest them was lined with windows overlooking the pool.

The deafening noise of the helicopter and its high powered weaponry was somewhat muffled as the door closed behind them. Greg managed to clear the area of all but one of the zombies. The last of them raced up the stairs, across the catwalk and jumped at his hovering machine. Its foot caught the upper railing and it pushed off, propelling itself toward Greg, who was hovering just fifteen feet from the side of the ship.

One of the large caliber rounds hit the zombie and it disintegrated into a mist of black. The fine black particles entered the air intakes under each side of the helicopter, just under the rotor. The great machine began to sputter. Marion watched in horror as it lurched forward and descended rapidly, falling past the catwalk and down into the pool area. The large blades splintered and shattered as they struck the deck.

Marion instantly turned, opened the door leading to the catwalk, and raced back out toward the pool. Everyone followed suit, pointing their freshly loaded firearms down at the pool.

They sprinted down the staircase to the helicopter that was lying sideways in the pool. The water was causing steam to bellow from the engine compartment but there was no sign of flame. Marion scrambled up the side of the warm machine as the rest of the group circled her location, keeping an eye out for infected.

Just as Marion reached for the handle of the cockpit door, Greg opened it from the inside and climbed out. Marion hugged him with enough force to almost force him back inside.

"Well that was one way to make an entrance," he said to his wife.

"Let's get working on that exit. We are pretty exposed out here," she said, as she helped him onto the side of the helicopter and back down onto the deck of the ship.

With Greg now safely on the deck of the ship, they scrambled up the staircase to the catwalk and back to the hallway they had just exited. Wilfred took over from there and led them down the hallway toward the bridge.

They were twenty-five feet from the door to the bridge, which stood open, when a zombie dressed all in white wearing an official looking cap appeared in the doorway. No sooner had it noticed them than it rocketed toward them at a full sprint. Greg lowered his weapon and fired one round, striking the zombie squarely in the forehead.

"Looks like we found the last captain," Wilfred said, quietly mourning his fallen comrade.

## *Unlikely Hero*

Greg led the group onto the bridge of the hulking vessel. Inside, two more infected were milling about. He dispatched them quickly and motioned for the group to enter and shut the door behind them.

"You're up, captain," he said to Wilfred, motioning to the amazing array of electronic equipment on the bridge. Wilfred went right to work, activating the emergency procedures that would cause the watertight doors on the ship to engage. He keyed the ship-wide intercom and made an announcement.

"This is the captain. As you know, this ship, and the entire city, are under the attack from an unknown contagion. I have engaged the vessel's emergency lockdown procedure. All of the hallways are now sealed by watertight doors. If you are in your cabin, stay there. Do not try to exit into the hallway. You are perfectly safe in your rooms and help will get to you as soon as possible. If you are in an exposed area, stay out of sight and stay quiet. If you can see a security camera, wave at it every once in a while so we can locate you. People in exposed areas will be rescued first. I will be back with further instructions shortly."

Wilfred turned to Greg. "We are going to need help. In order to get this ship moving, we need to get those mooring ropes cut."

"There is a team of Seals en route that will have this ship locked down inside half an hour. One of our scouts saw the massacre on the dock earlier and radioed in the order. They should be here any minute now," Greg said to the captain. During all of this, Madison and the rest of the group found a place to sit down along the far wall of the bridge. They were all now completely exhausted.

Greg walked off momentarily to radio base camp to check on the status of the Seal team. When he returned, he filled Wilfred in on the situation. "The Seals will be here in thirty seconds, but we need to give them some help. They can rappel directly onto the ship, but the pool area is overrun again," he said, pointing to the monitor that covered the pool area. Infected were once again pouring out onto the deck.

"I have an idea," Wilfred said as the sound of a helicopter

could be heard approaching the ship.

"If you've got a plan, now's the time," Greg said.

Wilfred reached up high on the command console and pushed a red button. A loud, low, penetrating horn erupted all around them. The infected that were around the pool dropped to the deck in a fit of involuntary spasms.

The Seal team could be seen dropping down on ropes dangling from a helicopter hovering over the pool area. The expert marksmen made quick work of the incapacitated zombies before they could return to their feet.

Greg turned to Brooke. "Thanks to you, young lady, the military is using low frequency sound waves to our advantage. The colonel's granddaughter saw your picture online and asked her father what you meant by "Drop D." Turns out our bright scientific minds ran some tests and verified that very loud, very low frequencies were indeed effective at subduing this threat. Something about causing an oscillation or something like that. You may have saved us all," he said.

Brooke smiled.

Greg turned to Madison and said, "Hello, Madison. It's about time we met. We have been looking for you for quite some time now. It is very nice to finally meet you." She looked up at the man staring at her. His face was kind and patient.

"Very nice to meet you too," she said, shaking his hand.

Just then, there was a banging on the bridge door. Greg could see in the monitor that it was the Seal team. He raced to the door and let them in.

The team entered, quickly getting down to business as they laid out a plan to clear the ship with Wilfred and Greg. The first goal was to disconnect the mooring ropes and move the ship away from the dock.

The Seal team divided in half and, within ten minutes, Wilfred had the large vessel in motion, moving it several hundred feet offshore. Greg and the Seal team then began clearing the hallways and passages down to the entrance the tender boats used to bring passengers to shore when a particular island destination lacked a deep water port.

Once cleared, Wilfred brought the large ship close enough to the garbage scows that several of the onboard lifeboats could be used to shuttle the survivors from the barges to the ship.

\*\*\*

Two hours later, the cruise ship sat motionless in the center of the harbor. As word of the floating sanctuary spread, small watercraft bearing other survivors began approaching the large ship from all directions.

Marion and the exhausted children left the bridge for the relative comfort of the captain's suite, located just one door down the same hallway from which they originally entered the bridge. The large cabin was unoccupied, save for a few of the previous captain's personal possessions, and it had plenty of room for everyone to stretch out and get some rest. A private balcony ran the entire length outside the cabin. It wrapped around to face both sideways and forward.

Connor went down to where the survivors were boarding. He found Morgan and Michael and brought them back to the room. For what seemed like the first time in a month, they all felt safe and began to get comfortable.

Marion and Connor had made their way out to the balcony. As Madison was about to join them, a knock came at the door. She opened it to find Jeremiah standing before her.

"It's time," he said.

Madison knew what he meant. She looked back at her aunt and brother on the balcony.

"One second," she said. "It wouldn't be fair to just leave without saying goodbye. I can't put them through that."

Jeremiah watched as Madison walked out onto the balcony and over to where her brother and aunt were sitting. He watched as Marion got up from her chair, walk over to Madison, and give her a hug and a kiss on the top of her head. Connor looked back toward where Jeremiah was standing and then back toward his sister. He waved goodbye to Madison as she left them, entered the cabin and crossed to where Jeremiah was standing in the doorway. "I'm ready. Let's go."

## *Fond Farewell*

Jeremiah led Madison down a hall that ran perpendicular to the length of the ship towards a cabin directly opposite theirs on the other side. As they entered the room Madison immediately recognized the black guitar case that was laid upon the bed. She could not contain her yelp of joy as she rushed over and picked up the Reaper.

"How did you do that? It was gone. I dropped it into the ocean," she said. Her brain could not wrap itself around the fact that she was once again holding her best friend.

"Wilfred's not the only one who has trinkets of technology. A small variation of the same instrument that moved us from the falling building to the sidewalk worked on moving the Reaper from just above the ocean surface to the balcony of the cabin I was residing in. I watched the whole thing unfold. That was quite a sacrifice you made for your family," Jeremiah said.

"You want to know what's weird? I didn't think twice about it. It wasn't until the Reaper was actually falling toward the water that I realized what I had done. I only knew my family for less than twelve hours and already I was willing to give up the Reaper for them. Very strange," Madison said, sitting on the side of the bed.

"Well, we have much to do today. We can't stay here in this cabin all day. Let's go out to the balcony and be on our way," he said.

"Jeremiah? Do you think it is wrong that I made this decision because it was the one that will make me the happiest, even though I have no way of knowing if it is the right one or not?" she asked her old friend as they approached the doorway that led out onto the balcony.

"There are very few absolutes in life. Trust your instincts. They haven't let you down yet." He said to his young friend.

Jeremiah held the balcony door open for Madison and they both stepped out of the cabin. The door closed behind them. Sixty seconds later, a bolt of lightning shot silently skyward.

## *New Beginnings*

Marion and Connor sat quietly on the deck, listening to the sound of the ocean and the seagulls flying overhead. The sun was beginning to set on the horizon and there was a slight breeze in the air. Other than a brief, random flash of lightning, it was a beautiful sunset.

The horrors of the day began to wash off them as they sat in quite solitude. Below, in hallways throughout the ship, and in all parts of the city, the fight for survival continued. However, their part in what was to become known as the MAR uprising of 2014 was over.

They had both slowly drifted off to sleep only to be woken by the sound of a guitar. As they opened their eyes, they saw Madison, sitting between them on a deck chair, looking out at the water and strumming the Reaper. The young girl was not singing. She sat silently, playing the guitar as she looked out over the water. She was smiling as tears rolled off her cheeks.

"I know how hard it is to say goodbye to a friend. Are you OK?" Marion asked as she reached out and put a hand on the girl's shoulder.

"I've never been better."

# Epilogue

# Still Spinning

Thanks to a thunderous Gibson Thunderbird, a well-timed selfie, and an inquisitive granddaughter, the MAR uprising of 2014 did not result in the desolation of mankind. Nearly the entire state of South Carolina was eventually evacuated before the threat could be contained.

Aid from all over the world came pouring in to help fight the threat, especially aid in the form of amplifiers and stacks and stacks of loudspeakers. A barricade of noise was formed two hundred miles in all directions of Charleston, South Carolina. When authorities were sure no infected had gotten beyond the perimeter, the wall was slowly pushed forward, shrinking the infected zone until, six months after it began, the last of the zombies were eradicated from the city.

As for the MAR, a cure for the disease proved to be elusive. Scientists identified the virus as a non-organic parasite. It was mechanical in nature and was obviously not engineered on this planet.

World governments began doing what they did best, scaring their populations into spending obscene amounts of money on bloated programs that were destined to make little or no headway into the problem. Laws were passed that required all government buildings to have low frequency acoustic devices at every entrance.

Private capitalist enterprises did what they do best. They spent as little as possible making protective acoustic devices that they, in turn, charged obscene amounts for on the open market. Charities raised money for underdeveloped countries around the world to fund the purchase of low frequency acoustic devices for impoverished communities. Their goal was to have at least one safe house within a mile of every population center on the planet.

It became commonplace for small MAR uprisings to spring up at random places around the globe. In the developed world, the MAR became little more than a nuisance. With all the protections in place, a person was more likely to win the lottery than become infected with the disease.

However, there were exceptions. Lawsuits were brought against manufacturers of shoddy acoustic equipment when people died inside of safe houses that were supposed to be protected. Government testing showed that well over a third of the equipment being sold did not actually protect the public at all.

Laws were passed that allowed private companies to take convicts off of death row and intentionally infect them with the MAR virus. The subsequent zombies were used to test new acoustic designs and to try cutting edge injectable solutions thought to provide a new way to reverse the effects of the disease.

On the internet, many homespun remedies were discussed. The most popular of these was to continuously hum. The humming, it was said, discouraged the virus from entering your body. As with all of these internet remedies, it was hogwash, having no scientific basis whatsoever.

In the end, no cure was ever found. It wasn't until human technology again caught up with the sophistication of the MAR that the world finally understood the nature of the disease. Embedded in every MAR nanobot was a signature written in individual molecules of carbon.

"Property of Omni. Illegal possession of this technology is punishable by death."

CPSIA information can be obtained at www.ICGtesting.com
Printed in the USA
LVOW07s2236290316

481330LV00001B/60/P